NOT QUITE THE BOSS

AMY LARK

CHAPTER 1

"Is this seat taken?" A dark rich voice came from over Phoebe Butler's shoulder, shattering the din of voices and soft music in the crowded hotel bar on a Friday night. Everyone packed into the air conditioned bar to escape the heat of summer. The city had its fair share of bars and most people preferred other ones over a hotel bar, but this bar had its advantages.

She turned around on the bar stool to face the man whose whole demeanor screamed rich businessman. From his shiny wingtip shoes to the perfectly tailored Armani suit to his gold cufflinks, this guy had wealth. Not to mention, a hot, tall body Phoebe wouldn't mind climbing. His face was sculpted with an artist's eye from his sharp jawline to his high cheekbones to his aristocratic nose. Even his blond hair was perfectly styled, not a strand out of place.

All that perfection made Phoebe want to mess him up. Her fingers itched to loosen his tie, ruffle his hair, and smear his perfect lips with her red lipstick.

After seeing all he had to offer, she lifted her gaze to meet his eyes. They were a shade of green she'd never actually encountered in the wild before. Sure, she'd seen photos of eyes like this, but never on an actual real-life person. In the dimmed light of the bar, she couldn't begin to see all the colors that made up his shade of green.

His lips quirked up in a smile at her perusal and he cleared his throat. "The seat?"

Phoebe flashed him a quick smile and held out her hand to the empty bar stool next to her. "You're welcome to it until my friend shows up."

"I appreciate it." The man nodded and shrugged out of his suit jacket. His light blue dress shirt hugged his broad shoulders down to his narrow waist. She hoped he'd roll up his sleeves so she could determine whether he worked out or was just thin. He draped his jacket over the back of the bar seat before settling into the chair. "I didn't figure the bar would be this crowded tonight."

Phoebe laughed lightly. "You must not be from around here. The Indigo Hotel bar happens to serve the best half-priced margaritas north of the border on Friday nights."

"Good to know." The man's eyes gleamed with interest as they travelled from her high heels to linger on her long legs on display as they disappeared beneath her light blue wrap dress. She took a sip of her margarita and his eyes paused on her "No Walk of Shame" red lips. The heat in his green eyes when they met hers damned near scorched her.

Interesting.

The bartender chose that moment to come and get the guy's order, of course. She'd have to keep Hot Business Guy in mind for later tonight if he was still around. If she was interested in the long haul, he'd be way out of her league. But for one night, he might be just what she needed. It depended on how much she wanted to work for it tonight.

Besides, wealth didn't matter when it came to sex. And sex was her playing field where she was a star player.

Phoebe picked up her phone and texted Morgan. *Are you on your way?*

Tonight was supposed to be a much needed girls only, no Drew allowed, night out. Given how busy the Indigo Hotel Bar tended to be on a Friday night, Phoebe had slipped out of the office early to stake out a spot while Morgan wrapped up the Bradbury account.

The startup of Taylor and King, the boutique ad agency Morgan and Drew created, had taken up all of Phoebe's and Morgan's spare time for the past few months. With the company finally in the black, everyone could take a breath. Well, almost everyone. With only Phoebe in sales, Drew and Morgan had to step up to keep on top of it.

Adding to an already crazy work schedule and Morgan and Drew spending every other waking moment together, Phoebe desperately missed her best friend. And frankly, that made her feel like shit. Even though they saw each other every day at work, it wasn't the same anymore.

Morgan had found love with Drew King, of all people, but Phoebe couldn't help miss nightly wine binging and gossip sessions after work. If anyone deserved to find happiness, it was Morgan Taylor. Drew might have been a total asshat to begin with, but even Phoebe had to admit, he'd turned out to be a standup guy.

Phoebe was happy for Morgan, even if it left her lonelier than ever.

Her phone buzzed on the counter. A text from Morgan. *Shit. I was just about to text you. I'm so sorry. Call ran long. Have to wrap up a few other accounts here at the office before the new hire starts on Monday. Will probably work all weekend. Rain check?*

Phoebe took a healthy chug of her margarita. She shouldn't be surprised Morgan was ditching her again. Business came first. Drew came second. And apparently

Phoebe came last. But that was kind of the story of Phoebe's life.

Maybe she should have stuck around the office for a little longer to help. After all, the new hire would be working with Phoebe as the account executive. Not that she wanted any help, but ideally, it would free up some of Morgan's time. That had been the plan. Instead, the new guy had stolen some of Phoebe's time with her best friend. He hadn't even started and he was already pissing Phoebe off.

But she wouldn't put that on Morgan. This was all part of the deal of being best friends with a workaholic. After the new guy started Monday, she'd get some time back with her friend.

No problem, she texted back, even though her chest hurt. Fuck.

She shoved her phone away from her and scanned the bar, looking for easy pickings. She hadn't forgotten Mr. Tall, Hot Business Guy, but someone else might be easier or at least require less talking.

The usual amount of lower-level business guys drank in clusters, occasionally with a woman or two present. Phoebe was positive she could have any one of these guys balls deep in her with a few words of encouragement and not much effort.

Normally, Friday nights were happy hour night at the bar with the whole team. Well, mostly the creatives and Phoebe. Morgan and Drew tended to be too busy to join in. But tonight everyone else had to back out.

So here she was, looking for someone to bang one out to take her mind off her best friend standing her up. Especially after Phoebe finally convinced her to take a night off from Drew.

Phoebe studied the groups trying to decide which guy would do for the night. If she were lucky, she might even get an orgasm out of the deal, without having to give detailed instructions and a roadmap.

"Excuse me." Hot Business Guy's deep voice, right next to her ear, shook her in a very good way. Just that voice could definitely get her there.

Phoebe returned her attention to the well-dressed man beside her. She'd avoided looking in his direction, as he most likely would not be easy. He might have pre-conceived notions of someone like her, sitting alone at a bar. As long as he didn't offer her money for sex. . . .

He wasn't even her usual type. She generally stuck with guys who were in the same socio-economic sphere as her. Professional working class.

Her kind of guy. No fuss, no muss. No commitment required.

Besides, she couldn't possibly be this guy's type when her rent probably cost the same as one of his cufflinks. She'd found this dress on the clearance rack for like twenty bucks. This guy probably only fucked women dripping in diamonds and who laid perfectly still so no one messed up their hair. She almost chuckled out loud.

Still, there'd been a spark between them, and she did like a challenge. If it didn't pan out, she could always track down the leftovers in the bar. His cologne reminded her of a cool morning in an ancient forest: damp moss, rich wood, and fresh greens. Light but substantial and intoxicating.

She met those green eyes and they fed into the fantasy his cologne provided. Gah, he could be one of the fae her Irish grandma warned her about during her bedtime stories. So damned pretty. He would definitely do.

"Yes." The fact that she hadn't posed it as a question wondering what he wanted must have thrown him off because he opened his mouth and closed it.

He cleared his throat and tried again. "Do you think I'll have time to order food while you wait for your friend?"

"My friend just cancelled on me, so the chair is all yours." Phoebe gave him the smile she'd give any good-looking man sitting at a bar near her. A little invitation and a whole lot of sin.

His eyebrow raised, but he held out his hand. "Aiden—"

"Phoebe," she interrupted, not wanting to know the guy's last name. If he said Rockefeller or some other rich guy's last name, she'd lose all her nerve and possibly the lady boner this guy was giving her. Not that she had anything against rich people per se, but she knew her lot in life. She did okay, but she'd never be wealthy.

His warm hand engulfed hers, sending tingles through her system. She needed to burn some energy, and Aiden was quickly becoming her number one candidate. Men and sex were her territory. She didn't need anything but his hot body against hers for a good time. No pedigree required.

"Sorry about your friend." He lifted a finger to get the bartender's attention.

"She's busy with work. We'll get together another time." Phoebe brushed it off, even though it still stung that she'd been stood up. Phoebe and Morgan had started as newbies together at Hart Associates. Morgan had been the star as a workaholic while Phoebe had been happy to let her blaze their trail up the corporate ladder. They became best friends over wine and commiserating about their sexist boss. They had a system until Drew came along.

She had no one to blame but herself for her friend's relationship. One accidental text had set the whole thing in motion.

When Morgan and Drew started their own ad company, Phoebe had happily followed. The opportunity to grow a business from the ground up sounded exciting, and it would be the only way she'd still have see her workaholic friend.

"I'm sure I don't compare to your friend, but I'd love some company while I eat." He smiled and Phoebe could see that hint of loneliness in his eyes. Not surprising for a businessman in a hotel. His loneliness wasn't boldly advertised like some people's, but she recognized it.

"You're in luck because my evening just blew wide open." She held up her margarita to him. He lightly tapped his amber drink, maybe a scotch on the rocks, against it. She met his eyes while they each sipped their drink. Heat poured through her, settling low in her belly as her body climbed on board the Aiden train.

Fuck, he'll do.

The bartender returned when they set their glasses down.

Aiden turned to her. "Can I buy you dinner? I hate to eat alone."

"I never turn down a free meal." Her heart melted a little, but she shut that feeling down. The guy was being nice because she had a banging body and by all accounts was a hot commodity. Romance didn't come Phoebe's way. She didn't want it or need it. She liked playing the field. No man told her what to do or when to do it.

The bartender handed them a couple of menus. After they placed their order, he moved off to do his job.

"So, Aiden," Phoebe began, twirling her straw in her drink, "are you here for business or pleasure?"

"Business." His long fingers curved around his short bar glass. Damn, she'd been hoping he'd say pleasure. Because she was all about pleasure. "What do you do for a living?"

"Can I be honest with you, Aiden?" Phoebe smiled a little and placed her hand over his forearm. A little spark wound its way through her system at the contact. She stopped herself from squeezing the hard muscle beneath her touch.

Under those clothes, he was likely ripped. She wanted to shred his clothes to get at that body.

"I appreciate honesty." His gaze dropped back to her lips for a brief second, making her pulse throb.

"I had a hard week at work and was looking forward to spending time with my bestie tonight, but she's busy with work. Can we skip the bullshit of getting to know each other by our jobs? As if that tells anyone who we really are."

"Would you prefer we stick to the weather?" His full lips quirked into a half smile that completely disarmed her, sending a little thrill down her spine.

"Maybe not the weather." Phoebe tapped her finger against her lips. "What about favorite movie? That would tell us more about each other."

"Okay." Aiden paused and looked thoughtful as he sipped on his drink.

Watching his throat muscles work mesmerized Phoebe for a second. His skin was taut. Freshly shaven. Every part of this guy was gorgeous. She was almost afraid he was too good to be true. It was hard to tell how a guy would be in the bedroom or if he was lacking in certain qualifications until it was too late.

Please don't have a micropenis.

"Not necessarily my all-time favorite but one I've watched a few times. *10 Cloverfield Lane.*" Aiden rubbed his hands against his thighs as he looked over at her. "I hope you weren't expecting me to say *Citizen Kane.*"

"I wasn't expecting horror, but not classics either. Maybe *Wall Street* or *Wolf of Wall Street,*" she teased. Phoebe turned her chair a little toward him. "I happened to enjoy *10 Cloverfield Lane.* It's a fairly busy plot with so many threads to hold onto but has a suspense vibe that makes your heart almost stop."

"Exactly. And John Goodman's character. So perfectly

portrayed." Aiden smiled. "I tend to like suspenseful horror movies, but I watch pretty much everything."

"I adore a good suspenseful horror. I'd rather be afraid to look over my shoulder than watch blood and guts fly everywhere." Phoebe gave a small shudder.

"Do you have a favorite?"

Phoebe pursed her lips as she thought about it. "I'm pretty open to movies. But my favorite horror is a series. *The Haunting of Hill House.* I could watch that over and over and pick up on new things each time. The creep factor is so strong."

"I haven't had time to watch that one yet." Aiden leaned back as the bartender brought their food. Aiden had ordered salmon with vegetables and roasted potatoes, while Phoebe's burger and fries looked decadent and lowbrow at the same time.

Just like her. She didn't need to pretend to be more than what she was. A simple woman working to make a living. Currently, staring down a perfectly cooked burger. She grinned. She wasn't sure how she would wrap her mouth around the huge burger, but she was looking forward to it.

"That's quite the burger," Aiden remarked as he placed a napkin across his lap. "I'm a little jealous."

"I'm glad I worked through lunch now." Phoebe smiled at him. "Thank you for dinner."

"Thank *you* for the company." Aiden cut into his fish. "I feel like I haven't talked to anyone since I got here."

She wanted to ask if he travelled for work often, but she really didn't want to bring up work again. Recently her whole waking life revolved around her job. When she hung out, she hung out with people from work. Her best friend was a part owner. Sometimes she wished she'd find someone outside of their sphere to be friends with, but who had the time for that.

They slipped into a comfortable silence as they ate. Phoebe started on her fries before attempting her burger. After managing a huge messy bite, Phoebe groaned.

"This has got to be the best burger I've tasted." She glanced next to her at Aiden. He had the table manners of a royal while she had sauce running down the side of her hand. Yeah, this was definitely a mismatch, but hell if she didn't want to see how the other half fucked. Particularly this guy.

Would he be polite or demanding? Would he fold his clothes as he removed them or rip his shirt off so buttons went flying everywhere? She pressed her thighs together at the thought.

She ran her tongue along the sauce drip on the outside of her hand next to her pinkie. Her eyes caught Aiden's heat-filled gaze. Instead of feeling embarrassed by her lack of manners, she gave him a naughty smile. He swallowed.

"I'm glad you're enjoying yourself." His tone was a little deeper and a lot more intimate.

"What's not to enjoy? Good drink, good food, and good company." Phoebe gave him a small smirk as he lifted his glass. "The only thing that would make it better would be good sex."

AIDEN KINGSTON almost choked on his scotch. This woman didn't seem to possess a shy bone in her fantastic body. He'd never had a one-night stand before, but Phoebe definitely tempted him. New city, new life away from his family. Nothing to hold him back. No one around here gave a fuck about his last name being Kingston. It was liberating.

"The night is still young." Aiden set his glass down. He hadn't ruled out inviting her to his room, but he wasn't sure how to go about it. He didn't have much in the way of "game."

Her brown eyes sparkled as she wrapped her red lips around the burger again. Her light red hair hung loose around her shoulders. The blue dress clung to her curves, just enough to entice. He was grateful the bar covered the evidence of what she did to him.

"Mmm." She delicately dabbed at her mouth with her napkin. "Did you have plans for the evening?"

Her eyes flicked over his suit with a question in them.

He'd considered changing into more casual clothes before heading down to find some food, but because of the time of day, he figured most people would still be in their business attire. Being able to blend in was a novelty to him since he'd come to this city. His wealthy family was well known in Chicago and the expectations were always high there. Here on the east coast, no one knew of him. That had been part of the lure.

His father had married the heiress of the Hunt family, Aiden's mother, earning his father a spot as CEO of the family company. Dragging Aiden and his brothers into the family business behind him. A company Aiden had thankfully left behind.

"I figured I'd try to get some research done for work on Monday." He shrugged. "I've been told I work too much, but since we aren't talking about work. . . ."

"That's my friend's problem too." Phoebe leaned back in her chair and crossed her legs toward him. Damn, she had magnificent legs. "It seems like the only thing on her mind these days is work or her boy toy."

He couldn't stop his smirk. "Boy toy?"

"You know, girl meets boy and he aggravates the piss out of her, but then they accidentally hook up and end up falling in love." Her grin was mischievous as she leaned toward him.

"Honestly, I don't know how she gets any work done as they are constantly on each other. I'm pretty sure their office isn't just for working. If you know what I mean."

"Must be an intense office. How do you get any work done?" He cut some of his vegetables and took a bite. The bar food wasn't as good as some of the restaurants he usually went to, but it was decent.

Her eyebrow cocked up. "I'm talking about sex in the office and you think the office is intense and ask how we get work done? I mean, if you want to talk about work, I guess I can play along. But I'd rather figure out how to ask you, *your place or mine.* A girl might begin to wonder if you have any interest in her at all."

She gave him a once over and his cock twitched. This woman would be the death of him, but what a way to go. She'd be worth a night of debauchery.

He closed the distance between them, breathing in her lavender scent, and confessed, "I'm not sure what I'm doing. I don't normally pick up women in bars."

"Where do you find them then?" She popped a French fry into her mouth, her lips still that sinful red color. She had lush lips and he'd already fantasized about them pressed to his, or parted in ecstasy as he gave her an orgasm, or wrapped around his cock. . . .

Pulling himself back to her question, he took a bite. He'd prefer to continue to think about her rather than think about the women he'd been with before. He lifted his gaze to her dark eyes. They held a hint of amusement and desire. His insides twisted at that look and he had to clear his throat before he spoke.

"Charity events." What he didn't add was his family had vetted the women in his life before he even had a chance to meet the women. God forbid Aiden bring a woman home they didn't know everything about. Only once had he done that and the memory of her made him smile. "I guess my first girlfriend, I met in high school. I flirted and teased her until she went out with me."

He hadn't thought of her in years. She definitely hadn't received his family's approval. Their relationship hadn't lasted long after that.

"Since high school. Damn, that's a long time ago. Do you even know how to flirt?" Her perfect lips tilted into a smile.

"Probably not," he admitted, pushing his plate back. He rubbed the back of his neck. He had no game. Sex was easy, flirting not so much.

She pushed her plate away and turned toward him. Her skirt parted over her knee, revealing her long legs. "Tell you what."

Her eyes sparkled when he met them.

"What?"

Leaning in, she gestured for him to come closer. When he moved in, her red-nailed finger tipped his chin to the side so that she could speak in his ear.

"If you want me, you can have me. For you, I'm a sure thing." Her lips brushed against his ear. He almost groaned at the rush of lust that crashed through him. He definitely wanted this woman. She pulled away and tipped his chin back toward her. Her nose grazed against his. One of her eyebrows arched high and her smile was cocky. "You can practice trying to pick me up though."

Her lips were close enough he could close the distance and satisfy his curiosity of how she tasted. He leaned in slightly, watching her smoldering eyes. Her warm breath caressed his lips. He drew back slowly, increasing the gap between them reluctantly.

"You haven't said whether or not you'll be taking me up on the offer?" Her voice held a hint of curiosity but nothing else. No remorse or regret or fear. Fierce came to mind.

"I guess I need to know more about what you are offering." Years of training couldn't be ignored. His family had money. *He* had money and that brought along with it women who wanted him for what he could provide them. He let his family find him women who weren't trying to trap him. At least not for his money, those women wanted his name and the power that came with it. The money was just a bonus.

Phoebe smiled and didn't look offended at all. "You'd be a fantastic catch for most women, I'm sure. But I'm on the strictly catch-and-release program. We *will* use protection. I'm not going to claim to be in love with you and stalk your ass. Or punch holes in the condom so I can pop out your brat. I don't want your money if that's what you're worried about. I just want a good time, a few orgasms would be nice, and then I'll be on my way."

Aiden nodded and sipped his scotch. Her statement didn't startle him. He couldn't be too sure, but she knew exactly what to say to put him at ease. He had his own condoms to ensure no claims of pregnancy afterwards. As a teenager, his father had instilled in him the necessity of always having contraceptives on him, even if he didn't plan on needing any.

The attraction between them was irresistible. She seemed fun and definitely not uptight like the women he'd dated. His family would never approve, but he'd moved away so he could do what he wanted. And right now, he wanted Phoebe.

"Unless you have a room here, my room is closer." He handed her one of the mints that came with their bill and popped the other one in his mouth.

"That's convenient." She straightened her skirt and took a sip from her margarita. "Give me your best pick up line."

"I'm not exactly prepared." Aiden wished he knew some creative ways to win her or at least some pick up lines. He wanted to impress this fiery woman.

"How about I give you some examples?" Her dark eyes twinkled with mischief.

"Sure." He wanted to run his thumb over her lush bottom lip. The noise of the bar had faded into the background with Phoebe talking to him. But when the bartender yelled something at a server, it made him aware of the people surrounding them. He wanted to drag her out of there to somewhere he could unwrap that awesome body and taste every inch of her. But they had time.

She straightened up like an actor preparing to go onstage. She flicked her hair over her shoulders and took a deep breath in and out. Her breasts rose and fell. "It's important to prepare."

"Of course." He reclined in his chair, swirling his drink in his hand.

She winked at him and then leaned in, touching his arm. "If I told you you had a beautiful body, would you hold it against me?"

A laugh burst out of him before he could stop it. He'd expected some rehearsed moves, not some corny line.

"Good, right?" Her grin filled his chest with lightness.

"What else you got?"

She held out her hand. "Hi, I'm Phoebe."

He took her hand. Heat raced through his veins.

She leaned in close and winked. "But you can call me. . . anytime."

He shook his head as his grin widened. "I think I'm getting the idea."

"Okay." She spread her arms in front of her. "Give it a go then. Wow me."

He couldn't believe he was going to say this to this beautiful creature, but what the hell. "Do you have a little Irish in you?"

She smirked. "No."

"Would you like a little Irish in you?"

She snickered. No woman he'd dated had ever snickered. Even when they were alone. "Are you actually Irish?"

"A quarter on my mom's side." He tapped his empty drink on the bar. Should he get another drink or suggest they take this upstairs?

A group of guys moved behind them and bumped into Phoebe's chair. She didn't seem to notice, but the bar was even more crowded than when he first sat down. The noise level crept up every few seconds it seemed.

"Do you want to come upstairs for a nightcap?"

Her eyes danced in amusement. "Is that another line? Who says nightcap?"

"My drink is empty. So is yours." He gestured to her glass. "We could get refills and stay in this moshpit, yelling at each other to be heard. Or we could go up to my room where we have quiet, space, and a bar."

She took hold of his tie and tugged him closer to her. She tilted her head like she was going to lean in for a kiss, but she stayed where she was. Her dancing eyes met his. His breath caught. "Lead the way."

CHAPTER 2

WHEN AIDEN ASKED her up to his room, she'd expected a simple room with a huge bed. Of course, when he pressed the top floor button in the elevator, she'd upgraded the room in her mind to one of those suites with a TV/couch area and a separate bedroom. This was a hoity-toity hotel after all.

As the last ones in the elevator, Phoebe glanced at Aiden. His green eyes were utterly captivating. He'd loosened the knot on his tie and casually slung his suit jacket over his shoulder. Leaning against the wall with one foot hooked over the other, he looked like he'd stepped off the page of *GQ*. This guy was high class all the way.

Thinking of her own hand-me-down furniture in her one bed apartment, she knew she was sparring way out of her weight class tonight. This hotel was expensive. He probably had more cash on him than she had in her bank account. Of course, his work could be paying for the hotel.

None of that mattered in the short term. It was only one night, and the attraction was intense. One-night stands were her thing. It gave her power even here in this place that dripped luxury. She just hoped he wouldn't be a wham-bam-thank-you-ma'am type. Because her anticipation had been climbing with every moment in his presence.

"Do you come here often?" She wiggled her eyebrows at him, needing to break the silence and her internal nagging voice.

"Do the cheesy lines work?" He looked at her. He towered over her, which was impressive, given her height with her heels was around five ten. Her head barely reached his chin. Guys rarely made her feel small and delicate, but this guy. . . . Heat worked its way from her center to radiate throughout her.

"What do you think?" She gazed through her lashes up at him.

"I don't think you need the cheesy lines to get what you want." His hand reached out for hers, but instead of taking her hand in his, his fingers trailed over hers. Shivers went down her spine, settling between her legs.

She stepped toward him as the elevator dinged for his floor. He lifted her fingers to his lips and placed a kiss on her knuckles before leading her out. Phoebe's heart fluttered. She almost pressed her hand over her heart because that never happened. Fluttering usually occurred much lower.

He held his phone up to the door. The snick of a lock filled the quiet hallway. She shook off the weird feeling and smiled at him. He was just another man, another notch on her lipstick case.

He led her through the door and she gasped. He released her hand as she walked ahead of him.

"Holy shit, Aiden, you didn't tell me you were loaded." She spun in a circle and moved into the space. This wasn't just a hotel room; it was a really fancy apartment. Floor to ceiling windows with a view of the city skyline drew her toward them. The darkness was dotted with city lights. There were double doors leading off to what she assumed was the bedroom. Leather furniture and a table for eight spread around the space. A fucking baby grand piano sat in a corner. *Tucked* in a corner! It didn't even take up all that much floor space. "This is *Pretty Woman*-level shit. Please tell me you have a bathtub you can practically swim in."

"Drink?" Aiden had moved behind the bar, not a minibar, a fully stocked bar with actual glassware.

"You aren't a mob boss, are you? You have to tell me if you are, right?" Phoebe slipped off her shoes next to the couch and walked over to the bar. Her toes curled into the plush carpet. "Wait, if you tell me, will you have to kill me?"

Aiden chuckled and pulled out a bottle of wine and a couple of glasses. He uncorked the bottle and filled the glasses. "I'm not a member of the mob."

He came around the bar and held out a glass to her. Man, he was tall. She wanted to climb him like a tree.

"Hmmm, I'm not convinced." She gave him a wink and clinked her glass to his. "To interesting evenings."

She took a drink at the same time he did. He lifted her glass from her hand and set both of them on the bar. Her breath caught at the look in his eyes. He closed the distance between them. His lips claimed hers. No hesitation. Not a little peck, but a full-on, pressed body to body kiss. Her insides lit up like a slot machine hitting the jackpot. His hands grabbed her ass and pulled her into his impressive erection.

Thank God. She nearly sagged in relief.

His kiss was firm as his rich scent made her knees buckle. She pressed up into the kiss on her tiptoes, sliding her hands around his neck and running her fingers over his short hair. Velvety hair tickled her palms as his tongue sought entrance. She opened for him and everything focused down to the feel of his tongue sliding against hers, triggering a lightning bolt of desire to electrify her whole system.

Scotch, wine, mint, and something rich and earthy that was all Aiden filled her senses. When he lifted his mouth from her, she almost pulled him back down, craving that intensity, wanting to be carried away with passion.

Instead, she drew in a breath to slow her racing pulse. His green eyes had darkened. They were truly beautiful in this lighting. She could see flecks of gold and brown blending into the green. His hands were still on her ass. Oof, she needed to take back control of this situation.

"Was that okay?" His voice was rich and heavy with desire.

Okay? Swallowing, she nodded, trailing her hand down his neck to his chest. "Perfect."

His lips tipped into a smile. "I'm not sure what the rules are."

She concentrated on tugging his tie loose to keep herself from grinding on the man until he took her hard and fast or she got off, whichever came first.

"The rules are whatever we make them." Her voice was softer than normal. She cleared her throat. As she lifted his tie, he bent his neck for her to take it off. It was a really nice tie, soft and silky in her fingers. She laid it on the bar next to the wine glasses. She went to work on the buttons of his shirt. "We can do whatever you want. If you want to play Little Red Riding Hood and the big bad wolf, or if work trips your trigger, secretary and the boss. We can get down to business or if you want to talk a bit beforehand...."

He had an undershirt on, still hiding his muscles from her. She trailed off as she pushed the dress shirt off his arms. Damn, maybe she was an arm lady now. His were all corded and hard.

He lowered his face until his lips brushed her ear. "I want you, Phoebe. Only you."

Pleasure trickled through her at his words. He'd barely

touched her and she was ready to go. Nothing snarky came to mind. She couldn't make fun of his sincerity, even though it made her uncomfortable. Most men she could share a laugh with, but Aiden wasn't joking with her anymore. His words swept through her like a heat wave. She nodded, not trusting her voice.

He searched her eyes. She wanted this. She wanted him. Satisfied with whatever he saw, he led her through double doors into a darkened room. Releasing her hand, he went to turn on a lamp. Without his touch, she drew in a breath and the weight of the previous moment lifted off her.

The room was huge for a hotel room with a king size bed taking up the majority of the space. Not able to help herself, she glanced over her shoulder at the door to the bathroom. Excitement welled within her.

"Please tell me there is a huge tub in there and bubble bath and an old Walkman with Prince's 'Kiss' in it." She turned to see the amusement in his eyes.

"You are something else."

She smiled, feeling more comfortable. "At least I'm better than work."

"You most definitely are."

"Now don't lie to me because I don't like liars." She pressed her hand against his firm warm chest. "Is there a bathtub or not?"

Dude, she needed to get this T-shirt out of her way. She knew what muscles that felt like the ones beneath her fingers looked like and she wanted to see them all. But damn, his ripped arms had her insides doing flips. She let her fingers trail over the ropy muscles.

He gestured for her to lead the way to the bathroom with said arm. The bathroom was huge and yes, it definitely had a swim-worthy tub. And a shower big enough for a party. Her mind went to all sorts of naughty things they could do just in this room.

"Bubble bath?" she asked as she looked through the soaps and lotions lined up along the tub.

"I'll get you some."

"Really?" She spun to look at him. Her heart skipped a little.

He smiled and nodded. Guys didn't do things for her. To her, yes please. For her. . . not so much. Especially if it had nothing to do with sex, but then again, sex in a tub could be fun.

"Give me a second." He went out to the bedroom, and she heard him pick up the phone. She stared in the large mirror at herself. Yes, *Pretty Woman* was her favorite movie of all time and this place sent her spiraling into memories of watching that movie growing up.

Man, if she could get him to order some champagne and strawberries and some black and white reruns. . . . Remembering his thick cock pressed against her, shivers raced up her spine. She'd definitely recreate that scene between Vivian and Edward.

Phoebe checked her makeup and hair quickly before turning to join him in the bedroom. He sat on the bed and hung up the phone. She stepped in between his legs and held his face in her hands as she leaned down to kiss him. It was a gentle, exploring kiss meant to thank him for being considerate.

Yes, bubble bath wasn't diamonds, but to her, it meant a lot. What would she do with diamonds anyway?

Of course, there were many ways to thank him. She wanted to get to all of them tonight. Her hands went to the tie on her wrap dress but his hands stopped her. She wanted them both to get naked. Wasn't that what he wanted? Lifting her head, she gave him a questioning look.

He pressed a kiss to her fingers before releasing them. "I've been wanting to do this since I met you. It's like gift wrap."

Her arms dropped to her sides. "I'm yours tonight. Whatever you want to do."

He raised an eyebrow. "Whatever?"

Her insides turned to liquid. This man, lord, he was something else.

"I mean within reason. Obviously, I don't have my riding crop and black leather boots with me, so if you're into crawling around on all fours and licking my boots, it'll have to be another time. Though I suppose you could use the magic hotel phone to make anything appear. So whatever. If it tickles your fancy."

He chuckled. His rich deep tone tantalized her with the sound of his laugh. A bubble of lightness filled her chest.

She stroked her finger along his jaw, feeling the light stubble there. "I'm open to whatever experiences you want to give me. And what I can give you."

"Quid pro quo," he said.

"Abso-fucking-lutely."

He lifted his T-shirt off over his head and threw it to the side. His chest was perfectly sculpted like the rest of him. She traced her hand over his pec to assure herself he was warm flesh and blood and not cold marble. His skin was smooth beneath her touch, making her fingertips buzz with energy.

The room was tidy and his shirt on the floor was the only thing out of place. She'd worried he would be the kind of guy who would take the time to fold his clothes into a neat stack before politely asking to fuck her. She'd never been so glad to be wrong.

With his hands guiding her hips, he positioned her between his knees. There was no uncertainty or hesitation from him. His confidence made her damn near melt. The heat in his eyes almost scorched her as he focused on her dress's tie.

"When I was young, our presents always had bows and ribbons on them," he said softly. His deep voice resonated through her bones. His fingers stroked down the tie holding her dress closed, and her core clenched as if he'd stroked her naked flesh. This anticipation would kill her. "Birthdays and Christmas. Those presents would be waiting for us to come and rip them to shreds. The twins always did. My younger brothers."

He pulled one string, slowly unraveling the bow, unraveling her at the same time. "But me, I liked to savor it. Take my time to untie the bow and delicately open the gift wrap to see the present waiting for me. It was torture and pleasure all in one."

His words were hypnotic. She could almost see him there in the past. A young boy, anxiously and patiently unwrapping one gift at a time while his brothers ripped into theirs.

He lifted his eyes from the bow and met hers. There was nothing boyish about him. Definitely all man. She pressed her thighs together against the aching pulse. Damn, she wanted him badly.

Desire and longing were her old friends. Find a hot guy and she was usually good to go. But this anticipation, this guy, was on a whole new level for her. It scared her a little, but not in a flight way. She wouldn't run away if she wanted to. She craved his next move more than the air she needed to breathe. He pulled the knot loose and the dress opened slightly.

"There's another knot inside," she whispered, afraid if she spoke too loudly the spell would be broken.

"The more ribbons and wrappings, the sweeter the prize." He opened the dress to find the knot, and she swore her knees went weak with want. She wasn't a cliché. She didn't go weak in the knees for guys. She used them for a good time and made sure they had a good time in return. But with Aiden, everything felt amplified. Obviously, it had been too long for her if he affected her this much.

His fingers grazed her side, leaving fireworks sparking across her skin, as he gently undid the other tie. Her dress fell open, revealing her light blue bra and panties. Her breath caught as he stood and slowly pushed her dress over her shoulders until it slid to the floor. His bare chest skimmed her lace-covered breasts and the soft skin of her stomach brushed his hard muscles, leaving her branded with his heat. Her eyes fluttered closed.

Way too long.

Opening her eyes, she lifted her hands to his sides, enjoying his warm, firm flesh beneath her fingertips. His eyes devoured her greedily. She had to work out to maintain her figure and still be able to eat what she wanted. This made those hours worth it. The way he looked her over made warmth seep into every inch.

He drew his fingers up her arms and closed them over her shoulders, turning her away from him. Shivers raced up her spine as he slipped his fingers beneath her bra straps and traced them down her shoulder blades to the band. She released a shuddering breath as he unclasped it.

She wanted to say something to disrupt the spell he was weaving over her. Something snarky and playful, but she couldn't find her voice. Completely wrapped up in him. Aiden lifted the bra from her, cupping both of her breasts. She filled his large hands. His skin was tanner than her own and the sight pushed all the right buttons for her.

Her eyes flickered shut and she leaned back onto his chest. His warmth surrounded her, making her feel languid and on edge, willing to stay in this moment, but anticipating the next. Her flesh tingled where it touched his, ready and waiting for more.

She wrapped her arms around his neck behind her to hang on. Taking his time, he explored her breasts and nipples until she ached. Need flooded her. This slow exploration drove her nearly insane. She rubbed back into his covered erection, longing for him to move on, but at the same time, craving what he was doing to her. He pinched and caressed her nipples, holding her breasts until he was the only thing keeping her upright.

He leaned down to whisper in her ear, "Only one more wrapping to go."

Warmth rushed to her core. Finally. She opened her eyes to watch his hands move over her. Her breathing was uneven and her heart felt like she'd run a 5K at top speed. She was more than ready for him.

His fingers slid down her waist and under the satin of her panties, cupping her butt.

She gasped at the tingles spiraling through her from his fingertips. If he stopped right now, she'd scream. She needed him. Her eyes drifted shut and she whispered, "Please."

He linked his thumbs around the sides of her panties and lowered them slowly down her thighs. Her breath caught. His mouth kissed the nape of her neck. He nudged her forward and slowly knelt behind her, kissing his way down her spine as he went. All the while lowering her panties to the floor until she was bared to him.

"Phoebe." Her name was a command on his tongue.

She turned and looked down at him, kneeling before her. Her fingers dove through his hair. As he stood, he ran his hands up her sides. She brought her hands down to his chest.

"You're gorgeous."

She flushed with warmth. "You're not so bad yourself."

Trailing her fingers down his sculpted abs, she stopped at

his waistband. She looked up at him for permission. Not her usual, but something about Aiden made her seek his approval. He bent and took her mouth. Slowly lingering, cradling her face in his hands.

Taking that as a yes, she undid his belt and pants. Already hypersensitive, her breasts were stark peaks as they rubbed against his chest. She wanted a little control back in this dynamic and knew how to get it. She slid her hand under his boxers and ran her palm along the smooth, hard length of his cock. Her core clenched in anticipation at his size. His breath caught and she smiled against his lips.

Stroking her thumb across the tip of his cock, she caressed his tongue with hers. A rumble formed in his chest like a low growl. Shivers raced through her. Shoving his pants down, she broke off the kiss to push them free. When she finished, she was kneeling on the floor, looking up at Aiden.

All of him and his perfect body. His beautiful erect cock throbbed before her. He was breathing heavily as he stared at her. But he was still in control. Holding himself in check.

That just wouldn't do. She leaned forward and licked his cock from base to tip, all while holding his gaze. That rumble started again, but he held himself still, his gaze hot as he watched her. His control impressed her, but she also knew what to do to make him break.

She leisurely explored him with her mouth and hands, never dropping her gaze from his. Loving the salty taste of his skin. Watching those green eyes grow darker and darker. When she took him deep into her mouth, he groaned and lifted her to her feet.

"Enough," he rumbled.

"Is it though?" Her hands stayed on his cock, the smooth skin and firm length of him hot in her grip. She only wanted one thing. His cock buried deep inside of her.

He turned with her and crowded her backwards until her knees hit the mattress. He lowered her to lie on the bed, hovering above her. "I want to be inside you when I come the first time."

Before she could wrap her legs around his waist, he dropped to his knees. His mouth closed over her sex, and she arched off the bed. Her body buzzed with sexual energy. She was beyond ready to come. He explored her slowly as if he hadn't almost been ready to come in her mouth. This man's patience was incredible. When he added his fingers to her torment, she lost the ability to focus on anything except the sensations coursing through her.

Her breathing came in short, uneven bursts. His mouth and hands were overwhelmingly brilliant, pushing her closer and closer to the edge. Slowly, he started a rhythm that her body followed as though he were a pied piper. It didn't take long before she fell apart under his wicked tongue and long fingers.

"Fuck," she breathed out as her heart raced.

Before she could come down, he thrust his fingers into her again, driving her higher as he hit just the right spot with his tongue. She arched up off the bed and cried out at the unexpected rush of a second orgasm.

He slowed his fingers, still keeping her on the wire.

"I should have asked earlier," she said between breaths. Her body pulsed around his fingers. It wouldn't take much to go over the edge again. Every touch hit exactly the right spot to make her crescendo.

He joined her on the bed, taking her nipple into his mouth. She could feel her body building again. She needed to get out her question before they took this any further.

"Do you have condoms?" she forced out, waiting until he lifted his head to meet her eyes. She'd hate to leave him to go all the way back to the living room and grab some from her purse.

He appeared determined to drive her insane. Those fingers of his tweaked and played with her sex, keeping her right on the edge.

"Please," she whimpered. "I want you inside me."

His eyes darkened. "I have some."

He opened a drawer on the nightstand, keeping one hand working her.

"Thank goodness. I have some, but not sure they'd be big enough." Phoebe fell back against the bed, riding the wave as his hand pushed her toward the brink, closing her eyes against the almost painful pleasure. "Size matters, you know."

He chuckled darkly and his hand left her. She turned her head and watched him roll on the condom.

Sitting up, she pressed her hand to his chest, pushing him until he sat against the headboard of the massive bed. She straddled his hips and lowered herself onto him, slowly, taking him in, inch by inch, until she fully engulfed him. So deep and so full she wanted to stay there. He was not a small man and she could feel the stretch as her body accommodated him. His hands went to her hips and helped her glide back up.

Aiden's gaze held hers. His green eyes locked her in as she rode him. Somehow the eye contact forged a connection that made this more intimate than any guy she'd had before. Their breaths synced with each thrust. This didn't feel like an ordinary one-night stand.

Aiden led her in a slow dance at first as he guided her hips. The pace dragged against every nerve ending within her. Her orgasm lay just out of reach but built with each slow stroke. She needed more, wanting to race toward the peak again. As he relinquished control to her, moving his hands to cup her breasts, her hands anchored on his shoulders and she followed the rhythm she craved. All while he held her gaze, those green eyes of his tracking her every expression.

Her orgasm hit her suddenly and she sank onto him, feeling every inch of him inside her. Her mouth latched onto his shoulder, tasting the salt of their overworked bodies. She never wanted to move again.

Before she could catch her breath, he rolled their still-joined bodies until the bed hit her back. He hovered over her and continued to thrust. Her body lit up again as she followed the rhythm of his hips.

She didn't think she had another orgasm in her, but as he thrust into her, it built again. He claimed her mouth with his. Finesse left him as he lifted her leg to allow him to penetrate her deeper and harder. The new friction proved too much and she let go. Her orgasm hit her harder. Her whole body tensed against his.

He stiffened above her and she could feel his cock pulse, adding aftershocks to her already spent body.

He collapsed on her, bracing himself so she didn't take his whole weight. She didn't mind. She loved this part of sex. Not cuddling, but the rawness right after when both of them struggled to return to normal. His weight and warmth on her felt amazing.

"Am I too heavy?" His voice sounded gravelly next to her ear.

Her core clenched weakly around him. "No. It's good. You're good."

He lifted his head and brushed her hair away from her face. "You're good too." He dropped his head and kissed her, soft and satisfied. He moved to get up.

"Not yet," she protested, and if her muscles weren't made of jelly, she would have wrapped her legs around him to keep him there longer.

He chuckled and left her in the middle of his bed while he

went into the bathroom to take care of things. She stared up at the ceiling. Good? Who did she think she was kidding? That was better than good. She seriously hoped he was up for a round two. Hell, she hoped she was up for round two. Maybe a little while later. Her body was a little achy already, but it felt divine.

He joined her back on the bed, lying next to her, his head propped up on one elbow. He trailed a fingertip down her breastbone. "What now?"

She smiled up at him. "I have an idea, if you're game?"

CHAPTER 3

AIDEN SAT on the floor in his boxers while Phoebe, beside him, had claimed his button-down shirt. The shirt hung to her knees. She looked a hell of a lot better in it than he did. Champagne, strawberries, and bubble bath had been delivered to his suite. On her request.

With her hair tousled from sex, her red lipstick non-existent, and her body engulfed in his shirt, Phoebe seemed younger and less femme fatale than she had in the bar. Especially when she smiled up at him like a kid in a candy store. They had moved the coffee table out of the way and were having a "floor picnic," she'd called it, in front of the television.

"It doesn't have to be *I Love Lucy*." Phoebe sipped from her champagne flute. "Anything would be fine."

He shook his head and flipped through channels, looking for something that would make her laugh. He settled on reruns of *The Office*. He would have never imagined he'd be spending Friday night trying to recreate *Pretty Woman* scenes. But Phoebe's enthusiasm was contagious. And the joy on her face made everything worthwhile.

"Mmm." She finished the strawberry bite in her mouth before adding, "I know this episode. It's a good one. Though my office has never been this fun."

"I imagine most offices aren't this fun. After all, work has to get done at some point." Aiden grabbed a strawberry from the tray. They were small and sweet and the color reminded him of Phoebe's nipples. He didn't know if this was all they would be doing or if they would have sex again. He couldn't even remember enough about *Pretty Woman* to know if this was a sexy scene. Maybe he could google it on his phone.

"I suppose our office has fun sometimes. Most of the time it feels like we are more of a dysfunctional family rather than an office. Being creative can be fun. But no warehouse to have warehouse games." She laughed at the punchline of some joke. He was too busy watching her to pay attention to the show. Could she possibly be this carefree? Most women wanted more from him, especially when they found out he had wealth, things like diamonds and gems, not just bubble bath and strawberries.

They always wanted more, but Phoebe hadn't even wanted his last name.

"Would you want a boss like Michael Scott?" He wanted to know more about her, but that wasn't part of the deal. They were essentially strangers having a one-night stand. He figured there were unspoken rules like no details or emotional connection of any kind.

"Um, no." She met his eyes. Her brown eyes danced with amusement. "He doesn't do anything. I wouldn't want to have to carry my boss's workload too."

"But he makes things fun, right?" He hoped he'd be able to be a good leader. He didn't need to be friends like Michael Scott. But he wanted their respect. A little fear crept into him thinking about work on Monday. He needed this job to work out. Prove that he could succeed on his own. Build his own space without his family's wealth backing him.

"Thankfully, he only exists on a TV show. I can't imagine having to work with someone like him day in and day out." She gave a little shudder. "But on TV? Comedy gold."

He smiled and she went back to watching the show. When the next commercial hit, he asked, "How does this work?"

"How does what work?" She turned to face him, sitting cross legged, which, given her lack of undergarments, drew his attention in multiple ways.

"Sleeping with a stranger. Hooking up. One-night stands. I'm kind of a newbie at it." He settled his back against the couch and watched her expressive face.

"First off, well done." She smiled and held up her hand for a high five. He gave her a look that said are you serious. She looked at her hand and back at him and shook it. He gave in and slapped her hand. "Excellent."

"I wasn't looking for praise," he grumbled.

She raised her eyebrow at him. "It's kind of up to us how this goes. Sometimes I'll exchange numbers with someone in case we'd like to get together for a booty call down the road, but there are no expectations. I'm not looking for a date or a regular thing. Very rarely a guy doesn't quite get that. I had to ghost someone hard about a year ago."

She gave a shudder but then smiled. "Work keeps me pretty busy. I'm just in this for tonight and wherever we want to go from here. But I'm not going to become emotionally attached to you."

He nodded. "I think I understand."

"Physically though." She smirked and drew her knees up. His gaze dropped lower. "I have to say I've never been so in tune with someone before. I don't always come when I have sex, at least not with intercourse, but. . . ." She blushed. "Let's just say I lost count, but I'm pretty sure I owe you a few."

"I'm not keeping track." The tension eased out of his shoulders. "But I wouldn't be opposed to repeat performances."

When she smiled that naughty smile of hers, his cock leapt to attention. When she'd gone down on him, he thought he was going to lose it. He didn't want to stop her and ask if she was okay if he did, but maybe that would have been okay to ask.

"I'm willing to stay the night and see what else might come up." She sucked on a strawberry while looking at his obvious erection.

He could feel the rush of blood flow through him. Nothing in his life had prepared him for this woman, but he liked the direction of this night so far. "I'd like that."

"A few questions." She moved up onto her knees and hit mute on the TV remote.

"Okay." Not sure what she'd bring up, but willing to just be in this moment. Not worry about the future. Just tonight.

"How sexually active are you?" She lifted his hand and traced the lines on his palm with a featherlight touch. A shiver rippled down his spine.

"I haven't been with someone in months. My ex and I were together for two years before that."

She nodded and scooted closer. "Have you been tested since?"

"All clean, why?" He got caught in those brown eyes of hers. They seemed ancient and innocent at the same time. He didn't have sex without condoms, too many risks. Even with his long-term girlfriend. His father had drilled into him to never trust a woman who might want to hook you in by getting pregnant.

"Just determining whether we can do this without a

condom." She lifted his hand to her mouth and sucked on his finger.

His brain stirred from the sensual fog. "This?"

She pulled his finger out of her mouth with a pop. She hit unmute on the TV and smiled at him. "Enjoy the show."

She reached for his boxers and pulled them down. He helped her take them off, and she unbuttoned his shirt, revealing her magnificent body inch by inch, and slipped it off. Completely naked, she met his eyes. "Only this."

Kneeling before him, she leaned over and slid her mouth down over his cock. Aiden lost focus on the TV as she used her lips, tongue, teeth, and hands to drive him wild. He gathered her hair in his hand to watch her move over him.

Her breasts swayed as she bobbed up and down. He reached with his other hand, teasing them gently, even as she tormented him. He wouldn't last much longer. The episode ended and another began on the TV.

Most women he'd been with preferred him not to come in their mouths. If he didn't say it now, it would be too late. He bit out, "I'm going to come."

Her dark eyes met his and held him locked in place. She didn't pull off but sucked hard on his cock. The energy he had used to hold on released. He threw his head back and let himself go. All the tension from the weeks leading up to this eased out of him as he let this woman drive him wild and he came in her mouth.

Phoebe sat up and took a drink of champagne. Her pupils were huge and her breathing stilted. Fuck, going down on him had turned her on. Some women he'd been with had treated it like a chore. One more thing to do to get those diamond earrings for Christmas.

But not this woman.

"Come here." He pulled her to him, catching her lips with his and tasting the strawberries and champagne as well as himself on her tongue. His fingers glided over her wet sex, and she moaned against his lips.

He lifted her onto the leather couch, pulling her bottom to the edge. Kneeling between her knees with her on display before him, he licked his lips before he said, "Watch your show."

~

SLEEP HAD NEVER COME SO FAST for Phoebe or lasted so long, outside of her own bed. She woke up wrapped in sheets in Aiden's huge bed with blackout curtains doing their best to hold back the morning light. She stretched and looked around for Aiden but didn't see him. Tenderness and soreness tugged at her in the most delicious places, bringing a smile to her lips.

His ancient woodlands scent surrounded her, making her want to snuggle down deeper within the sheets. Honestly, the man had to be part robot. Lately every other guy she hooked up with were all wham, bam, thank you, ma'am.

Rarely did she actually spend the whole night with a guy. She almost never slept over. And she never came so many times in one night in her life. She wouldn't have been surprised to wake up in her own bed, having dreamt the whole thing.

She grabbed his shirt from the floor and slipped it on. The living room was empty, except for the remains of their makeshift picnic. Her skin heated thinking of how he'd definitely given as good as he got before they'd ended up back in bed. Tingles raced down her spine, settling at the juncture of her thighs. She couldn't even remember going to sleep. Just orgasm followed by orgasm.

After last night, she should be satiated, but something about Aiden made her want more.

She strolled back into the bedroom and knocked before entering the bathroom. Empty. She sighed and spotted the bubble bath waiting on the side of the tub. Next to it was a note and a small speaker. The note said, "Hit play when ready. -A."

"Aiden?" she called out, feeling a little silly as she knew that unless he was hiding in a closet (which would be weird, but she might overlook it after last night), he wasn't here.

She shrugged and pressed play. The undeniable beginning guitar strains of "Kiss" played. Grinning, she hit stop. Okay, this guy not only gave her one amazing ride last night, but he was also kind of sweet. Especially given how weird her obsession with *Pretty Woman* was. She'd actually never shared that with anyone but his suite had brought the confession out of her and he'd played along. She wondered if he played piano.

With a grin, she turned on the faucets to fill the tub and dumped in a healthy amount of bubble bath, followed by another healthy amount given the size of the tub. The smell of lavender permeated the room as the water crept up the side of the tub. Checking the temperature, she dragged her fingers through the bubbles.

Not going to lie, this bath excited her in more ways than one. Her apartment had something that was supposed to pass for a bathtub, but it was so shallow, it was little more than a shower basin. Definitely not soak worthy.

She wandered through the suite to double check for Aiden, but he still wasn't there. It felt a little odd to be in his suite without him, but she wouldn't turn down a gift bubble bath for anything.

When the tub finished filling, she turned off the faucets. She dropped his shirt to the tiles and lowered her body into the warm water. She hit play on the Bluetooth speaker and skipped back to the beginning of the song. Letting the warmth ease her aching muscles, she sang along to the music. Her voice filled the huge room. When the song ended, it began over again. She laughed, the sound echoing through the bathroom.

She lounged in the tub for a while, playing with the bubbles, and listening to Prince's *Kiss* on repeat. The water stayed delightfully warm, but when she started to wrinkle, she decided she should probably get out. Only slightly disappointed that Aiden didn't show up and offer her three thousand dollars to spend the week with him. Not that she was a prostitute or even longed to be, but that was the linchpin in the movie. She wouldn't have minded sharing the bath with him either.

After a quick shower to rinse off, she slipped on the terry cloth bathrobe that hung on the bathroom door and wrapped her hair in a towel.

Surely, he had to be back by now. It was Saturday morning after all. Not a workday. Not that she knew what he did. It didn't matter because this was only a one off. He wasn't the kind of guy who would text at two in the morning two words: *U up?*

Even before she left the bedroom, the smell of coffee and fresh baked bread hit her nose. She smiled. Living a fantasy wasn't a bad thing. Aiden sat at the table in the living space. It was set for two. He read an honest to God newspaper.

She laughed as she crossed the space. "You know you don't have to keep up the fantasy."

He put the paper down and gave her a half smile. "Only if you explain your fascination with *Pretty Woman*."

Taking the chair next to him, she took a croissant from the tray. He lifted the coffee pot and gave her a questioning look. She nodded and smiled, while he poured.

"My mom and dad got a divorce when I was around eight." She took a sip of coffee, enjoying the rich brew. She could get used to the decadent life. "Mom got custody because Dad moved out of town."

She tore off a corner of the croissant and chewed on it thoughtfully. That part of the story she'd told many times. She rarely shared more than that. They divorced and tore apart their little family because Dad fell in love with someone else and Mom was supposed to be happy to see his cheating ass go. But her dad had left Phoebe behind too. The *Pretty Woman* part of the story she hadn't told anyone about.

"You don't have to tell me, if you don't want to." He lifted the cover off a tray of eggs, bacon, and hash browns. Her stomach rumbled. He dished some out onto his plate and offered her some. She nodded. Bribing her with bacon was a sure way to get her to confess.

"After last night, I want to share. After all, it isn't every day a stranger fulfills my crazy fantasies." She pulled the towel off her hair and ran her fingers through the wet strands. She draped the towel over an empty chair and took a piece of bacon off her plate. "Mom didn't take the divorce well. She didn't move off the couch for a week. I didn't know what to do, but I knew *Pretty Woman* was one of her favorite movies."

She chewed thoughtfully on the bacon for a moment, remembering how scared she had been. Her mother, her rock and now her only parent, had been a weeping mess on the couch. The man who had claimed to love them both had just left them behind without a second thought. And it had looked like she would lose her mother as well. But she knew her mother always smiled and laughed when they watched *Pretty Woman* together. Even if it wasn't the most appropriate film for an eight-year-old.

Aiden ate his breakfast, quietly waiting for her to continue.

She took a deep breath. "So I put the DVD in and played

it. Every day for a week during that summer. By the end of the summer, Mom was back to laughing and promised she would get her shit together. From then on when one of us had a bad day, we'd pop in the DVD and watch it until we felt better."

Phoebe shrugged. "It's not something I talk about, but it's not that groundbreaking either."

Aiden reached over and placed his hand over hers. She lifted her gaze to him. He said, "Thank you for sharing with me."

A warmth spread through her that wasn't sexual. She returned his smile. "Thank *you* for helping me recreate it. Champagne and strawberries, a huge bubble bath with *Kiss*, and even breakfast with fucking croissants. You are making me want the whole fairy tale."

He sat back in his chair. A flicker of concern crossed his face. "I thought you weren't into happily ever after?"

She laughed. "God, no. Not the happy ever after. That's for chumps. I'm talking about the Fairy Godmother makeover. Or in Vivian's case, a load of money and Rodeo Drive, baby."

He chuckled. "I'd have to charter us a flight to Los Angeles and still find a way to be at my job on Monday."

She shook her head, disappointedly, while smiling. "And here I thought you were the real deal."

"Probably a good thing I'm not." He filled his coffee and offered her some more. "So what's the plan then? Do we exchange numbers for future calls? Call it one and done? Negotiate terms in bed? What *are* you wearing under that robe?"

She gave him a wicked smile and stood up. "Nothing. And look, I even tied it in a bow."

His green eyes glinted with heat as he stood slowly. "Have I ever told you how skilled I am at negotiations?"

"I don't think that ever came up." She backed toward the bedroom as he stalked her. Her heart pounded with each of his steps. "Did I mention the bubble bath was lavender scented?"

She backed past the doors of the bedroom and her knees hit the bed.

"I've been smelling it all breakfast and have to say it's become one of my favorite scents." He stopped in front of her and reached for the bathrobe tie. Using the belt, he tugged her closer and leaned down until their lips were so close she could feel the warmth of his breath against hers. "How about the first one to cry mercy buys lunch?"

"You're on."

CHAPTER 4

"Do you forgive me?" Morgan showed up at Phoebe's door bright and early on Monday morning. Morgan's blond hair was pulled up into a bun. Some tall heels finished off her usual business wear of blouse and pencil skirt. She held two Starbuck's cups in her hands.

"For waking me up?" Phoebe backed up so Morgan could come in. She'd also disrupted a very naughty dream staring Aiden.

"For ditching you Friday night. I stopped by on Sunday morning to see if you wanted to run, but you weren't here." Morgan held out a coffee cup and wiggled it back and forth. "And forgive me for waking you up but I brought coffee."

"Oh." Phoebe could feel the heat flooding her cheeks, thinking about Friday night, Saturday morning, Saturday afternoon, Saturday night, Sunday morning. The things that man could do with his mouth, tongue, hands, and cock should be illegal in at least twenty states. Their one-night stand had gotten way out of hand.

Fucking Sunday morning. He'd been slow and methodical, driving her out of her mind with need and want. Something more had sparked in her at his tenderness, and it frightened her. Whatever was happening between them had been dangerous and addictive.

"Maybe it didn't turn out so bad?" Morgan lifted her eyebrow as she sat at Phoebe's little dining table that Phoebe had found while curb shopping. Sure, she had to put a few pieces of cardboard under the legs to balance it out, but someone had thrown out a perfectly good table. Morgan prompted, "Friday night?"

"Yes, Friday night didn't end badly after you ditched me. But that doesn't make it okay. We had plans." Phoebe ran her fingers through her hair and reached out to take the coffee. It was way too early in the morning for confrontations.

"Bradbury wants another proposal on a new flavor for their vodka." Morgan took a sip of her coffee. "If it had been any other client and we didn't have to spend some of this morning with the new guy, I would have dropped every-thing. I swear."

"Thank you for the coffee." Phoebe pressed her lips together. Work had to come first. She knew that. It was one of her reasons for her one-night stands instead of relation-ships. But that brought up another question. "Why are you here so early?"

"New guy starts today. I'm here to make sure you're early for once." Morgan lifted her coffee cup to her lips. "You'll be working with him the most and you are pretty much the only one able to catch him up to speed."

"Ah yes, my lacky who will do my bidding." Phoebe snick-ered as she headed toward the closet in her small bedroom.

"Not your lacky," Morgan grumbled. "He's coming in to be our dedicated account executive. Not be your slave. You've done a great job in sales, but we still need you to split your time between production management and sales. He'll be all sales with your help."

"That may be what he thinks he's walking into, but I guarantee I'll still be running the sales department too. I'll have him wrapped around my finger in no time." Phoebe grabbed her clothes and went into the bathroom to get ready. She might look like she fussed about makeup and hair, but she had getting ready fast down to an artform.

"Just meet the man. We really think the two of you will be able to work together and help grow our client base," Morgan yelled back to Phoebe.

"Teamwork is my middle name," Phoebe muttered as she applied her lipstick.

Within minutes, she and Morgan grabbed an Uber to get them to the office.

"Did you actually sleep at your apartment last night?" Phoebe asked on the way. Morgan had an apartment down the hall from hers, but she rarely stayed there these days. Drew's was closer to the office.

Morgan's cheeks flushed with color. "No, but Drew wanted to go in early, so I came to make sure you'd make it in before nine."

"It's not even eight yet." Phoebe rolled her eyes and finished her coffee.

Their office was on the middle floor of an older high rise. The building wasn't as fancy as their previous employer had been in, but it worked for them. They rode the elevator up and Phoebe swore she caught a hint of that ancient forest scent of Aiden's. It must have clung to her somehow. She needed to stop thinking of Aiden. He was long gone and out of her life. Just a slight detour. A very nice detour.

"Teammates, right?" Phoebe wanted the confirmation from Morgan without all the teasing. She was a little nervous going into this. She'd worked on building their client list without having to answer to anyone, and she couldn't be under someone's thumb again like at Hart Associates.

But the new guy would take on responsibilities she hadn't wanted and didn't have time for. "This guy and I will work together. He's not in charge of me."

Morgan nodded. "He has more experience than you with sales, but we were clear in the interview process you would be working together. Technically, on the org chart, he's ranked above you though."

Phoebe took a deep breath and pushed her sunglasses up her nose. "I don't like org charts. If he's like Thomas Baker, I get to fire him."

"No one is like Thomas Baker," Morgan scoffed. Their previous boss was a misogynistic jerk. Phoebe had smiled when she finally got to tell him where to shove his touchy-feely hands.

"If he is, though, I get to fire him," Phoebe insisted as they entered the office.

"Fine, but he's not." Morgan disappeared into her and Drew's office.

Phoebe looked around the shared space. No one else was here this early. They'd even beat the receptionist, Emily, in. They had four creatives plus Drew and Morgan.

The door opened behind her and Ben Clarke, the accountant, walked in, grumbling to himself.

"How's it going, Ben?" Phoebe casually leaned against Emily's desk.

He stopped and stared at her as if she had magically appeared in front of him in a burst of glitter. She smiled at him. He was actually an attractive man, but most of the guys in their company were hot stuff. Ben had an air of distinction to him. He couldn't be much older than them, though. Maybe it was the touch of gray in his dark hair and closely shaved beard. His eyes were a startling shade of blue.

He shook his head. "My ex-wife is coming back to town, so. . . ."

"That sucks." She hadn't known the guy was divorced.

"Yeah." He adjusted his laptop strap over his shoulder. "It sucks."

With a shrug, he disappeared into his office, closing the door without another word. And she probably wouldn't see him until next week some time.

"Hey, Phoebe."

She spun to see Emily taking her jacket off.

"Did I miss Ben?" Emily bit her lip and glanced toward the closed door that he'd disappeared behind. Her long blond hair fell in waves around her shoulder, half was pulled up into a messy bun. She was a few years younger than Phoebe and a lot sweeter too.

Phoebe nodded. "Not a good day apparently."

"I figure a smile will help anyone's day." Emily looked down at her desk and then smiled at Phoebe. "You're in early."

"New hire is due in today."

"I'll get the coffee going then." Emily nodded and put her stuff away before heading to the breakroom.

Phoebe took in a deep breath and took off her sunglasses. Mornings weren't her best time of day. Morgan typically respected that. Coffee. She shook off the tiredness and headed to the breakroom. One cup hadn't been enough for today.

"I'M SORRY I'M LATE." Morgan strode into the office and held out her hand to Aiden. "It's good to see you again."

"I'm glad to be here and can't wait to get started." Aiden shook her hand and waited for Morgan to sit next to Drew behind the desk before continuing. "You guys have made a lot of ripples in the industry. I'm sure I can help you make even more."

Aiden had been impressed by the small startup. Even more so, after his video interview with Drew. He had messy curly hair with intense blue eyes. On first impression, Aiden had thought Drew might be one of those guys who just went through the motions. Always ready with a smile and putting everyone at ease, but when it came to work that kind of guy usually passed off the actual work and took credit in the end. But then Drew had talked about the business and the future he wanted for it. Sure, they'd gotten off track a few times talking about college and the fraternities they'd belonged to, but being at the beginning of something great made Aiden want to be a part of it.

"We can't wait to see what you'll be able to do." Drew smiled and turned to Morgan. His smile softened when she met his eyes. It wasn't a colleague type look. Shifting uncomfortably in his chair, Aiden almost felt like he was intruding on an intimate moment just by being there.

He couldn't imagine being like that with anyone he'd been with in the past. Of course, he could be whoever he wanted to be now. His past wouldn't hold him back. His family's name wouldn't dictate his moves anymore.

Thoughts of the red-haired vixen from this weekend flowed through his head. They hadn't exchanged numbers. But that was probably for the best; she would have been a huge distraction. Those lips. That body. Fuck, he needed to stop thinking about her.

"We weren't sure if you would like to be in the pool or in a separate office." Morgan crossed her legs in her pencil skirt, running her hand over the wrinkle free fabric. Her hair was in a tight bun without a single lock out of place.

"The pool?" Aiden asked.

"Our creatives work in the large area with open desks.

Our other sales rep has a desk out there." Drew gestured toward the open doorway to the desks in the main area of the office. "We've got an office ready for you, but we can always make room in the pool."

"That won't be necessary." Aiden glanced over his shoulder at the open room. "I probably would be more efficient in an office."

"We can move—" Drew started.

"I don't think that would be wise." Morgan touched Drew's sleeve. "At least not until we figure out how well they work together."

"Coffee didn't win her over?" Drew arched his eyebrow at Morgan.

"It softened her edges, but I don't think we should make any changes until we see how they get along." Morgan turned and smiled at Aiden. "Do you need any coffee?"

"No, I'm good."

That didn't bode well if they were discussing the person he was supposed to work with. Working for the family business had been trying enough. Even though they were younger, his brothers had wanted to assert their dominance. Their father hadn't put up with it though, so constant strife filled the office. If Aiden had stayed any longer, the stress would have cracked him.

He loved his family. So he moved far away because he wanted to continue to love them.

"Why don't I show you to your office, and we'll get you settled in before introducing you to the rest of the staff." Morgan stood and gestured toward the door.

Aiden followed Morgan through the pool and into the smallish office. It would definitely work. Damn it, he needed to take a piss. He may have overdone it with the coffee this morning, but he hadn't gotten much sleep over the weekend and wanted to be focused this morning. "Where are the restrooms?"

"We have a single bathroom in the office, but it's currently out of order." Drew gestured to the outside doors. "Down the hall and to the left are the office building's."

Aiden nodded. "Excuse me."

A slight blonde sat behind the receptionist desk now, but she had the phone to her ear. She smiled up at him, but he didn't want to interrupt her. He'd be introduced to everyone before the end of the day.

Two other businesses were on the same floor as Taylor and King. A lawyers' office had glass doors that revealed a nice lobby. While the other office was a door with a tag beside it that said, Winston Publishing, LLC.

The bathrooms were nice at least. He washed his hands before heading out into the lobby area. The door to the women's bathroom opened, and his heart about stopped as Phoebe walked out of it. Her attention was focused on a damp spot on the side of her skirt until she lifted her gaze to him.

"What are you doing here?" they both said at the same time.

Aiden inhaled, catching her lavender fragrance and almost went hard from just her scent.

"Did you follow me here?" Aiden asked, looking over his shoulder at the door to his new job. Of course. He'd finally let down his guard and had a one-night stand with a crazy person.

"Yes, I'm a stalker and followed you from your hotel to here to what? Boil your bunny? Kill you?" The look she gave him should have shriveled any erection he had. Phoebe threw her hands in the air. "I work in this building."

"So do I." Aiden rubbed the back of his neck. Why did he

ask her that? Coincidences did happen. He hadn't just conjured her with wishful thinking.

Her eyes narrowed on him, and she crossed her arms under her magnificent breasts. "You didn't work here last week. How do I know *you* aren't a stalker?"

"I just started today."

Her mouth opened and closed like a dying fish a few times, as her eyes widened. "Nooooo."

She walked right into his new place of employment. Fuck, was she going to ruin this for him? He took off after her and came into the office to hear her talking to Morgan.

"Him?!" Phoebe pointed right at him.

"What am I missing?" Morgan looked back and forth between the two of them.

"Nothing," Aiden rushed out. He couldn't lose this opportunity.

"Nothing?" Phoebe glared up at him.

He couldn't tell his new bosses that he'd fucked this woman, who was apparently one of his coworkers, over and over all weekend long. How would that look?

"Aiden Kingston, this is Phoebe Butler. Though you two may or may not have already met?" With raised eyebrows, Drew walked up and put his hand on the small of Morgan's back. "Is that going to be a problem? You two will be working together. Maybe we should take this back to our office?"

Oh, shit. Aiden's stomach dropped like a really bad roller-coaster ride.

"Fan-fucking-tastic," Phoebe muttered.

Morgan stepped forward and put her hand on Phoebe's arm, in what looked like a comforting gesture.

"Come on, best to get this out of the way." Drew led them back into their office.

Three chairs were in front of Morgan's and Drew's desks.

Phoebe took the farthest one from him. She folded her arms over her chest and crossed her legs away from him. This wasn't a good start.

"Look, I'm not sure what history the two of you have," Morgan said with a quizzical look to Phoebe, "but our objective is to have the two of you work as a team."

Phoebe's lips were pressed tight together.

"If that's not something you two can do, then we need to know now so we can reevaluate things." Drew leaned forward with his hands clasped before him on his desk. "Is that something you both feel you can do?"

"Of course." Aiden straightened and glanced over at Phoebe's mutinous posture. "I'm sure we're both professionals and can separate work from personal."

Morgan's eyebrow raised, but before she could say anything, the phone rang.

"You should get that." Phoebe gestured to the phone. "Emily wouldn't have put it through if it weren't important."

Drew blew out a breath but picked up the phone. "Drew speaking. . . . Yes, we worked on it over the weekend."

As Drew focused on the phone call, Aiden let his gaze sweep over Phoebe. She looked just like she had Friday night with the exception of her hair being tied into a knot now. Her skirt and shirt highlighted her curves and showed off her gorgeous legs. He swallowed and turned back to face front again.

"Can I call you back in a minute?" Drew said and waited a moment before hanging up the phone. He met Aiden's gaze. "I'm really sorry, but we had a client who required a proposal as quickly as possible. We thought we'd have time this morning to go over some things with you, but apparently not."

"That's fine. Business comes first." Aiden felt Phoebe's gaze land on him.

Drew's smile filled with relief. "Phoebe, would you please show Aiden the basics? Introduce him around? Show him our software?"

Phoebe's dark eyes narrowed on Aiden again before she gave a mutinous look to Drew.

"Please," Drew added. "I swear we'll try to sort this out later."

Phoebe glanced at Morgan who nodded subtly. Some of the fight went out of Phoebe and she stood. "Of course. It would be my job after all."

When Aiden stood, Phoebe's hand wrapped around Aiden's arm. She pulled him out of the office and shut the door. No one sat at the desks as she tugged him through the office area and into his office before shutting the door behind them.

She released him immediately and put her hands on her head. She strolled around his new desk.

"I hate fucking Mondays." Phoebe sagged into the chair behind the desk. "So this is happening."

Instead of protesting her sitting in his chair, Aiden sat in the chair across the desk from her. Distance was a good thing when it came to Phoebe. "I'm beginning to see why people avoid one-night stands."

She chuckled. "Usually I avoid anyone that could possibly be a coworker. But you are fucking wealthier than Midas, so why would you need a grunt job?"

Aiden flinched. "Can we keep that between us?" Yes, he had a trust fund. Yes, he had his career because of his family, but he could have worked anywhere out of college and been at the same position he was in today.

"You mean keep it quiet that your one cufflink could probably pay for an entire year's worth of rent at my apartment building?" Phoebe didn't look impressed. No, she looked pissed at that thought.

"You aren't going to blackmail me, are you?" All the lessons his father had taught him about being careful where women were concerned were coming back to haunt him a weekend too late.

"Are you being serious right now?" Phoebe leaned forward on the desk. Her lips pressed together into a thin line and her eyebrows lifted.

The look she gave him would turn a lesser guy into stone, but even though he usually wasn't, it made him feel like a lesser guy. He shook his head, afraid to add more fuel to the fire by speaking.

"Is this ideal? No." Phoebe sat back in the chair. "For the record, I don't want a damned thing from you, except for you to do your job and I'll do mine."

Aiden nodded his head. "Fine."

"I don't play where I work." Phoebe straightened and stood. "It's unfortunate we didn't know before Friday, but what's done is done. And it is done."

Her voice left no room for protest. Not that he had planned to protest. He could take a hint. Sex would just complicate things more.

Aiden stood and got hit with her lavender scent again. They'd been all over each other all weekend. He'd thought about giving her his number multiple times, but she hadn't asked for it. He figured she must be finished with him. Fine.

"I'd appreciate you showing me around then, Ms. Butler."

She rolled her eyes. "We aren't that formal here. Phoebe is fine."

He held himself stiff as she walked past him to the door. His cock hadn't exactly gotten the message because seeing Phoebe again had made it too damned happy. This would be hell.

CHAPTER 5

It was almost noon when Phoebe finished introducing Aiden to everyone and showing him the ropes. Not the kind of ropes she would have gladly shown him over the weekend. Ugh, no more dirty thoughts about Aiden allowed.

"I'm going to lunch," she announced to Aiden as she stood. They had reviewed some of the clients she had her hooks in, but she'd had enough. His scent wove around her like a siren song while they sat in his office, and she couldn't handle it anymore. Her body hadn't received the memo that Aiden Fun Land was closed for the foreseeable future.

"We'll continue this in an hour." Aiden's eyes stayed on the report in his hand.

He'd better not be this bossy after today. She was tempted to curtsy and tell him to fuck off, but she managed to restrain herself. Instead she nodded curtly and headed into the office pool. Lacy and Jonah were working together at her desk, while Logan and Claire were across from each other at their own desks but discussing a recent Olly's dog food campaign. While Lacy and Jonah made an office relationship look easy, Phoebe knew no relationship was a cake walk, which is why she always avoided them.

Logan and Claire were besties which even Phoebe wondered if there was more going on there, but on the down low. Also probably not a wise choice. They had a small office. What happened when one of these couples inevitably imploded?

Phoebe shook her head. Drew and Morgan hadn't had a chance to talk with Phoebe and Aiden yet, but Morgan had texted Phoebe she might be able to slip away for a quick lunch.

Morgan and Drew's office door stood open, and Phoebe headed that way. She stopped in the doorway.

"Lunch now." Phoebe snapped her fingers at Morgan. "I have an hour according to my new boss."

Morgan rolled her eyes. "You're being dramatic."

"You don't want to see dramatic, so grab your purse and let's go." Phoebe stepped out of the doorway and leaned against the wall outside their office. This morning she'd been prepared to face the day after a fun weekend . Now Aiden was here and had become the person who murdered fun.

"Everything okay?" Lacy's soft voice made the whole office pause their conversations and look at Phoebe. Lacy was like everyone's little sister, except Jonah's, and everyone wanted to protect her.

On a normal Monday morning, there would have been a meeting. Then Phoebe would have worked out in the pool the rest of the morning, instead of being locked away with Aiden.

Phoebe forced a smile to not upset Lacy. "Of course. Just getting some bestie time in."

Morgan came out and grabbed Phoebe's arm, tugging her

toward the front door. Initially they'd bonded at Hart Associates because they were both working in the Luxury Goods department. Then they discovered they both enjoyed running and when an apartment became available in Morgan's building, Phoebe had moved in from her shared apartment. The nightly wine drinking had started after that.

Aiden's head lifted as they passed his office and his eyes locked with Phoebe's. It was over in a second, but damn, she needed to go find someone else or she was going to end up having hate-sex all over Aiden. At least she'd get orgasms out of the deal.

She bit her lip in the crowded elevator and waited until they were finally seated at their favorite lunch spot before saying, "Him?"

Morgan quickly ordered for both of them and handed the menus back to the server. Phoebe hadn't even bothered to pick up her menu. The server scurried away. Morgan put her hands flat on the table and sighed.

"Okay. What happened?" she said. "The guy just moved here from out of state."

Phoebe scoffed and ticked off on her fingers. "Friday night. Saturday morning. Saturday afternoon. Saturday night. Sunday morning."

Morgan sat back with her eyes wide open. "For real?"

Phoebe nodded and took a drink from her water. Morgan knew all about Phoebe's philosophy when it came to sex. Sure, she hooked up multiple times with a guy when the sex was good, but she'd never spent an entire weekend in one man's bed. Maybe a whole night, but usually in the light of day, the spark faded and she was ready to get back to her normal everyday life.

"Oh shit." Morgan grabbed her water and downed some of it.

"You're telling me." Phoebe blew out her breath. Her one-night stand had crawled into a weekend of debauchery. She'd barely managed to tear herself away on Sunday. Even now, her spine tingled thinking about it.

"It was that good?" Morgan leaned in with an eyebrow raised.

"Phenomenal."

"You had no idea who he was?"

"No last names and I didn't know the new guy's name anyway." Phoebe rubbed her temples. She definitely wouldn't have thought he'd be wealthy. "I just thought of him as new guy."

"Fuck." Morgan tapped her finger on the table. Her face screwed up as she returned her gaze to Phoebe. "Are you okay? Do you want to talk about it?"

"I'm fine. It's over." Phoebe wanted to laugh it off, but she could still feel the imprint of his fingers digging into her thighs.

Morgan chewed on her bottom lip. "Is this going to be an issue at work?"

"It's not like we have a policy against fucking coworkers." Phoebe gave Morgan a pointed look. "That's the reason you two founded this business, so you could work together and still fuck like bunnies. And don't get me started on Jonah and Lacy. Pretty sure they've christened the offices, and Lacy is one of the tamest chicks we have. Who knows who will be next? Claire and Logan are besties, but they are both attractive. I wouldn't be surprised if they were bumping uglies on the down low."

The server stopped with their drinks at Phoebe's last sentence. The server's cheeks burned bright red, and Phoebe almost laughed. Good timing.

Morgan waited for the server to run away before asking, "So you aren't going to continue to have sex with him?"

"No." God, that word made her lady bits protest. She forced a smile for Morgan. "You know me. I'm not into commitment, and I don't have many fuck buddies. Besides it would mess up the work vibe."

Phoebe wouldn't have minded adding him to her roster before, but she worried. Sunday morning had almost hit something she didn't want to think about. His libido had practically matched hers all weekend, which would make him ideal for hookups. And the orgasms had been beyond expectations.

But Sunday morning, she'd woken to soft caresses and a tenderness that had been missing before. His kisses had made her ache but not just in a physical way. They were saying goodbye, and it had damn near broken her heart. If she even had a heart left to break.

"I don't see a problem then." Morgan took a sip of her soda. "You don't get attached, so if there's a problem, it will come from him. This is a new job for him so my guess is he won't let this thing get in the way."

"Okay. Maybe. But this guy is way too dominant and bossy. This isn't going to be a partnership." Phoebe shivered remembering how he took charge of her pleasure. She really needed to get whatever this was in check.

"I'm coming back to this as a friend, but first as coworkers, you two will be able to work through this. Drew and I can bring you both in this afternoon between appointments to talk things over. All partnerships need work at first until the two of you figure out how you can come together."

"He's got that down," Phoebe mumbled.

Morgan raised her eyebrow and then shook her head. "Stop trying to distract me. Give him a chance. I'm sure down the road you guys having sex will just be a distant memory."

Phoebe made a disbelieving noise as the server brought

their lunch. The server dropped their plates in front of them, quickly asked if they needed anything else, and then ran away as swiftly as possible. Phoebe stifled a chuckle.

Morgan sat up straighter and leaned forward. "I'm not usually one to ask for details but you usually are really eager to give them. All weekend long? How did that happen?"

Phoebe opened her mouth to spill the tea about everything that happened this weekend, but the words caught in her throat. She'd promised to not tell anyone that Aiden was loaded and that would be half the story. The hotel room. The fantasy. As much as she loved Morgan, she wasn't about to share her *Pretty Woman* story with her. Morgan knew about her mother, but she didn't know the particulars about Phoebe growing up. Morgan and she shared a job and being fresh out of college in the real world together. They'd talked a little about growing up, but Phoebe hadn't wanted Morgan's pity over her sad childhood.

Besides, Aiden wasn't supposed to exist outside the bubble of the weekend. She wasn't sure she would have shared him with Morgan like she always did with other guys, even if Aiden hadn't shown up at her work. He had been a fantasy brought to life in a lot of ways.

"Come on, Phoebe." Morgan took a bite of her sandwich. "You told me all about Alex's crooked penis. The bartender that coughed when he came. Don't get me started about the guy whose spunk tasted slightly lemony. I'm not asking for details like that. I never ask about details but you always give them."

Morgan was right. With every other guy, she'd been more than willing to spill all the details, so why was she clamming up about Aiden? She shook off the memory of his soft kisses on Sunday morning. Fuck it.

"We met at the bar. He bought me dinner. We went to his room and screwed our brains out all weekend. The end."

Phoebe held up her hand. "Wait, not the end. Monday morning he's suddenly my coworker or boss, depending on who you ask, so it will never end."

"He's your teammate, but he'll have more responsibilities in the sales team than you. You still report to us and not him."

Phoebe could almost see Morgan take off her boss hat and put back on the friend hat.

Morgan frowned and took a few more bites before she met Phoebe's gaze. "It must have been good for you to stay all weekend."

Phoebe laughed. "Either that or he tied me up as his sex slave the entire time. I just happened to get away Sunday so that I could come in to work on Monday, because he's considerate like that."

Morgan rolled her eyes. "Okay, so you don't want to talk about Aiden and sex. He is good looking though."

"I do have good taste," Phoebe admitted. "But I'm finished with him. We didn't even exchange numbers. If he hadn't shown up at work, I never would have seen him again."

"You've run into hookups before." Morgan shrugged.

Mostly because Phoebe went to the same bars and clubs. Aiden had been different.

Phoebe thought about those gold cufflinks, his silk tie, and Armani suit. She shook her head. "Trust me, we would have never seen each other again."

AFTER LUNCH, Phoebe spent a total of fifteen minutes in Aiden's office. She showed him what files to look at even though it meant leaning next to him at his desk and taking in his scent and heat. It was worth it when she went back to her own desk in the middle of the chaos that was their office pool.

She put her head down and worked on the new accounts. She also worked as project manager on the other end. Once the client approved of the concept, she helped coordinate the vendors they needed because they didn't have a full-time art department.

"Is this the sexy redhead at Taylor and King?" Jason McAlister answered his cell phone.

Phoebe grinned. "Is this the tall, dark, and gorgeous photographer for hire?"

"What's up, sweetheart?" Jason's voice was a nice tenor, and after the morning she'd had, Phoebe could use a relaxing flirt with the photographer.

"Got a job. You interested?"

"For you? Always."

She could practically see his wink. Jason was classic tall, dark, and handsome. His brown hair had an unruly wave to it and laid haphazardly over his almost black eyes. He probably wasn't as tall as Aiden, but she still had to look up at him when he showed up in the office. She hadn't lied when she told Aiden she didn't mix business with pleasure. As long as he worked with their company, Jason was officially off-limits and that suited her just fine.

"Want to meet for lunch tomorrow to discuss?" Jason was quick to add. It didn't stop him from trying though.

Phoebe opened her mouth to turn him down, but at that moment Aiden walked out of his office. His green eyes stopped on her. He leaned against his doorway just looking at her. All arrogance and cockiness that only made her want him more.

"I think lunch sounds fantastic, Jason. We have a scenario in mind for the photoshoot." Phoebe leaned back in her chair and held Aiden's gaze. "We want the kind of sexy that smacks you in the face when you see it on the page."

"Well, bring it, darling," Jason practically purred in her ear. "How about I get there a little before so we can look over comps before heading out."

"Perfect. See you tomorrow." Phoebe ended the call but still didn't drop her gaze from Aiden.

"Can I see you in my office?" Aiden's voice rippled through her, pulling at the desire he sparked within her and holding it tight.

She nodded sharply, grabbing her tablet. "Of course."

No one else in the office paid attention to them. It was late in the afternoon and a Monday so most of them would be leaving shortly. Right now the company had a balanced load of client work. So most of the staff got to go home at a regular hour.

Drew and Morgan had gotten sidetracked with the Bradbury account again, so they hadn't found time to have a talk with Aiden and Phoebe.

Phoebe stepped into Aiden's office.

"Close the door please." He gestured absentmindedly, as he took his seat behind his desk.

"I feel like I've been called to the principal's office," Phoebe said and closed the door.

"I don't know how you work out there." Aiden rubbed at his temples. "The chatter is constant and aggravating."

She shrugged as she sank into the chair across from him. "I started on the creative side so it helps me think."

Straightening her skirt over her knees, she crossed her legs and lifted her gaze to Aiden. His eyes were locked on her legs. A pulse hit between them.

"You needed me?" The words were meant to be innocent, but her voice came out breathy.

His darkened gaze lifted to hers. Clearing his throat, he

closed his eyes. When he opened his eyes, he looked at his computer screen.

"We should coordinate how we approach these clients. Develop a strategy." Aiden sat back in his chair. "I understand that you also help with project management, but we need to be on target with new clients."

"On target?"

He'd been here a day—what the hell was he talking about. What target?

"I've gone over the past few months to figure out where we should be at the end of the year. We need to put together a plan for the next five years if we want to see any real growth." Aiden rested his linked hands on the desk. "I want to come up with a list of clients we want on our roster and how we can go about winning them over."

Phoebe bristled. She couldn't help it. The growth they'd seen had been due to her, Morgan, and Drew, but mostly her. She'd agreed they should hire an Account Executive to manage new business, because frankly the long hours wore on her. She also hoped it would free up Morgan so they could at least find a few hours to hang out.

She'd been freed from working beneath their past employer's thumb. No more having to run everything past him or avoiding being alone with Thomas Baker. No more snide comments about how well she was doing for being a woman. Now she had autonomy in her work. Morgan and Drew trusted her to get things done and to do them well without breathing down her neck.

Granted, part of the bristle was likely because she'd been on her knees for this man more than once over the past weekend. Sure, he'd returned the favor, but now he wanted to come in to her business and tell her what *they* needed to do. After one fucking day on the job. Arrogant much?

"We can do that when you are caught up to speed and

know what the fuck you're talking about." Her voice may have been calm but a hint of disdain tarnished her tone. Phoebe recrossed her legs, knowing it would draw his gaze. She knew how to use the weapons in her arsenal and wouldn't shy away from her sex appeal. "We've had a solid growth curve, but we can't take on more without growth in other areas, such as the creative team and administrative. Eventually we'll need to internalize our art department or those costs will overrun everything. Those types of discussions should be held with Morgan Taylor and Drew King because it directly affects their finances."

"I wasn't brought in here to twiddle my thumbs, Phoebe." When he said her name, the way he said it was exactly how he'd said it over the weekend. Worse, he pinned her with those green eyes. Her body throbbed. Fuck, she'd given him weapons against her without even realizing it. "I'm here to do a job and that job is managing the accounts and determining when we need to grow or scale back. I don't need permission to do that."

"Bullshit." Phoebe stood and leaned her hands against his desk. "This is a team not a fucking dictatorship. *We* didn't bring you in here to lead shit. We brought you in to keep me from having to work ludicrous hours to keep up with everything."

Aiden rose slowly from his chair to tower over her. "Obviously one of us is under a misconception of what is going on here."

"If you say it's me, I'll fucking scream." Phoebe straightened and puffed out her chest. "I've been with this company since the beginning. I'm the one who had to use my savings to make sure I didn't starve when we started out. I had to claw tooth and nail to get each of our initial clients, and I'm not about to let some rich fucker come in and lay claim to my department."

Aiden's lips pressed into a line. "We should talk with the owners."

"Damn straight we should." The heat in this room must be boiling because Phoebe wanted to fan herself. She wasn't being rational, but after less than a day, the guy wanted to take on all this extra work. He should pick up the slack. Not bury them further. What the fuck?

CHAPTER 6

"HOW CAN WE HELP YOU?" Drew asked, warily, as he nudged Morgan to make her look at the doorway where Aiden and Phoebe stood together.

Not exactly together, Aiden noted. Phoebe held herself away from him so they wouldn't touch. She rolled her eyes at his look and moved into the office.

"Apparently, we need to have that talk about what exactly you want the two of us to do." Phoebe dropped elegantly into one of the chairs in front of their desks. She gave Morgan a pointed look.

Drew's brow furrowed. "What do you mean?"

Aiden cleared his throat. "The nature of our department and who does what is up for discussion."

"All right." Drew leaned back, rocking in his office chair for a moment. Aiden could almost see the wheels turning in Drew's head as he closed his laptop. "We have time for this now. I'm sorry we've had to put it off."

"Clarity would be good," Phoebe said with a biting tone.

Drew's gaze sought Morgan's, and she gestured at him to

take the lead. He leaned forward, bracing his elbows on the desk.

"We are a small business and want to grow, but slowly, at an acceptable rate without stretching our resources. Including our current leased office space."

Phoebe gave him an, *I told you so* look. Aiden tried to ignore it and focus on Drew.

"The past few months have been good to us and we were able to expand our employees and give some bonuses to those who took a chance on us from the beginning. As part of that expansion, we decided we could use someone specifically in the sales department. Which would be you."

Aiden restrained himself from smirking at Phoebe and saying, *see*. He was a professional, after all.

Phoebe scooted to the edge of her seat. "Of course, he's the one working full time on sales, but I have more experience in this company. Even though I also work in creative, most of my energy goes to sales. The department is still both of us, and one of us isn't above the other."

She gave Aiden a look that said she was most definitely above him. Unfortunately, his brain spun that to the image of her taking him into her that first time. Losing himself in her dark eyes and that amazing body, he blinked a few times to get his mind back to the conversation at hand.

"Yes, Aiden, you are technically the account executive." Morgan folded her hands on top of the desk. "But Phoebe has been with us from the start. We've worked with her for years, and she knows what our goals are. We can't force too much growth until we are ready to expand our resources. You two should be able to find common ground or at least a mutual understanding."

Morgan's gaze stopped on Phoebe.

"Before we make any changes, why don't you two figure out how to make the department work for you both?" Drew straightened in his chair. "Spend two weeks figuring out where we are at and how you two can work together and get to know our way of doing things. Phoebe knows what we've done and how we've been doing it. If you guys have problems, come to us. Otherwise, we'll revisit this then and if we need to, figure out how to divide the work. But I'm hoping you two are adult enough to hash this out."

Well fuck. That didn't go as well as Aiden had hoped. Had he not fucked her all weekend maybe he would have suggested that to Phoebe from the beginning but seeing her here had put him on edge.

"Of course," Aiden said. "We should be able to sort things out and then move on. I would love to discuss strategic planning with all of us after that time frame, so we can all be on the same page going forward."

"We can definitely schedule something," Morgan said. "Are we good to move forward from here?"

"Apparently that's it for now." Phoebe gave both Morgan and Drew a sour look before she rolled her eyes and turned to Aiden. "Can we go now? Mom and Dad want us to sort out our own fight."

"Phoebe." Drew shook his head. "We're all trying to be professionals here."

She stuck her tongue out at him as she stood. "I still have that Tinder profile ready to go and I even have an updated photo."

"I told you to delete that," Morgan said. Her eye twitched slightly.

Drew just laughed. "What is it this time? Are we done with Furries? What's next? Burly men with huge cocks or maybe, chicks only into feet need apply."

Aiden blinked as he looked back and forth between the other three people. What were they talking about? Did he even want to know?

"I still think the photoshopped chains add that certain something that you're lacking." Phoebe moved to the door. "You should really look at investing in some. Not the necklace kind though. I'm sure Morgan wouldn't mind. She likes being tied—"

"Out, Phoebe." Morgan's face glowed red as she pointed to the door.

Phoebe gave them a wicked smile and turned to the door. "Just remember who holds the cards in this relationship. Hint, it's not you two."

Aiden stood as Phoebe strolled out of the office. "Any helpful advice with that one?"

Drew shook his head. "Don't make her your enemy. Honestly, I think you two could make a good team or I wouldn't have brought you in."

Morgan smiled. "Phoebe just needs time to adjust. She doesn't deal well with change and our last boss tried to undermine her whenever he could. Both Drew and I feel you two could make a difference to this company."

Aiden nodded and drew in a breath before he followed Phoebe. She'd settled at her desk. The rest of the pool was empty so Aiden took the nearest chair and sat.

The door to Drew and Morgan's office closed softly behind them.

"You and I have to figure this out," Aiden said.

Phoebe kicked off her shoes and put her feet up on her desk. Her hands rested on her stomach and she tipped her head back. Her eyes shut like she was going to take a nap. "When you admit this is my circus and my monkeys."

Aiden studied her. He didn't know much about his opponent. At least not how she worked. He'd learned plenty about her appetite for sex. His previous lovers hadn't been as into sex as Phoebe seemed. He and Phoebe had spent hours figuring out each other's bodies. And even after their weekend marathon, he still wanted more of her. Craved to know more.

Of course, now that would never happen. He wouldn't start his new career with such a mark on his record. Having sex with Phoebe in the recent past was fine. It complicated things, but eventually they'd work through it. To continue to have sex though—he couldn't afford to be labeled as the guy who has sex with his coworker, in addition to the one who only got as far as he did because he went to work for daddy out of college.

Aiden sighed and ran his hand over his jaw. "What does that even mean?"

"Meaning, we'll run the show my way until you get the hang of it. Just like Drew said." Her eyes opened. Her gaze ran down the length of him, making his cock twitch. Her gaze settled on his groin like she knew what she did to him. "Once you know how our ropes work, then maybe I'll let you play with them."

Her gaze lifted to meet his. Would she be like this every day? The innuendos. The low-key flirting. Was that just who Phoebe Butler was, or was she the woman who got excited over bubble bath and "Kiss?" The one thing he knew for certain was Phoebe wouldn't hold her punches. If she wanted something, she went after it. Which in sales was a good thing.

"We need to learn to work together. Figure out a strategy as a team. Even while I learn the ropes. But I have a stake in this, too. It's not just your circus anymore. It's ours."

"Are you sure you want to play? It would be easier if you just sat back and watched." Her eyebrow cocked up and her lips parted slightly. Her fingernail traced the opening of her blouse.

This woman could make a monk throw off his robes and disavow God to be with her. And Aiden was no monk. But this was part of Phoebe's power move. He was beginning to understand her. Unfortunately, it wasn't a game he knew how to play. Yet.

"Yes, Phoebe."

She bit her lip when he said her name. If she didn't fascinate him so damn much, he might have missed it. He took note of the reaction for future use.

"We have two weeks to figure out if this 'partnership' will work." She stood and stretched. Her clothes clung to her curves he was intimately familiar with. His gaze stopped on her dancing brown eyes. "You have a lot of catching up to do. I'm sure everything will eventually sink in."

He stood, forcing her to tip her chin up to keep meeting his eyes. "I'm a fast learner."

She gave him a smile and patted his chest with her hand. "Good."

~

Day two, Phoebe decided to stroll in after nine as usual. Carrying her Starbucks, wearing her shades, and having no fucks left to give. Sleep had been elusive last night but she'd finally gotten some after she let herself work out some of her issues with Aiden.

Her favorite toy hadn't been quite as effective as the man himself, but it had done the trick.

"How are you this morning, Emily?" She paused at Emily's desk knowing she couldn't walk past Aiden's office without him seeing her. *If* his door was open. So the other purpose of stopping was to determine if his door was open. Unfortunately, the angle was wrong and she'd need to lean back to see. He might see her trying to look.

"I'm good. Do you think Ben will go to happy hour this Friday?"

Phoebe had been so distracted trying to see Aiden's door she almost missed Emily's flushed cheeks and downcast eyes. Interesting.

"You know it's my life mission to get that guy to come out with us." Phoebe tapped her finger on the counter. Now more than ever if sweet Emily had a little crush. "Leave it to me. I have my ways."

Emily gave her a small smile. The phone rang and she picked it up.

The check for Aiden's door plan didn't pan out, but now Phoebe had a little matchmaking to do. She took a sip of her Starbuck's and pushed her sunglasses into place. She'd worn a different wrap dress today just to torment Aiden, but she still wanted to make it to her desk before he called her into his office.

She wanted him to have to come to her.

She also didn't want to look like she was sneaking past his door though. She gave her hair a little fluff and strolled into the main office.

"Looking good, Butler." Logan smirked at her. He was a couple of years younger than her, but hot with short dark hair and golden-brown eyes. One hundred percent her male equivalent. She gave him a blinding smile as she set her stuff on her desk.

"Right back at you, O'Connell." She gave him a wink before lowering herself into her seat. "Anything pressing this morning?"

She glanced around at the four others in the pool. Various nopes or shrugs were all that she got.

"Great, an easy day then." Phoebe's gaze was drawn to the very closed door of Aiden's office. She didn't want to ask if he was in. Nope, that gave him too much power. Besides, if he was anything like Morgan, he'd be in.

If he wanted Phoebe, he could come and find her.

She slipped off her sunglasses and put them on her desk while she started her computer. Before long, she was knee-deep in the latest acquisition that Jonah and Lacy had brought in.

She reached for her coffee cup and found it empty. Grabbing her mug, she headed into the breakroom. Lacy stood holding her own cup, watching the slow drip of the coffee machine.

"How's it going?" Phoebe asked as she leaned against the counter to wait.

"Good." Lacy's brown eyes lit up and she sat down in one of the chairs. She'd always seemed like a little sister you had to look out for until Jonah came along and pried her out of her shell. "How's the new guy? I haven't even seen him at the coffee machine yet."

What could Phoebe say about Aiden? He was a spectacular lover, but too damn serious at work. Probably not wise to spread that around. The lover part.

"Yeah." The door closed as Claire stepped into the breakroom. Claire looked like a model with her high heels, perfectly coiffed dark hair, and makeup that accented her dark eyes. "What is his deal? Is he going to haunt the joint like Ben or actually come out once in a while?"

Phoebe laughed at the idea of him haunting the office. "I'm sure he'll make his presence known."

"Why do we keep hiring hot guys?" Claire stepped forward as the coffee stopped dripping and held the pot out toward Lacy first. As she poured Lacy's and then hers and finally Phoebe's cups, she bemoaned, "A woman can only handle so much man candy before she's forced to indulge."

"I always thought you and Logan—" Phoebe stopped as Claire burst out laughing.

"Logan's a good friend, but that's it." Claire leaned against the wall. "Jonah obviously always had a thing for Lacy, but Aiden is positively yummy."

Phoebe's chest burned as she forced a smile to her lips. "That he is."

Claire could tempt Aiden easily. She was attractive and smart. She was also a huge football fan.

Lacy smiled and sipped at her coffee. "He seems nice."

Phoebe's chest eased as she thought about how considerate Aiden had been over the weekend. Of course, they'd also had sex which made a lot of guys nicer. He almost seemed standoffish with her in the office.

She glanced at her phone and noticed the time. She frowned. She needed to finish getting ready for her appointment with Jason.

"Gotta get back to work." Phoebe slipped out of the breakroom and glanced toward Aiden's closed door. Her brow furrowed as she sat at her desk and picked up her pen. Almost eleven o'clock and she hadn't heard from Aiden yet. He had shown up for work today, right? He didn't seem like the type to give up easily.

The others followed her out of the breakroom and settled back into work. She pulled up the information for her meeting and made a few notes.

She bit the end of her pen and studied his door to see if she could see light underneath, which would mean absolutely nothing since the window shade could be up even if he wasn't in there.

Setting down her pen, she turned back to her computer screen. A notification popped up in the corner. She clicked on it and an instant message from Aiden showed.

Need to see you in my office.

The fuck?

Not unless you say please, she typed back. He didn't even have the decency to come out of his office to get her.

Please. Though we are coworkers and shouldn't need to waste time.

She grinned. *It took you longer to explain that then it did to type please.*

I assume you have time in your schedule now since the only thing in your calendar is your meeting with the photographer.

I'm very busy. You shouldn't assume.

She almost heard his sigh through the door. She shouldn't be getting a buzz from this conversation but it struck her in a way that tickled her insides.

Please come into my office.

She considered it for a moment. *Maybe you should come to my office.*

Jonah and Logan were discussing the latest dog food campaign and which dog breed was better and why. Great Danes vs. German Shepherds. Drew and Morgan were arguing over the final ad copy on a perfume campaign with Lacy and Claire at the conference table. It was chaos and she thrived in it.

The door opened to Aiden's office, and he leaned against the doorjamb. His eyebrow lifted at her and the noise level out here. She shrugged and gave him a smile. *My circus. My monkeys.*

He looked good today in his slacks and dress shirt. He didn't have a tie on so the top buttons of his shirt parted at his throat, and she could just see the edge of a hickey she'd given him on Saturday. That shouldn't turn her on, but it did.

Who was she kidding? The guy turned her on full stop.

Backing up a step, he gestured for her to enter. She stood and closed her laptop. Her skirt swirled around her knees as she walked toward him. His eyes took in every inch of her, pausing on the tie to her dress, which almost made her knees buckle.

His heated gaze lifted to hers as she reached the doorway.

"Please," he said and bowed his head to her.

If her panties hadn't already been wet, that word would have soaked them. He had that effect on her. She nodded at him as she took the chair in front of his desk. He closed the door and the office chaos dampened to a light murmur.

"How much of your time is spent on project management?" Aiden's voice sent shivers down her spine as he moved around his desk to take his seat.

"Depends on the week. At the beginning of a campaign, it could take a few hours to a few days to arrange everything, and that depends on the size of the campaign." Phoebe crossed her legs and rested her hands on her lap. "Why do you want to know?"

"I want to get a handle on how much time you have to devote to sales." Aiden typed something into his computer.

She couldn't see the monitor from this angle. She opened her mouth to ask him what he was doing.

"Do you keep track of your time by client?" Aiden paused in his typing to ask.

"What do you mean?" She narrowed her eyes at him and leaned back in the chair, trying to convey an ease she didn't feel. She knew full well what time tracking involved. They'd had to do it at Hart Associates and she continued to do that. But what she didn't know was what was he trying to get at. Was he still trying to convince Drew and Morgan that he should be in charge? Because her time varied depending on what needed attention.

"Basically, it's a time sheet where you keep track of what you are working on to the quarter of an hour or by specific time." Aiden didn't turn to look at her, so he missed her quizzical brow. Like she needed him to explain time tracking. Fine, she'd continue to fuck with him.

"I don't even keep track of how many hours I work in a

day." She did. She had a full Excel sheet dedicated to her time tracking.

Aiden took his hands away from the keyboard and finally turned to meet her eyes. "That needs to change. We both need to keep track of what we work on and for how long. By client and by task."

Phoebe's insides clenched in protest because he was the one asking. "You want me to keep track of when I use the bathroom and get coffee too?"

Aiden shook his head. "Of course not."

"Oh, well, good then because I thought you might be a little unreasonable." She rolled her eyes. "Besides being a huge pain in my ass, what exactly will this prove?"

"I want to figure out how to best allocate responsibility. To do that, I need to know how much time certain tasks take us." Aiden's gaze dropped down to the knot on her dress.

She ignored the heat that pooled inside of her because the heat from her temper spiked at his words. Raising her eyebrow, she gave him a look of disdain. "Is that all you need? Because honestly this could have been communicated over IM instead of beckoning me like I'm your personal secretary."

Aiden leaned back in his chair. His gaze floated over her as he thought about his next words.

She crossed her arms under her chest, highlighting the cleavage she had showing. She lowered her voice slightly when she said, "What else do you need, Aiden?"

His gaze flicked to her lips before lifting to her eyes. "I'd like to sit down this afternoon and go over the client files together."

"We can use the other office. It's easier to spread out in there." Phoebe gave him a tight smile as she stood. "By the way, if you look in the administration directory on the server, you'll find mine and all the others' time tracking spreadsheets."

His lips pressed together. "I'll message you when I'm ready to go over the files."

Phoebe clenched her fists at his order but kept her smile. "Of course it will have to be after my lunch date."

CHAPTER 7

Lunch date. Those words kept spinning around Aiden's head long after Phoebe sashayed out of his office. He'd heard her flirting on the phone yesterday with someone. She had photographer meeting on her calendar so maybe she did mix business and pleasure when she wanted to.

She'd left his door wide open which meant he had the perfect view of her profile at her desk. And that fucking dress.

He couldn't even get up to close the door. He'd been hard as a rock since she walked into his office. If she had a preference for that style of dress, he was fucked. When she'd been in his office, he had to focus on his computer screen instead of her perfect figure gift wrapped especially for him. Her lavender scent hung in the air, tormenting him.

Her lunch date had dinged his pride but didn't stop him from wanting her. Was this one of her usual hookups? Which brought up other questions that bruised his ego. Why hadn't she asked for his number after their weekend? They'd been fucking fantastic together in bed or out of bed. In the shower. That fucking shower.

Reminiscing about her luscious breasts with water cascading over them didn't help the situation below his belt. A voice drew him back to present.

A tall, good-looking man walked over to Phoebe's desk. His dark hair was long but stylish. He had dark jeans, a black shirt with a leather jacket over it. It was like he was trying to project the bad boy look. What a cliché.

Phoebe stood to greet him and gave the guy a hug. Her smile was huge and she laughed at something the guy said. Aiden's gut knotted. A couple of the others stopped and greeted the guy.

Phoebe drew him over to the conference table and set up her tablet. The guy sat directly next to her. What if it was more than casual?

Fortunately, Aiden calmed down enough that he could stand without everyone knowing what Phoebe did to him. Grabbing his coffee mug, he headed toward the breakroom, keeping one eye on the guy and Phoebe at the conference table.

"Oh, Aiden." Phoebe's voice startled him.

He stopped and made his way over to the conference table.

Phoebe looked up at him with a twinkle in her eye. "Aiden Kingston, this is one of our best photographers, Jason McAlister."

Aiden held out his hand. A little peeved at the way she emphasized *best*. Jason had a vibe that women tended to like. A lot.

Jason stood and took Aiden's hand. "Good to meet you. Are you one of the fantasy weavers in this joint?"

Jason's grip was solid, and Aiden released his hand quickly.

"I'm the Account Executive." Aiden dropped his hand to his side and glanced at Phoebe.

"Cool. I'd rather listen to Phoebe tell me the latest fantasy than some dude any day." Jason smiled and winked at Phoebe.

"This is part of your process, Phoebe?"

Her cheeks flushed pink for a second as she met his eyes. "The production manager side."

"Mind if I sit in?" Aiden flashed her a grin, daring her to say no. She'd have to make up some reason if she wanted to be alone with this guy.

"Of course not." She gestured to the chair on the other side of Jason with that mischievous look in her eyes.

Ignoring the place she wanted him, Aiden went to the other side of Phoebe and sat beside her at the table. He purposely brushed his knee against her legs. Jason resumed his own seat and Phoebe faced her tablet.

"This campaign is for a new cologne named Petrichor." Phoebe opened the client file and the vision board from Jonah and Lacy. "The idea is a hot day, dryness in the air, and those first drops of rain. They want several photos to choose from."

"Sex that reaches up and smacks you," Jason's low voice said. Aiden noticed Jason seemed far more focused on Phoebe than on the campaign she wanted to hire him for.

"Definitely." She threw some sketches on the screen. "A couple caught in the rain. Making out. Clothes clinging to their bodies from the heat."

Aiden blinked a few times to get the image of Phoebe in the rain out of his head. His father's company dealt with a lot of family products. The type of ads they produced were family-friendly and cute. This was definitely new to him. Good thing he appreciated a challenge.

Besides, his job was to sell his team to the client to get their foot in the door. The team would be the ones to close the deal with their original campaigns.

"Any specifications on models?" Jason leaned in close to Phoebe, and Aiden almost couldn't hear him when he added, "You and me could make the rain steam."

"You know it." Phoebe laughed and moved a little so that her chair effectively pushed Jason back. She glanced at her screen. "We have reservations to make. We can finish discussing this over lunch."

Her gaze caught Aiden's for a minute. Molten pools of rich chocolate drew him in, making him want to drown in her. Her lips parted slightly and he almost leaned in to claim them as he had done so many times over the weekend. Kissing her was almost like art coming to life. Everything about it was perfection and temptation.

"Sorry you didn't get to watch everything," she said with a gleam in her eyes. "Maybe next time you can watch until I finish."

Her red lips curled into an inviting smile. She knew exactly what she was saying and what it would do to him. She had to.

Phoebe stood and he purposely stood at the same time, knowing she wouldn't back Jason's way and risk running into him. Her little tactic with the chair meant they weren't actually having sex, but Jason wanted to. She wouldn't play coy if she wanted someone. Aiden knew that firsthand.

Phoebe's body brushed against Aiden's. Her eyes widened as she looked up at him.

"I'm always available to watch." His voice was low to keep this to her ears only. "Any time."

Heat flared in her eyes. She sucked in a breath, moving away from him. Her plastic smile formed on her lips as she turned to Jason. "Shall we head out?"

"Sounds good." Holding out his hand, Jason stepped closer to Aiden. "Good to meet you, man."

"Same."

They both became distracted when Phoebe leaned over to pick up her tablet. Her ass displayed beautifully under the flowing skirt of her dress. He wanted to grab those hips and sink into her until they both needed to catch their breaths.

Realizing they were still holding hands, the guys both withdrew at the same time. Jason flashed Aiden a knowing grin, but Aiden kept his smile small and professional. Leering at a woman's ass wouldn't bond Jason and him. Especially when that ass was Phoebe's.

"See you later." Phoebe winked at Aiden before she headed out the door with Jason.

The only good news from that interaction was that those two wouldn't be having sex. Jason might be interested, but Phoebe wasn't. Aiden stood there for a moment and released a long breath. With a slight smile, he headed back to his office.

WORKING with Aiden hadn't been as much of a chore as those first few days. They found almost a rhythm for the rest of the week. Phoebe walked into the office Friday morning actually feeling good about the day. Not only was it the end of a stressful week, but it was the beginning of the weekend.

Happy hour Friday. And because Aiden was the new guy, everyone would be coming. Including Ben. After much sweet-talking from yours truly. But first she had to get through the day.

Busy on the phone, Emily smiled at her as Phoebe passed the front desk and headed to the breakroom. She'd finished her Starbuck's before she got here and needed more caffeine to get through the morning meetings.

Everyone had already moved to the conference table or were heading that way. Glancing down at her phone, she opened the door to the breakroom and inhaled that ancient forest scent that went straight to her core. She looked up to lock eyes with Aiden's green ones.

Things hadn't been easier between them, just less of a chore as they figured out how to deal with each other and the lingering attraction between them. Ignoring the attraction during the day and getting herself off before bed every night seemed to help.

"Morning," Aiden said, his voice a little huskier than normal. The same tone his voice had been in her dreams. She'd woken up mid-dream last night as dream Aiden had continued to make her orgasm over and over. Her body had found release from the dream, and she had still throbbed when she woke up. Sleep had evaded her after that. Therefore, coffee.

"Morning." She moved to grab a coffee mug and waited for him to finish pouring his cup.

He lifted the coffee pot to indicate he would pour for her. She shrugged and held out her mug. She wished she could forget the feel of those fingers gliding over her skin. His lips against hers. That perfect cock of his as it slid deep inside her.

He cleared his throat, and she saw that he'd finished. Hell, she almost finished too.

"Sorry," she murmured and sipped some of the hot coffee.

"Big plans for the weekend?" Aiden's voice startled her. He rarely talked to her unless it was about work and even then, he was practically curt.

"Not in particular." She could feel the warmth spreading through her body. Only part of it was from the coffee. Getting laid was a high priority, but she wouldn't tell him that. "You?"

He shook his head.

"Still living in the hotel?"

"For now."

She sighed. The conversation between them last weekend had been much easier than this. But there were limits that even she wouldn't cross at work. At least when it came to Aiden. She didn't want to know if he had decided to explore hookups and one-night stands. If he would try out her cheesy pick-up lines on some random this weekend. If he would lure a woman back to his hotel and make her his over and over. She took a deep breath.

Seriously, with his money and looks, all he had to do was wink at a lady and she'd be willing to go. Fuck, if he winked at Phoebe, she might be crazy enough to go for another round. Things might be a hell of a lot more complicated, but he had been so in tune with her. And the things they'd done. . . . She sipped her coffee and let its heat sink through her body. She could go for a repeat.

"We should probably join the others."

Had he been watching her while she was thinking? She glanced up at him and he shrugged. Maybe he was as tired as she was. She would power through the day and find some reserve of energy to get her through the happy hour.

She followed him out to the conference table where she wished she had her sunglasses. Dozing behind them had become a favorite pastime during some of these meetings. The meetings had become quite monotonous. Business was good. The wonder twins, Logan and Claire, were doing amazing. The horny couple, Jonah and Lacy, were doing awesome. And the bosses, Morgan and Drew, were thriving.

Aiden's knee brushed hers under the table, sending sparks along her skin. Of course he had to sit next to her. She definitely needed to get some tonight and probably tomorrow night and Sunday night and then maybe her body wouldn't act like a needy bitch every time he got close to her.

This level of attraction was new to her. Yes, she'd had

guys who made her see stars before, but usually once the initial appeal wore off, she was done. On to another target. She and Aiden had spent a whole weekend exploring each other, and she still didn't feel like she'd had enough of him.

The main reason she hadn't asked for his number was she was afraid she *couldn't* get enough of him. If she'd added him to her phone, he'd become speed dial number one as he could give her orgasm after orgasm. Even now, after he'd made her work life hell, she wanted him balls deep inside her, making her scream. She didn't need that kind of noise in her life. That was the kind of attraction that bordered on obsession.

The other reason? He was filthy rich. Probably even obscenely wealthy. Yes, slumming it with her had probably ticked some wish list item off some rich dude bucket list, but it couldn't last. Everything about them was different. When she was first out on her own, she'd struggled to make ends meet. Sometimes she had to choose which utility would have to be turned off for the month. It was better now, but that shit stuck with you.

He probably didn't even know what packaged ramen tasted like. Which was a shame because she still had it at least once a week. Things weren't as tight now that the business had grown, but she liked that being frugal kept her feeling real. He probably hadn't spent a minute of his life in a thrift store. Hell, he was probably rich enough that the stores came to him.

"Phoebe?" Morgan's voice drew her attention. Everyone looked at her like she'd missed something important.

"Yeah," she said, sitting up a little straighter.

Drew chuckled until Morgan sent him a look. "We were asking how production was coming along on the Petrichor print ad."

Work. Yup, she was still here.

"Hired Jason as photographer, and he's sent over a few

models he thinks might work as well as some scouting locations." Phoebe took a small sip of coffee. "I got those late last night, so I'll be forwarding them to Jonah and Lacy for a final look and approval."

Morgan smiled at her and gave her a slight questioning look, which Phoebe shrugged off. This week was long and hard, just like Aiden.

She had to stop thinking like this about Aiden, or she'd end up dragging him into the copier room to bang one out.

Her gaze flicked toward Aiden as everyone else got caught up in another campaign which was still in development. His green eyes hadn't left her. A little darkness lurked under his eyes which maybe meant he hadn't slept well either. That perked her up a little.

At least she wasn't suffering alone.

The meeting finished shortly after. Phoebe went to her desk to grab her things. The past few days she'd spent in the extra office going over files with Aiden. That was the plan for this morning as well. So she headed into the office to set up.

Aiden came in with his laptop and took the same seat he'd been using. Once she had everything properly hooked up, she sat across from him. Plenty of distance between them.

"Five more client files," she announced, ready to be done with this. At least they hadn't spent all day together the past few days. Plenty of other things needed their attention, but by the end of the next couple hours, Aiden would be caught up on all their clients so far. Including the ones they didn't win after the proposal. So confining themselves in an office together should go away next week.

"Violett Industries." She opened the file and went through the basics. Size, product range, scale of advertising. She even played the unedited advertisement Taylor and King had created for their new cologne.

"The majority of our clients' advertising needs seem to have more of a sexy edge than family-friendly." Leaning back, Aiden templed his fingers over his lips.

"Morgan and Drew tend to bring the sexy, so we do tend to draw clients who want that from us." Phoebe pulled up the next client. "However, we do have clients like Olly's Dog Food."

She pulled up the puppy food campaign that Claire and Logan came up with. "We can be cute and cuddly, too. Olly's was one of our first clients. They're a smaller company and couldn't afford the rates the full-scale advertisers quoted them. We were able to give them a more personalized approach at a much greater value."

"This is more on track with what Crown, Hunt & White does." Aiden shuffled through some of the papers he'd brought in. "I'm afraid I have a little bit of a learning curve with the sexy ads."

"Sex is easy. Show a little skin. Give the feeling the audience is viewing something they shouldn't, and you hook the target audience." Phoebe slipped her shoes off under the table. "Forbidden works well, but so does a little voyeurism. When we worked at Hart Associates, we worked luxury goods. Almost every ad was based on desire. Something just out of your reach that you need to have to complete your life."

Phoebe shivered and finally looked at Aiden. His darkened eyes captured hers. Just out of reach. Forbidden, not really, but not advisable. Obsession. That was exactly what Aiden was for her.

An obsession she needed to flush out of her system. Even if it took multiple hookups. . . .

"We should get back to work." Aiden broke their stare down first. Maybe they were both just tired and that made them vulnerable.

All she had to do was remind herself he wasn't that like-able in real life. Sure the fantasy had been amazing, but the actuality of him working with her and being her "boss. . . ." Or at least, trying to be her boss. Well, that guy sucked.

"Tell me about Olly's," he said, softly, drawing her attention back to him. The heat still lay banked in his eyes, but there was a softness too. Like he knew what she was thinking and how impossible it would be for them to be more than coworkers. Even if it was just sex.

Phoebe shook the thoughts from her head and focused on her screen. "Olly's."

CHAPTER 8

Happy hour. What else would Aiden do on a Friday night in a new town where the only people he knew were his coworkers. The bar hummed with noise from the press of people and the music playing on the jukebox. The jukebox was one of those new digital ones. He didn't know if it had a different name, but it performed the same function.

The whole office crowded around a long table. Morgan and Drew had gone off to buy the first round. Phoebe sat mixed in with the others from the pool, while Aiden sat at the end of the table with Ben from accounting. Emily sat on the other side of Ben near Lacy.

"Phoebe told me this is your first time to a happy hour?" Aiden couldn't think of anything else to talk about. He'd taken accounting classes in college, but it hadn't exactly been his favorite subject. This was his first attempt at a conversation with the man since he'd only seen Ben in passing at the office.

"Drinking seems like a good alternative to going home right now," Ben said. His eyes were focused on the door as if he were dreading someone might walk through them.

"We have that in common then." If Aiden had a drink, he'd hold it up to cheers with Ben. The thought of spending another night alone in his hotel room hadn't exactly filled him with joy. He still had the bottle of lavender bubble bath, but otherwise the cleaning staff had wiped away all traces of Phoebe.

Except they couldn't clean his memories, and she was everywhere. Her laugh, her smiles, her flirting looks, her sultry voice. Her naked body always within reach. He'd woken at two a.m. last night, reaching out in the darkness for her. Only to be met by empty sheets.

Maybe he could get her out of his head if she weren't with him every day. Dressed like a sexy vixen and arguing with him about the stupidest things until all he wanted to do was fuck her on his desk until the only thing coming out of her mouth was a delicious moan.

"You're new to town, right?" Ben folded a paper napkin in half.

Aiden nodded as he snuck a glance at Phoebe. "Moved from Chicago."

"My ex is from Chicago."

Aiden didn't know where to go with that, but just then Morgan and Drew brought pitchers of margaritas and beer to the table. Everyone passed around mugs and then the pitchers, filling up their mugs with either of the drinks.

Drew sat on Aiden's other side, while Morgan sat next to Phoebe.

"How did your first week go?" Drew asked and took a sip of his beer.

Aiden glanced over at Phoebe. She had her head thrown back laughing at something. It made him crave that abandonment she gave him during sex. Nothing artificial or contrived, just all Phoebe, unlike every other woman he'd had sex with. He could always tell when a woman was faking.

Phoebe rarely faked anything and definitely not during sex.

Aiden cleared his throat and turned to Drew. "Just the challenge I was looking for."

"Good, good." Drew took a drink. "You and Phoebe getting along better?"

"We're working on it." If he could keep his focus on the work instead of her legs, he was fine. That woman owned way too many skirts and dresses. He thanked God she didn't wear trousers that cupped her perfect ass. He probably would have gone home ill.

"She's an odd one, but she's part of the Morgan package." Drew nodded at Morgan, who smiled back at him. "Phoebe is loyal and savage in her defense of those she loves. Just don't get on her bad side."

Aiden raised his eyebrow at Drew.

"Morgan and I were up for the same promotion at our last company. Phoebe thought of some truly diabolic ideas to help Morgan 'take care' of me." Drew chuckled softly. "Fortunately, Morgan never let her go through with any of her schemes, but I learned my lesson. Stay on Phoebe's good side."

Should Aiden be worried? Phoebe hadn't exactly been singing his praises all week. She'd threatened Drew with posting a doctored photo to a dating website. That didn't sound horrible, but it would be inconvenient.

"I'm sure you've got nothing to worry about," Drew said after glancing Aiden's way. "Phoebe only gets upset when something important to her is threatened. Morgan is one of the most important people in her life, so she's very protective of her."

"She's very fierce." The words slipped out of Aiden's mouth. Fuck.

"That she is. Like a rabid raccoon." Drew nodded. "I'm

glad Morgan has her in her corner. I wasn't one hundred percent on board with her coming to work with us, but Morgan said it was a deal breaker. When we were reading resumes for your position, I told her you would be my deal breaker."

"What?" Aiden turned his head to look at Drew, surprised. He'd never been anyone's first choice. Of course, given his family connection, he hadn't had much choice when it came to work.

"We needed someone strong enough to take charge, but also adaptable enough to deal with Phoebe." Drew nodded his head toward Aiden. "I figured after working with family, you could deal with anything she'd throw your way."

Aiden glanced around to see if anyone was listening to their conversation. He didn't need to let everyone know his family owned the business he came from. He was fortunate his mother's maiden name was in the company name and not his father's. This was his fresh start to prove that he didn't need a job from his father to succeed.

"I really appreciate the opportunity," Aiden said. His chest felt full at Drew's words. He refused to let Phoebe run over him at work.

Drew clapped him on his back. "I can't wait to see what you do for our company."

Drew walked around the table to where Morgan sat. He straddled the bench she was on and pulled her into him. She softened and leaned against him while still carrying on a conversation with Phoebe.

He couldn't resist looking at Phoebe. A hint of jealousy played on her face so quickly that if he hadn't been watching her, he would have missed it. What was that about? Morgan or Drew?

～

PHOEBE LAUGHED at a joke Jonah told. Her laughter tickled Aiden's ears.

Morgan and Drew had left a while ago, followed by Ben and then Emily. It was just Jonah, Lacy, Logan, Claire, and Aiden left. The four creatives in the office besides Morgan and Drew. He knew them mostly by the various campaigns they'd contributed to, but tonight, he could get to know them a little more on a personal level. If he could get his mind off of Phoebe.

As the number of people grew smaller so did their table. Aiden now sat next to Phoebe, when for the earlier part of the evening, she'd just been in his frame of view. Now her scent wrapped around him, mixed with her heat, enticing him to come closer.

Jonah had his arms wrapped around Lacy as she leaned into him. Aiden couldn't help the flash of jealousy that hit him. He wanted what those two had somewhere down the line. Not now when he was just figuring out what he could be on his own. But then Phoebe's leg brushed against his and he wanted to slide his hand around her, pulling her into him.

Claire flicked her hair over her shoulder. "How are you liking Taylor and King?"

Aiden cleared his throat. "It's a good company. I can't wait to get more entrenched on the day-to-day stuff after I finish learning about our current clients."

"It'd be good to see you more than when you come and go." Claire smiled at him as she sipped at her margarita. Her dark eyes held his for a moment, but they didn't spark through him the way Phoebe's did.

He'd mainly stuck to his office this week, trying to catch up on all the company had done since its start. He had to admit how fast they'd grown impressed him and he knew Phoebe had made a lot of that happen.

Logan came back to the table with some sort of shots.

"None for me." Lacy waved him off when he tried to hand her one. She'd barely had anything to drink tonight, but she must know her limits. "I don't want to end up leaning over the toilet."

"I'd make sure you got home okay," Jonah said softly down to her. She gave him a bright smile before giving him a brief kiss.

"You better, since we live together, but I'm still going to skip the shot." She reached up and tugged on his beard.

Smiling, he squeezed her.

Everyone else took the offered shot. When Logan got to Aiden, he put two in front of him.

"New guy gets the extra." Logan smirked and took his seat next to Claire. Logan had been all smiles tonight. He'd tried to draw Aiden into a discussion on the upcoming football season, but Aiden didn't have a lot to say about it. "Hopefully now that Phoebe has hogged you for a week, the rest of us can finally get to know you. We will gladly provide the social lubricant."

Everyone smiled at Aiden as they lifted the shots and downed them. It was some mix of vodka and something sweet. Not his favorite, but palatable.

Phoebe turned his way and cast an exaggerated look at the other shot glass. "Come on, Kingston. Submit to peer pressure and take the second shot."

Aiden shook his head at her teasing but downed the shot. He'd only had a couple of beers and now the shots, so he was still doing pretty good. A few shots wouldn't floor him.

"Don't submit to the peer pressure, Aiden." Lacy's light voice drew his gaze to her. She had huge brown eyes and her brown hair was tucked away into a bun. She seemed tiny leaning against Jonah. He had longer blonde hair on top that came down to eye level and the rest of his head was shaved. He had a neatly trimmed, full beard. His blue eyes didn't stray from Lacy. Any fool could see he was smitten.

"Peer pressure?" Aiden asked.

"I tried to keep up with these four once before and it ended very, very badly." She gave a shudder.

Jonah wrapped his arms around her and rubbed her upper arm. "It didn't end all that bad."

"You weren't the one with their head in the toilet." She looked up at him with such adoration.

"Which you barely remember. Plus, I got to hold you." Jonah chuckled low.

She blushed hard when she smiled at him. Facing Aiden again, she said, "These people have iron stomachs and no sense of when enough is enough."

"Noted." Aiden nodded at her.

"Nonsense," Claire spoke up as she swept her long dark hair over her shoulder. Even with similar coloring, Claire and Lacy couldn't be more different. Lacy projected sweetness while Claire projected sin. "She just couldn't hang, but you'll be able to hang with us. Won't you, Aiden?"

A slightly evil glint lit Claire's eyes. Aiden wasn't sure which woman to trust.

"Stop, you guys." Phoebe leaned into the table and from his angle, Aiden could see a lot more of those magnificent breasts. "Let's be honest. Aiden couldn't keep up with us if he tried."

His brain was so fixated on her breasts he almost didn't hear what she said. She knew damn well he could keep up with her.

"After all" —Phoebe patted his leg under the table, making him almost jump from the contact— "he's probably used to drinking wine and scotch. Not tequila shots, like I'm going to get us a round of."

She got up when Jonah spoke, "None for Lacy and I."

Phoebe stuck out her tongue at him. "Spoil sports."

"How about it, Aiden?" Phoebe cocked her hip as she gave him a dare you look. "Think you can keep up?"

"With you?" He took her in from the top of her red hair to those killer heels she had on. "Anytime."

She smirked at him before she glanced at Logan and Claire.

"I'll help." Claire joined her and the women headed toward the bar.

"I'm going to the ladies' room," Lacy said before pressing her lips to Jonah's.

He smiled after her before turning back to the table.

"To think I knew you before you were whipped." Logan laughed.

Jonah just smiled and took a drink of his beer. "What can I say. The better man won the girl."

Logan shrugged. "Lacy and I would have never worked out."

"You're right," Jonah said.

They both laughed and Aiden didn't know what he could add. He hadn't really spent any time getting to know these guys yet. Maybe in a month he'd know all their inside jokes. Maybe not.

"Working with Phoebe is a trip, isn't it?" Logan said to Aiden with a wink.

If by trip he meant seeing the woman he'd spent all weekend in bed with at his work on Monday morning, then the answer was yes. "She has a colorful vocabulary."

"That's putting it mildly." Jonah leaned around his beer mug. "It didn't shock me, but I find I cuss a lot more around her."

"I think it's more the oozing sexuality that got me when I met her." Logan balanced the empty shot glass with his fingertip against the table. "I've met too many women who are shy talking about sex, but not Phoebe. I stand by my choice in Kiss, Marry, Fuck."

Aiden was lost about the last statement Logan made, but the rest he understood a little too well. However, he really didn't feel like he could partake in this conversation given his intimacy with Phoebe. He wasn't about to open up about the weekend with two guys he worked with. Not even if they could help him find clarity.

"Honestly, I would have picked Lacy for all of them." Jonah shrugged and lifted his beer to his lips. When Lacy returned, she sat next to him, leaning into his side like she fit there.

"Please tell me we aren't playing that game again. It really makes me uncomfortable." Her nose crinkled up and Jonah kissed the tip of her nose.

"No games tonight." He smiled at her. "We can go whenever you are ready."

Phoebe and Claire came back with a tray of shots, limes and salt. At least three shots a piece by the look of it. The effects of the two shots he downed hit him, easing some of the tension in his shoulders.

"I think that's our cue to leave." Lacy stood back up. The women all hugged each other, while Jonah shook the guys' hands. He tugged Lacy close to him as they headed out.

Aiden hadn't put much thought into relationships in years. But seeing those two, and Morgan and Drew sparked something in his chest. An emptiness he longed to fill. Maybe later, but right now, he was just finding his footing on his own. Away from his family and their legacy.

Phoebe's eyes glittered as she sat beside him. "Regular shots or body shots?"

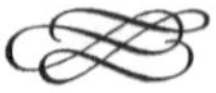

Aiden swallowed before he asked, "Body shots?"

Phoebe might have been a little liberal with her pours on her margaritas earlier. She wasn't drunk, but definitely buzzed. Which made her even more daring, especially with the rest of the office gone. Claire and Logan had been out with her before, so they knew her deal. And she wanted to torture Aiden for torturing her all week.

"Never done one before?" Phoebe winked at him. "Don't worry, the learning curve isn't that steep."

Standing, Phoebe went to the other side of Claire. "You'll help me demonstrate, right?"

Claire nodded and scooted over so Phoebe could sit beside her.

"You have done a tequila shot before, right?" Phoebe glanced over Claire's shoulder at Aiden.

"Of course." He looked slightly offended by the question.

Phoebe smiled. "Good. Same premise."

Maintaining eye contact with Aiden, she leaned forward and brushed Claire's hair over her shoulder. As Claire tipped her neck, Phoebe licked the spot where Claire's shoulder met her neck. Her eyes met Aiden's as she picked up the salt-shaker. Phoebe sprinkled the salt over the wet area and handed Claire a lime. Claire bit into the rind of the lime and held it with the fleshy part out for Phoebe.

"Lick." Phoebe licked the salt from Claire's neck. Her eyes remained on Aiden the entire time. Aiden's eyes had already darkened, and she couldn't help the desire swelling inside her.

"Drink." She took the shot and got caught in Aiden's dark green eyes.

"Suck." Her gaze swung to Claire's smiling eyes as she leaned forward and took the lime from Claire's mouth. Sucking the lime, she returned her gaze to Aiden. "Easy, right?"

She set the lime down and leaned forward to brush a quick kiss on Claire's lips. "You are such a good demonstration subject."

"Thanks." Claire winked at her, as Phoebe went back to her seat beside Aiden. Claire didn't blush or stammer like Lacy would have. If those two hadn't left, Phoebe never would have suggested body shots, but she knew Logan and Claire wouldn't object. They were always up to have some fun.

Aiden swallowed and cleared his throat. "I don't think this is work appropriate."

She raised an eyebrow. "Good thing we aren't at work then. What do you say, Aiden? Think you can keep up?"

The light of challenge sparked in his eyes. She had him.

She glanced behind her at Logan and Claire. They weren't an item, but they were both comfortable with sexual situations, so she wasn't concerned about the inappropriate nature of what they all were doing. Hell, Logan might brag about it to his non-work friends, but she doubted anyone would bring it up at the office.

"It's your turn, Aiden." Her voice was low enough for him to hear over the din of the bar. She tipped her head to the side for him and gave him a teasing look.

His green eyes drew her in and held her there as he leaned forward. His lips touched where her neck and shoulder met, and she almost whimpered. She'd misjudged her ability to stay unaffected by this man. If it were Logan or Claire, there wouldn't be this pulse of sensuality between them. The current always flowed when Aiden touched her though.

Even though it looked sexy when she and Claire had shared the shot, there was no heat or fire between them. With Aiden, her whole body went up in flames as he dragged his tongue over the area so slowly she ached. Her body was too in tune with his, and the longing too fresh. When he pulled back, his eyes were as dark as when he took her under him in his bed. She throbbed in response.

He sprinkled salt over the wet spot on her neck. As packed as the bar was tonight, it felt like they were the only two there. But Claire and Logan were behind her and she knew they might be watching so she'd have to behave. Even though everything in her wanted to misbehave, and badly, with this man.

Had he not brought her to climax over and over again, she might be able to brush off what happened between them. If there hadn't been that moment on Sunday morning where the urgency hadn't existed and things slowed down. He'd kissed her so softly and thoroughly that she gave up part of her being to him.

He owned a little part of her and always would and that was terrifying.

He held out the lime to her, stopping her crazy thought process. She smiled at him and placed it in her mouth.

"You sure?" His words were almost buried under the noise of the people surrounding them.

She wasn't sure, but she wanted him to touch her. No, she needed him to touch her. She'd ached for it all week and had been strong enough not to give in, but the buzz of liquor in her veins gave her just enough courage to face her attraction head-on. She gave him a smile around the lime and nodded.

Leaning in, he put his open mouth over the salt. Her hands tightened on her thighs to keep from reaching out to hold his shoulders and press herself against him. His tongue traced over the muscle there. She closed her eyes to savor the sensation.

Her eyes opened when he sat back. He took the shot and pressed his lips to hers to take the lime. She suppressed the moan that wanted to escape as the lime flavor burst in her mouth mixed with the tang of tequila and the taste that was purely Aiden.

She could kiss him for hours and had, which only made the brief touch of his lips more potent. She wanted more.

He took the lime with his tongue and sat back. Her heart raced, and her breath caught at the desire so evident in his eyes. He set the spent lime on a napkin with the one she'd used and looked over her shoulder.

She turned to see Claire taking the lime from Logan. When Claire leaned back, Logan's eyes burned for a second before he hid it. Maybe this was too much fun for everyone.

"Everyone had a shot?" Phoebe asked.

"Round two?" Claire turned to look at Phoebe with a mischievous look in her eyes.

Seemed like Claire was enjoying herself. From his look, Logan was too as he pulled over two more shots. Phoebe took two for her and Aiden.

She leaned into him slightly. "What do you think? Can you handle more?"

"Yes." His smile should have warned her. His hand slid along her leg beneath her skirt. Desire pulsed hot and heavy under his warmth. How much had he had to drink?

Her breath caught in her throat, but she gave him a flirty smile. She leaned in as if going for a kiss and at the last moment moved to the spot on his neck. He had already unbuttoned his shirt, but she released another button to pull it to the side. When her tongue snuck out to taste his salty skin, his hand on her thigh squeezed, triggering her core to clench in response.

She lifted her head as she reached out for a lime. Her thumb brushed over his lower lip as she pressed the rind-edge of the wedge against his lips. He opened his mouth and took the lime from her. She tried to calm her breathing as she salted his neck. His hand crept farther up her leg and she took the shot in her hand.

She could tell him to stop touching her, but she didn't want to. Glancing over her shoulder, she noticed the other two were in their own little world. She turned back around. Her curiosity of how far he'd take this made her part her legs more.

"You ready?" Her voice had deepened and was slightly breathless when she spoke.

He nodded in response. His eyes burned like green flames. She licked the salt from his neck and as she took the shot, his finger slid along the edge of her panties. She gasped as she slammed the glass on the table before she leaned in to take the lime. When their lips met, he drew the lime into his mouth farther. The lime juice burst into her mouth as his finger stroked along her panties, pressing against her intimately.

She almost came right then and there, but she pulled back and his hand retreated to her thigh again. He took the lime out of his mouth and set it on the napkin before grabbing another one off the plate. The hand on her thigh moved to hover over her panties and she held her breath and fought the urge to press forward. His other hand brought the lime to her lips, brushing against her lips with his thumb like she had. She flicked her tongue out to taste the lime juice on it.

His harsh inhale brought a smile to her as she took the lime from him, holding it for his shot. When his lips touched her shoulder, his fingers slipped under her panties to slide over her sex. Her chest rose and fell, but she maintained the façade that they were only doing shots in the middle of a crowded bar with their coworkers at the same table.

Fuck. He'd barely started and she didn't want him to stop.

When he lifted his head, his darkened eyes drew her in, holding her still as he salted her neck. He set the salt down and his fingers pressed between her thighs. He took the shot into his hand. As he leaned forward to lick the salt, his fingers slid along her until they slipped inside her entrance when his mouth made contact.

She bit into the lime as he stroked in and out of her while he sucked at the salt on her neck. She almost couldn't keep the sounds in. The throaty moan died in her mouth as he lifted his head. He smirked at her, knowing exactly what he was doing to her.

After last weekend, he knew the ins and outs of her body like the back of his hand. He threw back the shot and his mouth was on hers. His thumb brushed her clit while his fingers continued to move within her. She fought to keep her hips from rocking against his hand. His tongue took the lime, but he didn't pull away when he sucked on the lime.

He thrust at an angle that took her breath away. Her body responded to him, falling over the edge, and shook at the climax.

She responded to him. Everything in her wanted him to take this further. To feel his cock sink into her and push her over the peak again and again. Until she was finally satiated. Until the longing was gone. Until they were two halves of one whole.

He lifted his mouth from hers. As his fingers slid out of her, her core pulsed around his fingers trying to draw them back in. His smug eyes danced with the knowledge of her surrender to his touch. He pulled his hand from beneath her skirt to use it to take the lime out of his mouth.

His tongue licked her wetness from his fingers. Fuck. It hadn't been enough. She barely stopped herself from leaning in to taste his lips. To taste herself and the lime and the tequila and him. To straddle his lap and ride the rock-hard cock she knew he was sporting. He glanced over her shoulder and that seemed to sober him a little.

Oh, yeah, they were in a bar with their coworkers, and he'd just made her orgasm during a shot of tequila. Of course, those shots made her even less concerned about everyone around them. She turned back in her seat to face the table.

Logan had a goofy grin on his face, and Claire was shaking her head at him.

"It's bite the lime, Logan. Not my lip." Claire put her hands on the table.

"Sorry." He shrugged and looked anything but sorry.

"No more body shots for me. Unless you want to trade partners." Claire held up her hands. She gave Phoebe a look that said she was done. Phoebe gave her a subtle shake of her head. No trading partners. Claire raised an eyebrow, but said, "I vote regular shots from now on."

"All right, then let's finish the last one the old-fashioned way." Phoebe licked the back of her hand and salted it, passing the salt to Aiden. His eyes nearly burned her from the look in them.

They each took a shot in hand.

"Should we say something?" Logan asked. His eyes were glazed. They would all be cabbing it home tonight.

"Is anyone coherent to say something?" Phoebe asked.

Claire giggled. "Cheers?"

Aiden shook his head. "Sure."

They all said cheers before they licked the salt and downed the shot. Phoebe's hand brushed Aiden's when they reached for the limes. She sucked in a breath and her eyes met his. She bit into the lime and her body had almost a Pavlovian response. Her core tightened and her pulse throbbed.

Fuck.

"That's my last drink." Claire flipped her shot glass and put it with the others in the middle of the table.

"Maybe we should have asked Jonah and Lacy to stay as sober people." Logan rubbed the back of his neck. He slurred the word sober a little.

"Maybe we should have taken the shots a little slower," Aiden added.

"It's the weekend. We'll be fine." Phoebe patted Aiden's thigh under the table. The word *weekend* brought forth the memory of last weekend. Right now, sex with Aiden didn't seem like a bad idea. After all, he'd already gotten her off. She should at least repay the favor.

AIDEN'S HEAD swam as they talked about sports and a bunch of TV shows that no one had time to watch. Phoebe's lavender scent washed over him like a soft blanket that he wanted to pull over him. Her taste lingered on his tongue. Even the glass of water Claire had insisted everyone drink didn't wash it away. Besides, he didn't want it gone.

He wanted more. To bury his tongue into her eager core

and taste every inch of her wet pussy until she throbbed against him. Phoebe's hand had stayed on his thigh. Her thumb rubbed against the same spot, and he had to stop himself from moving her hand to his throbbing cock.

Somewhere in the back of his mind he knew they shouldn't be touching, but it felt so fucking good he just didn't care. Maybe he couldn't hold his own against this woman when it came to drinking. Maybe he didn't care.

He needed to go to the bathroom.

"I'll be back." Aiden stood abruptly.

Phoebe's fathomless eyes looked up at him and her full lips parted. That look only increased his desire for her. If he didn't sober up, he knew he'd invite her back to his place. For the life of him, he couldn't remember why that was a bad idea.

The crowd barely parted for him to get to the hallway where the bathrooms were. The noise dimmed and he could see that the hallway went on for a bit past the bathrooms. He slipped into the men's. After finishing, he washed his hands and headed into the hallway.

Phoebe leaned against the wall opposite the door and the look she gave him was anything but work appropriate. She held out her hand to him. He took it and she tugged him away from the bar down the darkened hallway. They rounded the corner. Farther down the hall stood a door marked employees only.

He opened his mouth to say something, but her finger touched his lips and she shushed him.

"No talking." She wove slightly as she pressed him back against the wall. He steadied her with his hands on her hips. They'd both had way too much to drink. Her hands went to his pants to unfasten them. Her dark eyes focused on her work.

He should stop her. They were in public. What if their

coworkers came to find them? Instead, he reached out and brushed a stray hair behind her ear. Her lips tipped into a smile as she opened his pants. She reached in and palmed his cock through his underwear.

She pressed forward until her lips touched his ear. "I knew you'd be hard for me."

His cock twitched against her palm.

"I need to return the favor." Her tongue traced along his ear and she sucked on his earlobe.

Pulling back, she looked into his eyes when she pulled his pants down a little to release his cock. She licked her lips and his cock wept. He should stop her, but fuck it, he wanted her. He hadn't threatened her job if she didn't suck him off and definitely hadn't asked her to do it at all. But damn it all, he wanted her to.

She lowered herself to the ground and looked up at him. "Hold my hair."

He complied and she gave him a smile before taking his cock into her sweet, hot mouth. He groaned. All week he'd been fascinated with her lips. The different shades of red she spread on them. He'd imagined the color smeared over his cock in bed at night as he stroked himself.

Now he watched those red lips closing over him as her tongue traced the underside of his cock. So much better than he remembered. Her hand cradled his balls gently as she began to stroke him with her lips. Her eyes locked on his, and he swore he could drown in them. Sink into darkness with her and never leave.

He shouldn't want her as badly as he did. He wanted to lift her, press her against the wall, and sink into her welcoming warmth. Fill her until he felt her shatter around him. The best part was he knew she'd be soaked from going down on him. It turned her on to do this to him.

She swallowed, sending ripples over his cock. He couldn't hold back any longer.

"Phoebe," he groaned, giving her an out. She'd swallowed before, but he didn't want to assume.

She dragged her head back and licked the tip of his cock. She smirked up at him and then took him down her throat again. He gently guided her head with his hand in her hair until he couldn't hold back any longer. He groaned as he came. She kept going until he was fully spent.

Swallowing, she stood and straightened his clothes. When she fastened his belt, she leaned in and kissed him. He could taste himself on her tongue.

"Come home with me," he whispered against her lips.

She shook her head. "We shouldn't."

He wanted to argue with her but he knew she was right. They'd crossed the line tonight and that could be blamed on the drinking. But if he took her home, he wouldn't want to let her go. He'd spend all night rediscovering her body and slaking his lust with her.

Monday morning would come and he'd be even worse off than before. Even this taste of what they were like together made him want to tear apart everything to be with her again. To have her in his bed all weekend long.

Leaning in, she brushed her lips against his before moving her lips to his ear. "You and I have this spark that is hard to deny. Giving in would be bliss. But I know you'd regret it."

When she stepped away, she gave him a knowing look. She was right. But that didn't make him want her any less.

CHAPTER 10

Kicking herself all weekend hadn't helped Phoebe to get over Aiden. Blaming it on the alcohol was a weak-ass excuse, but it was the only one she had. She was a needy bitch who couldn't help herself when it came to him.

She'd been tempted to fuck Aiden in that darkened hallway until she saw stars again, but it would have been the tipping point. She would have gone home with him. She would have stayed in his swanky hotel suite. Had breakfast on the bed. Taken a bubble bath with him. Fucked his brains out every minute of every hour until they couldn't even get it up anymore. She wasn't sure it was possible, but she would have wanted to try.

Phoebe stepped off the elevator and into the offices of Taylor and King. Her shades on and her coffee pressed to her lips, giving her life.

"Morning, Phoebe." Emily's soft voice should be a balm to her sorry-ass soul.

Phoebe nodded at Emily and leaned on the counter in front of her. "How was your weekend?"

"Pleasant. Grandma's doing so much better. It's like she

wasn't even sick at all." Emily practically beamed. That girl lived for her grandma which was sweet. The problem was she didn't really live for herself. Phoebe hadn't forgotten Emily's crush on Ben, but her own sex life was currently up in the air so she couldn't exactly work on anyone else's.

"I'm glad she's better." Phoebe smiled at her. That was all she could do. She couldn't fix Emily's life anymore than she could fix her own.

"Glad to see you finally made it in." Morgan met her in the front. "Monday meeting. Remember?"

"Again?" Phoebe whined. She really didn't want to do this meeting. She didn't even want to be at work. She should have spent the weekend in someone else's arms. Letting that dick erase the effects of Aiden on her. Instead she'd fantasized about Aiden and what they could have done if she hadn't been such a fucking stick in the mud.

"Come on. The faster you get there, the sooner it will be done." Morgan led the way to the conference table.

Aiden sat at the table with his laptop open, along with everyone else.

"I thought this was a creative meeting." Phoebe pulled her sunglasses down to look over Aiden. Fuck, he looked delectable in his dark gray suit with a teal shirt that high-lighted his eyes.

"Aiden asked to sit in." Drew's voice made her turn toward him. He looked way too chipper this morning. He and Morgan must have had morning sex. That put an even more sour mood on Phoebe's already sour mood.

"How am I supposed to sell these people if I don't know what they do?" Aiden's voice was almost sharp. Was he angry that she turned him down? She got off and so did he so what's his problem? She'd saved them a world of embarrass-ment at having to wake up next to each other sober. That, and stopped them from going at it again and again and again.

"Whatever." Phoebe sank into the seat next to him, the only seat available, and propped her feet up on the table. She pushed her sunglasses up her nose and waved her coffee in the air. "You may proceed."

She closed her eyes as she leaned her head back and listened to them discuss the current projects. She stayed up to date on everyone's progress because that was what a project manager was supposed to do. Any notes she needed to make, she would do once the meeting was over.

Throughout the meeting, she could feel Aiden's eyes on her. It was like being shoved under a spotlight each time it happened. Warmth and heat flowed through her until his gaze moved away again. She shifted restlessly and finally opened her eyes. She straightened in her chair and kept herself from tossing daggers Aiden's way.

Instead, she downed the rest of her coffee as Lacy finished up her status report.

"Phoebe?" Morgan said.

Phoebe rattled off the status of every project she was currently managing, along with the status on all the clients she was currently pursuing. When she finished, she glared pointedly at Aiden. His look of astonishment pissed her off. Just because she looked like she didn't care didn't mean that she didn't actually care. She had a job to do, and she did it with finesse.

"All right then." Drew clapped his hands. "Anything anyone want to add?"

"I have a question," Aiden said, scrolling his mouse on his laptop.

Phoebe groaned and shoved her sunglasses into place before resuming her nap-like posture.

"What kind of clients would each of you like to see brought in? It can be as specific or unspecific as you'd like. I just want to understand what will spark your interest."

Aiden leaned back as he contemplated everyone at the table.

Phoebe almost scoffed out loud, but the earlier groan was probably enough for now.

"I'd love to work with a small brewery or distillery," Logan piped up. "At my old job, we had a major brewer, which was exciting to work on, but I think something smaller would be cool."

"Great." Aiden made notes on his computer.

"There's this bakery downtown that makes the most perfect cupcakes." Lacy looked like she was imagining one in front of her right now. "They are small and just starting out. They may not have a large advertising budget, but I'd love to be able to help them grow."

"What's the name?" Aiden asked, while typing.

"Sweet Nothin's. No g."

"I'd like to do more in fashion." Claire leaned forward on the conference table. "Clothing, jewelry, shoes. I love the perfume and cologne ads, but I'd love to do something less eccentric."

Everyone else chuckled and nodded their heads. Phoebe straightened slightly. No one had told her any of this. Why did they wait for Aiden to ask them? She always tried to play toward the strengths of the group. And since they almost always won cologne and perfume ads, she focused her search there.

"Vacation stuff." Jonah stroked his hand down his beard and glanced at Lacy. "Hotels, restaurants, beds and breakfasts, travel destinations. Even a cruise line might be fun to develop ads for."

Aiden nodded as he typed then he turned to Morgan and Drew. "Anything for you two?"

"I've always loved luxury goods so anything along that

line wins me over." Morgan shrugged and looked to Drew. "You used to work in Beverage."

"Not by choice." Drew smiled at her. "I actually love everyone's suggestions. I'd also like to propose bringing in some not-for-profits. Like animal shelters or some sort of save the whatever. I think we've grown enough that we can do some work for less than standard rates to help our community."

Aiden finished typing and closed his laptop. "That all sounds fantastic. Phoebe and I will have to put our heads together to find some new opportunities."

"Let's get back to work then." Drew stood and offered his hand to Morgan.

Phoebe went to her desk and opened her laptop to turn it on. Aiden stopped next to her and after a moment, she glanced up at him.

"Can I help you?"

"Schedule some time this afternoon to come discuss these new ideas with me?" It was kind of posed as a question and almost a demand. It made her bristle.

She narrowed her eyes at him before she said, "Sure, why don't I put that in our calendars like a good secretary."

"That's not—"

"No, no. You go do all that work that keeps you so busy and I'll grab you a coffee, shall I?" She pressed her lips together.

He gave her a mulish expression. "Coffee would be great. Black."

He walked away. Well, shit, now she had to get him coffee. She shoved away from her desk.

As she walked into the breakroom, Logan and Claire were already in there, sitting at the table. Looks like the body shots hadn't changed their relationship at all.

"If the Packers would get off their asses this season, they

might have a chance with their new draft picks." Logan pushed his coffee mug back a little.

"You don't even like the Packers." Claire shook her head. "Hey, Phoebe."

"Hey." Phoebe got down two mugs and resisted the urge to spit in Aiden's, but it wasn't like they hadn't already swapped spit before. "What's happening in sports land?"

"Draft picks." Claire stood and stretched. "Of course, all my favs went to the wrong team."

"At least it wasn't the Packers like mine." Logan shook his head. He pointed at Claire. "We on for sports center tonight."

Claire nodded and took a sip of coffee. "As long as you don't mind watching at my place."

"Shouldn't be an issue." Logan headed toward the door but stopped before opening it. "By the way, you two should make out more often. That was fucking hot."

Logan winked before he headed out.

Claire just laughed. "Yeah, right. Like I'm going to give him more spank bank material."

"I was a little buzzed. Sorry if I put you in an uncomfortable position." Phoebe didn't usually push that kind of stuff on her coworkers.

Claire waved her hand and made a dismissive sound. "You aren't the first chick I've kissed. Besides, Logan was right. It was hot. But just so you know, I don't swing that way."

Phoebe laughed and held her hands out to the side and struck a pose. "I don't know. After all, you could have all this."

"Let's be honest. Both of us like dick." Claire winked at Phoebe.

"You're not wrong." Phoebe shrugged.

Claire blew her a kiss as she walked out the door. Phoebe couldn't wipe the smile off her face. She grabbed the two coffees and made sure to take a drink from both to leave lipstick stains on them. Schedule a time. Get him a coffee.

She'd show him who the secretary was in this relationship.

~

By Friday, Phoebe was strung so tight, she was ready to explode. There was no happy hour scheduled for tonight and by four o'clock she wanted to go home.

"Hey," Morgan said. Phoebe spun her desk chair around to face her. "Want to take a break with me?"

Phoebe glanced at Aiden's open door, where the bastard spent half the day watching her work. To think she'd gone down on him a week ago. She definitely blamed it on the alcohol. This week had been an endless hellhole of work. They had to find leads on all the new projects the staff wanted to bring in.

Oh, it wasn't Aiden's little side project. No. He wanted Phoebe to do most of the leg work. While she also had to manage the projects that were in progress and put out fires of potential new clients at the same time.

"Sure, I'll walk with you." Phoebe pushed away from her desk, making sure her skirt swirled around her legs. She'd worn another wrap dress because she knew it got under Aiden's collar. She smoothed it over her hips and played with the tie to make sure it was tight before lifting her gaze to find Aiden's heated one focused on the knot.

When he lifted his gaze, she smirked at him and then followed Morgan out of the office and down the stairwell. Teasing him was the only thing that made the day worthwhile.

"Is everything okay?" Morgan asked as they descended to the fourth floor where the vending machines were.

"Everything's peachy. Why?" Phoebe didn't want to tell Morgan that Aiden was driving her batty with all his requests. Or that she was so strung out on him that she couldn't even use one of her fuck buddies, because she knew she wouldn't get the same rush she got when Aiden fucked her. No one came close to the orgasms Aiden gave her. This better be temporary. He better not have ruined her for other dick.

"I know you and Aiden didn't start working on the best of terms, so I wanted to check in and see how everything was going." Morgan opened the door to the fourth floor, and they made their way to the vending machine room. "Monday we can touch base again and see how things are going, but as your friend, I want to know how you are doing with all this."

"Honestly, he's a lot, but things are starting to sort themselves out." He'd been hired to take the load off Morgan and Drew's shoulders so they could have a semi-normal life for two workaholics. Phoebe couldn't tell Morgan he was the devil incarnate, tempting her with sin and bossing her around like she was one of his minions. Or that part of her got off on his bossing her around. That was way too messed up to share. And she usually shared everything. "We're getting things done."

"You should come to dinner tonight." Morgan pressed the buttons on a vending machine and a brownie fell to the tray below.

"What?" Phoebe hadn't really been paying attention.

"Come to dinner at Drew's. We can catch up and pretend to be adults having a dinner party." Morgan collected her goodies and moved to the soda machine.

"This isn't an invite to a threesome. Because as much as I love you, I do not want to be party to yours and Drew's kinks." Phoebe smirked.

Morgan's face went beat red.

"Phoebe," Morgan admonished. "We keep our kinks between the two of us."

"So you *do* have kinks." Phoebe grinned. "What is it? Is he into feet? He wears your shoes? He wants you to spank him while he calls you mommy?"

"God, no. Stop. I'm not discussing my sex life with you." Morgan shook her head.

"Oh, but you wanted to know all about Aiden and me," Phoebe teased as she retrieved her own soda.

"You just don't usually have a filter when it comes to men. So color me curious when you suddenly don't want to say anything about him." Morgan shrugged and pulled open the door. "So tonight, yes?"

"Fine." Phoebe moved out into the hallway. "Should I dress to the nines?"

"What you are wearing is fine."

"But if I wanted to tramp it up, you wouldn't mind?" Phoebe winked while she pushed open the stairwell door.

"You do you."

"I always do."

CHAPTER 11

AIDEN DIDN'T KNOW what to expect when Drew invited him over to dinner. So when he stood at Drew's door with a bottle of wine in his hand, he felt very self-conscious. He knocked on the door and looked down the empty hallway of doors. He really needed to find an apartment of his own.

He could stay in the hotel indefinitely if he wanted to. It wasn't a matter of cost. He had the money in his trust, but he also shouldn't spend it all on living expenses. He should settle in and have a more permanent address. Besides the hotel only reminded him of Phoebe.

The door swung open and Phoebe stood there like he'd conjured her. The huge smile on her face fell when she noticed it was him. Her red hair grazed her bare shoulders. The dress she had on was another wrap dress but she'd changed since the office. This dress had spaghetti straps holding it up and left her shoulders wonderfully naked. Her cleavage was on display for any man to admire. All that flawless skin only turned him on more.

He was weak.

"Aiden?"

"This is Drew's apartment, right?" He lifted his phone to look at the address Drew had texted him. "You live in the same building?"

She rolled her eyes and shook her head before stepping back. "This is Drew's. I live in the same building as Morgan though."

Stepping inside, Aiden cleared his throat.

"Aiden." Drew came out of the kitchen with his hand out to grab Aiden's. Relief flooded him at the sight of Drew. When Aiden gripped his hand, Drew's other hand caught his forearm. "Great to see you, man. So glad you could make it."

Morgan smiled at him from behind Drew. "Good to see you again."

"What is this?" Phoebe crossed her arms under her breasts and glared at the two of them. She really didn't need to call more attention to her breasts. They were practically perfect and filled his hands nicely. He missed the weight of them in his hands and her perfect nipples in his mouth.

To avoid staring happily at Phoebe's breasts, Aiden's gaze bounced between everyone. "Drew invited me to have dinner with them since I was new in town."

"And I invited Phoebe. We figured talking outside the office would be a good idea." Morgan waved her hands like it was a magic trick. "Sorry for the subterfuge, but I figured Phoebe wouldn't come if she knew, and I wasn't sure about you, Aiden."

"Besides you both deserve a free meal for the time you've put in the past two weeks." Drew took the wine from Aiden. "Nice. We should let this breathe. Morgan, could you help me in the kitchen?"

Phoebe made a face at Morgan and mouthed something to her. Something that looked like a threat. Morgan ignored Phoebe.

"Make yourselves at home." Morgan followed after Drew.

Aiden moved to sit on the couch.

"I wouldn't sit there." Eyeballing the couch, Phoebe dropped into one of the armchairs. "I guarantee there's been monkey business on that couch. I'm not even sure the table is safe, but I assume they at least wiped it with a Clorox wipe."

Aiden nodded and took the armchair next to Phoebe. "So this was a setup?"

"Not to make us date or anything, but to make sure we've cleared the air and aren't ready to strangle each other anymore." Phoebe crossed her legs, showing off some red heels that he could imagine her leaving on while he bent her over that couch and took her from behind. Or maybe her heels up on his shoulders so he could go deeper.

"Like my shoes?" She held her leg over to him so he could inspect her heel if he wanted.

He'd love to run his fingers up her leg and under that skirt. She'd have on skimpy panties that he could shove to the side—Jesus, he needed to calm the fuck down.

"They're very nice." His voice was deeper but hopefully she wouldn't notice.

"They're my favorites." She dropped her leg back down. "I'm sure you could use the magic phone to get some in your size."

He shook his head and gave her a wary smile. "I don't actually use the magic phone all that often."

"Have you even looked at apartments? Or do you want to stay in the hotel for the rest of your life?" Phoebe's glance flicked toward the kitchen, but Drew and Morgan still hadn't come out. "It definitely has its perks."

"The hotel does have some benefits." He leaned closer to her. "I hear they have the best half priced margaritas on Fridays."

She grinned at him. "This side of the border."

He gave her a half grin. "Sorry, I forgot. This side of the border."

"But where do you put all your stuff?" Phoebe asked.

"Sold most of the furniture. The rest is in storage. I'll move it when I find a place. When I begin looking, that is." Aiden rubbed his hands over his slacks. "I haven't actually looked for an apartment before. My family owns buildings, and there were always places available in them."

"Must be nice. I live in a shoebox inside a shoebox, but at least it's my shoebox." Phoebe's smile still glowed. She seemed much more relaxed now than at work this week. Maybe Morgan and Drew were onto something with having a talk outside the office.

She'd been distant and snippy, so he'd given her space when he could. But she kept trying him and he couldn't help but rise to her bait. He'd felt like a complete dick a few times, but it kept him from thinking like he did when he got here. About all the things he wanted to do to her and with her.

It wasn't all sexual. He liked talking with her and watching TV shows, even without the extracurricular activities. Though they did make it more exciting.

"Sorry. We had to find the corkscrew." Morgan appeared with a wine decanter. Her lips looked a little fuller and her cheeks were flushed. Drew followed her out with four glasses. His lips quirked into a half smile.

"That's not the only screw you two found," Phoebe mumbled under her breath. Aiden bit back a chuckle.

"I hope you like lasagna because that's pretty much the only thing I can make," Drew said as he held out the glasses for Aiden and Phoebe.

Aiden took both and waited for Morgan to fill them before passing one to Phoebe.

"Thanks." Her voice was soft.

Morgan and Drew sat across from them on the couch. Obviously they weren't afraid of their own cooties.

"Did I overhear you are still looking for an apartment?" Morgan asked.

"He wouldn't want yours." Phoebe shook her head at Aiden. "Trust me it's small and you can do so much better."

"I wasn't going to offer him mine," Morgan insisted.

"Why not? It's not like you actually spend any time there." Phoebe sounded a little hurt.

"Drew's apartment is closer to work," Morgan tried to explain.

"I haven't actually started looking yet," Aiden interjected to stop them from continuing down this train of thought. Neither of them seemed comfortable with it. "I don't really know what areas are good and what areas to stay away from."

"You should have Phoebe go with you." Morgan smiled and took a sip of her wine. "She's lived here all her life and knows this city intimately. You want a good piano bar or the best club. Half price drinks or the best draft beer in town. Phoebe's your girl."

His chest tightened a little at that statement. She wasn't his girl. She was a woman he hooked up with and then ended up working with and then kind of hooked up with again last weekend. Except when he asked her to his hotel, she said no.

"She doesn't have to—"

"Sure, I've got nothing better to do tomorrow." Phoebe twisted in her chair toward him. "What about you? Busy tomorrow? Or are you working?"

She knew he didn't know anyone, so it wasn't like he had plans.

"You definitely shouldn't be working on the weekends," Drew said. "We hired you so we could have more days off, but not so that you would have to work twice as hard."

"It would be nice to have a tour guide to this city," Aiden relented. "If Phoebe wants to."

"Great, it's decided then." Morgan clapped her hands and the timer went off. "Oh, dinner's ready. By the way, fabulous wine, Aiden."

They all stood. Aiden grabbed Phoebe's arm to hold her back while the other two went into the kitchen.

Aiden leaned down to speak in her ear. "You don't have to give me a tour if you don't want to."

She turned her face up to him. "I've got nothing better to do. Besides, you're rich and I never get to go to those fancy places up close and personal. It'll be a trip."

He glanced down at her red lips, remembering them wrapped around his cock. His hand tightened on her arm. He couldn't stop himself. "Can we get a drink after this?"

She raised her eyebrow and turned into him. "Just you and me?"

Fuck. He wanted to drag her out of this apartment and lock her away in his hotel room until she couldn't stop screaming his name in pleasure. "You and me."

She patted him on his chest. Her fingers curled around his tie, tightened and tugged on it slightly. "Fuck it. Why not?"

Letting the tie slip through her fingers, she stepped away from him. He released her arm as she walked over to the table. Her hips swayed and he almost bit his knuckle to keep from groaning. Dinner was going to be torture.

DINNER WAS NICE. The conversation flowed because of Drew and Morgan, but all Phoebe could think about was after this ended. Aiden asked her for a drink. She hoped he meant in his hotel because she needed him to fuck her and fuck her hard.

If she couldn't forget him or fuck someone else, then she needed to get him out of her system. She couldn't even look at other guys. Even though at work he frustrated her to no end, she still wanted him.

Phoebe squirmed in her chair as Aiden's knee brushed hers under the table. It shouldn't be turning her on. She was a little girl flirting with a boy so no one else would notice. It was maddening.

"I haven't been watching the latest season of *Bachelor*," Morgan confessed.

"Has anyone?" Phoebe smirked. "Besides how can you watch anything when the business takes up so much of your time? You don't even have enough time to have a cocktail with your bestie. You better not be wasting time on a reality TV show that you only watch because of me."

"I would always choose you over TV." Morgan's eyebrows pulled together as she met Phoebe's eyes. "Things are calming down thanks to the new hires. We should be able to carve out time to spend together again."

Phoebe drew in a breath and that hollow feeling in her chest filled a little at Morgan's pleading look. Phoebe knew who her best friend was when they started hanging out. It was just an adjustment sharing what little free time Morgan had with Drew.

Morgan continued, "Jonah coming on board really balanced out the office dynamics, and we are both really excited to see what Aiden can do."

Phoebe choked on her wine. She'd seen what Aiden could do. It was impressive, but she couldn't say that here.

"You okay?" His dark voice caused a fissure of excitement to run down her spine. She'd never last to his hotel room.

"Fine." She cleared her throat. "Just went down the wrong pipe."

"Are you two finding a balance at work?" Drew picked up his wine glass but didn't drink. "Some growing pains are expected when building a new business. We do think you two are the best to help us achieve our goals."

Phoebe almost smiled at Drew's praise. She knew it wasn't his fault that Morgan was so busy. Well, mostly not his fault. Morgan had always been an overachiever. But she needed someone like Phoebe to keep her grounded and remind her that play was necessary too. Phoebe shouldn't be surprised that even as things calmed down at work, Morgan would always find more to do.

"I think. . . ." Aiden paused to look at Phoebe. His green eyes smiled, filling that hollow place in her chest again. "We are starting to figure out what we need to make this partnership work."

Yeah, he needed to give her lots and lots of orgasms. That would definitely make her less stressed about the work situation.

"I'm glad you two seem sorted out." Morgan smiled and turned to Aiden. "Phoebe has been doing such a great job on her own. She's always been an amazing project manager. It's why I insisted on bringing her with, besides the fact she's my friend and I enjoy working with her. Sales was new to all of us, but she's really picked it up fast. We hope you'll help take the company and Phoebe to the next level."

Warmth spread through Phoebe's chest at Morgan's words. She needed to hear that Morgan still appreciated her. Aiden's hand slipped over Phoebe's thigh and squeezed. She threw him a sharp look, but he wasn't looking at her. No signs of lust on his face as he faced the others.

"I've been figuring out Phoebe's strengths." He released

her thigh and his hand slipped away. "I'm confident we'll figure out a way forward that works for both of us."

"Good to hear," Drew said. He filled up their glasses with the last of the wine.

"I have to admit I was skeptical at first." Phoebe crossed her legs and met Morgan's eyes. "But I think we'll be fine. Asking the creatives what they want to work on was a good idea. Even if it adds to the workload."

"It's just nice to have a weekend where we don't have to worry about work if we don't want to." Morgan laughed softly. "We even found time to cook instead of ordering takeout."

"Dinner was great, you two." Aiden took a drink of wine before asking, "How long have you lived together?"

Glad for the change in topic, Phoebe snickered. She'd been wondering the same thing.

"We don't live together," Morgan said, glancing at Drew. "I still have my apartment, which is down the hall from Phoebe's. We haven't really talked...." She gestured vaguely in the air.

"When we move in together, we'll probably get a new place with a little more space," Drew filled in. "But our current leases aren't up yet."

Phoebe could see that happening sooner rather than later. Those two were attached at the hip. Blissfully in love. Not something Phoebe was comfortable with. For them, it was fine, but she'd never been part of a couple.

Sex, yes. All the time, please. But the idea of a relationship made her queasy.

"I've always lived on my own," Aiden said. A muscle ticked in his jaw for a moment. "One girlfriend practically moved in, but I corrected that situation before it got worse."

Interesting way to put it. She didn't care about his past relationships though. All she cared about was where his dick currently was and how she could be there. For her, this was about sex. Nothing more, nothing less. Aiden fulfilled her needs very emphatically.

"I've never even been in a relationship, so no troublesome man to boot out when they overstay their welcome." Phoebe shrugged.

Aiden seemed surprised, but he didn't say anything.

"You've had guys you kept for a while," Morgan said in a knowing way.

"They don't last, and they never stay." Phoebe leaned back in her chair and finished her glass of wine. "Besides this city is full of cocks just waiting for their turn. Who am I to deny them a taste."

Drew chuckled but Morgan smacked his arm playfully before giving Phoebe a look that she couldn't quite understand.

"That's not who you are." Morgan's blue eyes never left Phoebe's. "If you wanted them to stay, they would."

Phoebe's throat tightened. No, they'd leave like everyone else. She coughed lightly to loosen it before pulling a smile to hide her discomfort. "Haven't found one worth keeping. Not sure I want to."

Morgan's eyes softened. She glanced at the guys at the table and her lips pressed together. She gave Phoebe a look that said this discussion wasn't finished. But instead she said, "Well, I'm still here for you."

"Too bad you don't have a dick." Phoebe gave her a half smile. She really wanted to ask, are you really here for me? Because lately it hasn't seemed like Morgan would even try to make time for her. Phoebe didn't let people in for good reasons, but she needed someone, and Morgan was her people now.

"I'm pretty happy she doesn't. Would anyone like more

wine?" Standing, Drew gathered some of the plates, breaking the tension. "I think we have another bottle."

"I'm good," Aiden said. "It's been a lovely evening, but it's getting late. Want to share a cab, Phoebe?"

Phoebe relaxed slightly and stood. She was ready to get out of here. Morgan stood with her, looking like she wanted to give her a hug. Phoebe smiled at her and closed the distance between them, drawing Morgan close.

Morgan whispered for Phoebe's ears only, "I'm still here."

In her heart, Phoebe knew that. She felt that. But right now, it was hard to see that. Morgan had been there through a lot of the shit Phoebe had gone through. She knew the good and the bad. Even though Phoebe didn't need her friend's help right now, she still wanted to spend time with her.

Morgan rubbed her back, and when she pulled away, she brought her knuckle up to her eye. "Sunday run?"

Phoebe looked over her shoulder at Aiden. She planned to be in Aiden's bed tonight, but she didn't know what that would lead to, and she didn't really want to think much farther than tonight. She turned back to Morgan.

"Maybe? I'll text you."

Morgan grabbed her hand. "I want to spend time with you and talk."

They'd had this talk before. How Phoebe was worthy of more than just sex. How she only looked for men who only wanted her for one thing. Or if they wanted more, Phoebe finished with them so fast the guy never saw it coming. The thing was she needed to leave them. Because she couldn't wait around to be the one left behind again.

Phoebe smiled and squeezed Morgan's hand. "We'll see."

"Thanks for the food." Phoebe gave Drew a nod.

Drew acknowledged her with a nod and shook Aiden's

hand. Then Aiden shook Morgan's hand before they headed out into the hallway.

When the door shut behind them, Aiden and Phoebe moved toward the elevator. Phoebe let those thoughts fall behind her as they walked. Neither of them said a word, but they didn't need to.

She and Aiden had been on a collision course since that first night at the hotel bar. She needed tonight. Finding each other again just made her want him more. Had he not shown up at work, she would have regretted not getting his number. Everything had just been too raw Sunday morning. She'd been too exposed. Her insides screamed for her to run and she had.

But Monday, she might have changed her mind. She might have ended up back outside his room. Doing something she would never have done in the past. But she didn't know if that would have happened. Because he'd shown up at work instead.

The elevator opened and they stepped in.

"Do you want to go to a bar or. . . ."

Phoebe took a breath and smiled up at him. "Or your hotel room? I'm voting hotel room."

"You could stay since we're going apartment hunting tomorrow anyway." Aiden rubbed the back of his neck like he was afraid she'd say no like last weekend.

Her insides squeezed and she bit her lip. All night with Aiden? The decision was easy.

"I'm not doing the walk of shame, so we need to stop at my apartment to grab my things." Phoebe took out her phone to order an Uber. Noting it said five minutes, she slipped the phone into her purse.

"Okay." Aiden took her free hand in his. She glanced down at their entwined hands as if there was a foreign entity clinging to her.

"Is this not okay?" he asked, squeezing her hand. Butterflies took flight in her stomach.

"I don't think anyone has held my hand since grade school." She shook her head. Men took her hand to lead her to the bedroom or to tug her to them. No one held her hand just because. Those queasy feelings she'd had on that past Sunday made a quick appearance before she shut them down. She glanced up at Aiden and smiled. "It's not bad, just different."

"Different can be good." He smiled at her and tugged her into his side. He wrapped his arm around her waist. Her hand grew cold without his, but his arm felt nice wrapped around her.

"This doesn't mean I'll like you at work." She leaned her head against his strong heart, listening to the rhythmic thudding, drawing in his scent that she couldn't get out of her head. Moss, dirt, trees, something intangible. Something purely Aiden.

"I wouldn't expect you to." Chuckling, he kissed the top of her head.

"You better be serious about being a partnership at work."

"I wouldn't expect anything less." His arms squeezed around her. "How about tonight we just be Aiden and Phoebe and not worry about work? Just focus on each other."

Phoebe tipped her head to look into his eyes. "Just sex?"

"Just sex." His smile curled around her heart.

The elevator came to the first floor, and they walked out like a fucking happy couple. What was happening to Phoebe's life? This was weird, but she liked it and didn't want to fight it anymore. She wanted Aiden. What was wrong with that? They could use each other until the sparks died and then go on working with each other like they'd never had their mouths all over each other.

Easy peasy, right?

BEING HELD SHOULD FEEL awkward to Phoebe, but when it was Aiden, it made sense somehow. Still, she wanted more than to be held. If the Uber weren't almost here, she would have dragged Aiden into the nearby bushes and had her way with him.

Instead, she settled on tugging his tie to bring his mouth down to hers. It was a kiss filled with heat and desire and interrupted by the abrupt beep of a car horn.

"You Phoebe?" the driver shouted.

She reluctantly released Aiden's tie and pulled him by the hand to the car. "Yup."

Aiden held open the backdoor and slid in after her. His hand settled on her thigh and all that pent-up, frustrated sexual desire throbbed inside her.

Even the driver felt it as he yelled, "No sex in the car."

Phoebe laughed because Aiden looked really put out. Before Aiden could offer the driver an obscene amount to make him change his mind, Phoebe pulled Aiden's arm around her shoulders and held his hand. She relaxed into his side. She could just be in this moment without worrying he'd think it meant more than it did.

It wasn't far to her apartment, but the closer they got, the more nervous Phoebe became. She hadn't really thought about Aiden seeing where she lived. Not that she lived in a hovel, but it definitely wasn't the penthouse suite at a swanky hotel.

Aiden took her other hand and played with her fingers, making her insides ache and her breathing stutter. They finally arrived at her building, and Aiden handed the guy a twenty as a tip and got out. He reached back in to help her, and her heart skipped a little. Dangerous game indeed.

She led him through the lobby to the elevator. At this time of night, the apartment building was mostly silent. As the elevator doors closed, it looked like it would only be the two of them in it. He turned her to him and kissed her. Slowly, like they had all the time in the world to spend on this one kiss.

His tongue sought entrance, and she opened for him. All the pent-up desire from the week fed into this kiss. The things they'd denied themselves. Time seemed to stand still as he brought her body close to his. The heat of him swept over her. The scent of him, that ancient forest scent threatened her sanity as fantasy merged with reality.

The elevator stopped and Phoebe pulled back. She pulsed with heat. No longer worried about her apartment, she tugged him out of the elevator and pulled him down the hallway to her door. She struggled with the keys as he lifted her hair to kiss the nape of her neck.

"I like it when you wear your hair up." His lips slid against her spine, sending shockwaves through her system. Tingles tickled along her nerve endings.

"Why?" She finally got the key in the lock and turned it.

"Because I can see the spot that makes your toes curl when I kiss it."

She opened the door, and he spun her around in his arms. His lips reclaimed hers as he backed her inside and kicked the door closed behind them. His fingers pulled the string to her dress.

He lifted his head from hers and looked around. "Nice apartment."

She'd left a single lamp on so she wouldn't come home to darkness.

"Thanks." Her voice was breathless.

He moved her against the wall and took her lips again. His hand slid into her open dress and found the other knot. She pulled his shirt from his pants, feeling the urgency too. They had all fucking night.

Later.

Right now, they needed to put out this fire before it consumed them both.

His hands moved over the skin of her hips and she moaned against his mouth. He smiled against her lips as she worked on opening his belt and jeans. Finally she slipped her hand inside his boxer briefs and caressed his cock. It jerked in her grip and her core clenched in response.

He pushed down her panties and they slid to the floor. No backing out now. This was happening. Finally. His hand slid between her thighs and his fingers slowly parted her and pressed against the heart of her before sliding three fingers inside.

"Fuck," she moaned against his lips. Her head dropped back against the wall as she rode his hand, grinding into his palm. Needing the contact and craving the release, knowing he'd definitely get her there.

"Please tell me you have something." She had an assortment by her bedside but she didn't think she could make it that far.

"In my pocket." His mouth closed over her neck. The suction sent waves of pleasure through her.

"Hoping to get lucky?" Not that she cared, right now she was grateful. She put her hand in his pocket to search for the condom.

"Have it on me all the time since I met you. You fry my brain and I want to be prepared just in case you let me back in."

When she closed her fingers around the condom packet, she pulled it out. Then she went to work on his pants, getting them down enough that his cock was free.

"Good." She paused when he hit a spot inside her that made her whole body vibrate with need.

"Now, Phoebe." His voice was urgent, bringing her back to her task.

Tearing open the condom, she rolled it down on him. His hands moved to her hips and lifted her up against the wall. He entered her in one powerful move. Already on edge, she came suddenly, startling her. She wrapped her arms and legs around him as he moved in her, steady and hard, pushing her orgasm to last longer. Just when she thought she couldn't handle it anymore, she cried out as she peaked. He continued a few more hard moves and then groaned against her, his whole body shaking in release.

Exhaling a long breath, she squeezed him with her legs, resting her limp body against the wall and relying on him to support her weight. Their panting breaths filled the room until they slowly returned to normal.

"I guess our budding friendship is ruined," she said, patting him on the shoulder.

"We weren't that close to begin with." He kissed the side

of her neck as he lifted her off him and steadied her on her heels.

"I'm sure you say that to all the ladies." She bent down to retrieve her panties.

"Only you." He stepped away to take care of the condom in the kitchen trash.

She stepped into her panties. Tying her dress, she headed into the bedroom to grab some things. She could hear him wandering through her apartment and it didn't make her any less nervous, knowing he was looking with post-coital bliss at her stuff. Not even sex goggles could make her place look good compared to what he was used to.

It couldn't be helped though, so she just hurried to grab a change of clothes and toiletries. As she walked around her bedroom, she caught glimpses through the door of Aiden wandering around her living room.

The first time she passed, his fingers lingered over the knitted afghan on the back of her sofa that her grandma had made her. The next time, he looked over her DVD collection. And when she came back out with her packed bag, his long fingers cradled her crystal dragon.

"Please be careful with that," she said it without thought. Her heart willed him not to break it. But rationally she knew he'd be careful with it. He wasn't destructive. But she felt she needed to qualify her fear, "It was my mother's."

"It's lovely." He set it carefully back on the stand. "Was it a gift?"

Phoebe's throat constricted. She didn't want to talk about this. She shouldn't have brought him here at all. Especially when she hadn't had time to prepare. To hide the pieces of her that weren't for public consumption.

Aiden walked over and placed his hands on her shoulders. "Are you okay?"

She cleared her throat and nodded. At least this time tears

hadn't fallen. She must be getting stronger. Time to be bold and brazen it out. "Are we ready to go? Or should we have round two here?"

She wiggled her eyebrows at him.

He searched her eyes like he was trying to dig deeper into her mind. It made her uncomfortable. They didn't need to know each other better except what they liked during sex, and frankly he was already an expert on her.

He rubbed her shoulders. "Let's head back to my hotel. Maybe we can have a bath."

"Oh, that sounds good."

His hand traced her arm and he linked his hand with hers. If it distracted him from asking questions or looking at her like he wanted to see everything, she would hold his hand. Not because his warmth reassured her. She verified the dragon was on the shelf properly as they headed to the door.

SITTING ON THE TILED EDGE, Aiden drew the bath and added the bubble bath while Phoebe set her toiletries on the second sink in the bathroom, effectively claiming it. It made his chest warm watching her. He shouldn't want to know more about her, but he did.

She'd only referred to her mother in the past tense. But that could just be because the situations they'd talked about were in the past. But it felt like more.

Lavender steam filled the bathroom as she strolled toward him. Her red lips curved into a smile. Her feet and legs were bare. Her dress flowed around her bare legs. Those legs were amazing.

"You're lovely," he said as she closed in. Reaching out and holding her hips, he pulled her between his knees. He wrapped his arms around her and pulled her into a hug. His head rested against her breasts with her steady heartbeat in his ear. She wrapped her arms around his head and dropped a kiss on the top.

They stayed like that for a moment. Just being able to touch her was powerful. Sure the teasing and sex were awesome, but he missed holding her. She'd slept in his arms two weekends ago. Laid in them and talked to him about nonsense until they fell asleep. A dangerous thought occurred to him. What if he wasn't equipped for one-night stands? Her being here now signaled that might be the case.

"I think the bath is ready," she whispered.

He lifted his head and looked up at her. This was probably stupid to spend the night with her again, but he couldn't seem to help himself. Last weekend, he'd used the excuse that they had been drinking. Tequila shots made him stroke her until she came. Tequila had to be the reason she went down on him in the hallway. Now he didn't have that excuse.

All he knew was he wanted her, and the more he had her, the more he wanted from her.

He turned off the faucet. She reached for her dress's tie and he put his hand over hers and shook his hand. "Mine."

She put her hands on his shoulder. "Hurry up. I love it when I slip into a hot bath."

He raised an eyebrow. "Hurry?"

She gave him a playful sigh and an exasperated smile. He'd already rushed through sex at her apartment. That immediate need still lingered, but he could handle going much slower now. He had her all night.

He pulled the string and leaned forward to kiss her exposed stomach. She smelled like sin itself with whatever fragrance she'd put on. Lavender and something spicy teased his senses. Smoothing her dress aside to reach the other tie, he slowly pulled it loose, and spread the dress open. He reached up and held her lace covered breasts. She pressed into his hands with a moan. Perfection.

He'd spent all week with her right there in front of him but so far out of reach. He wanted to reexplore every inch of her.

Standing, he pushed her dress off her shoulders and draped it over the makeup chair. "Those dresses are a fantastic investment."

She smiled up at him. "I thought the heels were what did it for you."

"It all works for me." He kissed her ear. "You do it for me."

Her breath came out on a shudder. She unbuttoned his shirt as he worked on her bra and panties. When she stood naked before him, she pressed into him as she shoved his shirt off his shoulders. He hissed at the contact of her skin against his. It had only been two weeks, but it felt like an eternity. She added his shirt to the pile on the chair.

His hand swept over her bottom. She stepped back to work on his belt and pants while he explored her smooth skin with his fingertips. She was perfect; even the freckles that lightly dusted her chest were perfect.

He stepped out of his pants and helped her into the tub, following her in. He sat against the edge and pulled her down to sit between his legs.

"I think it was the other way in *Pretty Woman*." Phoebe leaned her head back on his shoulder. She'd knotted up her hair so it wouldn't get too wet. He lifted a stray strand from her shoulder and brought it behind her.

Slipping his fingers over her soapy breasts, he said, "They got it wrong then."

"You might be right." She smiled and placed her hands on his knees. Her fingers massaged his legs.

"You can say that all you want." He slid his hands down her stomach and along the inside of her thighs.

"What?"

"That I'm right." He kissed the back of her neck. "I like being right."

She chuckled. "What man doesn't?"

"Maybe, but how many men are actually right?" He massaged her muscles gently, hoping to release some of the tension she seemed to hold onto during the ride over here.

Her eyes closed as she released a breath.

He used his hands and fingers to elicit moans and sighs from her. Slowly, her body relaxed against his as his ministrations and the hot water eased the tension out of her. Her fingers played with the bubbles near his knees.

"This scene is where Richard Gere tells Julia Roberts about his father." Phoebe's voice was soft, but it was the only sound in the bathroom. "Something about never getting his father's approval."

"I don't remember much about the movie. It's been ages since I saw it. My family isn't that bad. My father gave me approval. More so than he gave the twins. But I didn't just want approval. I wanted to be able to prove myself worthy," Aiden admitted, resting his hands on her stomach.

"Worthy of what?" Phoebe's voice was quiet as she traced an infinity sign on his knee.

Aiden sighed. "Respect maybe. I wanted to do something because I did it and not because my family handed it to me."

"Yeah, that's not the reason Edward is screwed up."

"Sorry." Aiden smiled and hugged her to him. "But I did remember the croissants."

"Mmmm. Croissants." Phoebe drew a circle on his knee with her fingertip. Her head stayed on his chest and it felt good to hold her like this. "Why do you live in a hotel?"

"I don't have an apartment yet."

Phoebe sighed. "Obviously, but why haven't you actually looked for one? You've been here for two weeks, at least."

It was Aiden's turn to sigh. "Is this my therapy session?"

"Only if you want to switch places so I can put my eighty inches of therapy around you." She chuckled and lifted her leg up above the water. "I haven't actually measured the length of my legs, but that's what Vivian says."

"That's not what I want around me." He kissed the top of her head. Another *Pretty Woman* reference?

"Avoiding the question."

"Okay." He took a breath and thought about it. "I don't know. It's expensive to live here, but it's also convenient. Everything is taken care of. I don't have to worry about getting electricity turned on or hiring a maid service. If I want food, I can call room service. I'd have to shop for furniture."

"Didn't you have an apartment before?" Her fingers hit a sensitive spot on the inside of his thigh that made him jerk in reaction.

"Sorry, ticklish," he said and settled them back into position. "I didn't see a point in moving all the furniture. I have a few boxes of important stuff and a few pieces of furniture in storage, but I figured most of what I had probably wouldn't fit my new place anyway."

"I don't think I've thrown out anything since I moved out on my own." Phoebe rolled her head to the side. Her ear pressed against his heart. He could stay like this forever and be happy. "My furniture is the furniture I grew up with. Even my bed frame is an old one of my grandma's."

"I'm not sentimental about furniture."

She pushed up and half turned toward him, smiling. "It's not sentimental. It's practical. It costs a lot to live here and I like nice shoes, so compromises had to be made."

"I do like your shoes." Bubbles dripped off her breasts into the water. Touching her had been relaxing and arousing at the same time. He wanted to fuck her, but condoms didn't work well in soapy, hot water. "Is bath time over yet?"

"Only when you answer why you haven't really gotten an apartment." Phoebe rested her arm on his chest and her chin on her arm. Her brown eyes gazed up at him, compelling him to be truthful.

"I guess I wasn't sure if I would stay here." Aiden ran his palm down her back, swiping through the bubbles and loving how warm her wet skin was. "Committing to a year-long lease wouldn't make sense if I needed to go back."

"Why would you need to go back?"

He didn't know if he wanted to talk about this to anyone. But he didn't have to go into specifics. "My entire family lives in Chicago. My mom is hunting for the perfect Mrs. Aiden Kingston. After a while, I got sick of having my whole life controlled."

Phoebe nodded sagely. "You see, that's why I don't date. None of that drama. Just sex until it isn't fun or convenient anymore." Phoebe finished turning to face him and straddled his hips with her knees. His already hard cock settled between her folds, against her softness, but not inside her where he wanted to be.

"Sex sounds good." He wiped the bubbles from her nipple and took it into his mouth. She pressed down against his erection and slid along it. Her head fell back.

Her lack of inhibition called to a part of him he didn't even realize he had. For him, sex had always been the natural progression of a relationship. A few dates followed by some heavy make out sessions eventually led to sex, but by then they would be a couple.

Phoebe wanted none of that. No flowers or candy, just the best sex of his life. He caressed her wet breast with his hand while he ran his tongue across her other nipple, sucking gently. She was all softness and heat as she moved against him, the water gently lapping his sides. Her wetness rubbed along his cock. The sensation wasn't enough to get him off, but it was definitely making him harder.

"Have you ever had sex in a bathtub?" He lifted his head to look at her. Her eyes were closed as she focused on her movements.

"Never been in a big enough tub to have sex in." Her voice was soft, echoing in the bathroom.

He wanted to be the one to show her. To create a mess with water that he'd be ashamed for the maids to find tomorrow, but condoms were non-optional. Bubble bath could break down condoms.

"The shower works better for intercourse." He wanted to be inside her and that wouldn't happen in the tub. "We could rinse off the bubbles and stay wet."

He took her nipple into his mouth again and she rode him, apparently not quite able to get there herself in their current position. She opened her eyes and met his. The heat in her eyes damn near scorched him to the bone. "Okay."

He lifted her from him and stood in the tub with water running down his body. He dripped the entire way to the shower and turned it on to get hot. He grabbed a condom and placed it near the shower. When the water was warm enough, he went back over to get Phoebe. She stood and the bathwater slid the bubbles down her lovely form.

Swinging her into his arms made even more water soak the towels on the floor. "The other benefit to hotel life. I don't have to clean this up."

Phoebe glanced at the mess. "You don't *have* to. . . ."

"But I will. Later." His heart thumped happily as he stepped into the shower still holding her in his arms and set her on her feet. Filling his palm with soap, he rubbed his hands together and eyed her.

She stepped into the water to rinse off the remaining

bubbles and then stepped back to him. His hands captured her attention. "Is that for me?"

Nodding, he started with her neck, tracing the shells of her ears. Taking care to lather her entire body. Not neglecting any spot, though a few spots might have received extra attention. She held onto his shoulders. Her breathing had grown ragged by the time he moved her into the shower to rinse off.

He took the pins out of her hair and let it fall under the water, running his fingers through the red strands. "I've always loved a ginger."

"Lucky me," she said, a little breathless.

He grabbed shampoo and washed her hair, gently massaging her scalp. He rinsed and then applied conditioner. While she shook out the last of the conditioner under the shower head, he ran his hands over her, keeping the fire burning bright.

"My turn." She gave him a wicked look as she put a healthy amount of soap in her hands. He rinsed and remained still as she ran her hands everywhere on him. The amount of time she spent with her hands slipping over his cock almost made him lose it.

"Always so in control." She shook her head as she pressed into him to reach his hair. Their slick bodies rubbed in all the right ways. She shampooed and conditioned him, her fingernails lightly scraping his scalp. It turned him on but also made his heart skip a beat. He'd been with other women and even showered with them, but no one had spent as much time taking care of his needs as Phoebe did.

"Obviously not in complete control," he said, "or you wouldn't be here." He bent to kiss her neck before he rinsed off and pulled her under the stream with him as he took her mouth with his. When he was with her, his control faltered. He shouldn't be with her at all. They worked together and both wanted to be the top at work. But he couldn't seem to help himself.

He untangled himself from her and carefully put on the condom. He sat down on the bench under the water stream and pulled her down onto his lap. She straddled his hips and lowered herself onto him. He groaned as she sank down, fully engulfing him.

The hot water slicked their bodies. He rubbed her breasts while she rolled her hips over him. Her moans and sighs made him want to come right then and there, but he wanted more depth and knew she needed it to go over the edge. He stood, lifting her with him, and backed her against the shower wall, taking control and driving deep and hard, the way he knew would get her there. He kissed her and she met his lips and tongue eagerly.

She froze as her orgasm hit her. Exquisite in her pleasure. He captured her sigh with his mouth and let himself go, following her over the edge. Her body wrapped around him as he leaned into her against the shower wall.

"We definitely couldn't do this in my shower at home." She pressed a kiss to his neck. "First, we'd run out of warm water. Then, we'd end up on that show *Sex Sent Me to the ER.*"

"I haven't heard of that one." Aiden gently lowered her to her feet and took care of the condom before joining her under the shower stream again to clean off.

She turned off the knobs and reached for a towel.

He stopped her. "Let me."

She shrugged but grinned at him. "People go to the ER for all kinds of weird sex-related injuries. It's on late at night so I catch it once in a while. Usually after a late night at the office."

He moved the towel over her, catching drops of water. Every inch of her was divine. "You are very beautiful."

"You aren't so bad yourself." She grabbed a towel and

worked on drying him. He finished before she did and tried and failed to wrap her hair in a towel.

"It must be witchcraft." He shook his head as she quickly wrapped her hair and returned to drying him.

"An ancient secret passed down from mother to daughter. Yup, must be witchcraft to men." She chuckled. "There's so much more of you to dry."

She didn't stop and hand him the towel, just continued. It surprised him because women who had claimed to love him had never been so thorough as this woman who only wanted him for sex.

"Do you want some dessert?" he asked as they headed into the bedroom wrapped in hotel terry cloth robes.

"I'm always willing when it comes to chocolate." She flopped on the bed. Her robe parted and his body sparked to life again.

"I have an idea," he said.

She leaned up on her elbows and watched him as he placed an order with room service. When he hung up, he grabbed her leg and pulled her to the edge of the bed while he knelt beside the bed. "Let's see what comes first."

CHAPTER 13

PHOEBE WOKE up to gentle snoring in her ear. She lifted her head and looked down at Aiden's sleeping face. A living statue carved of warm marble. Her chest throbbed. She reached up and ran her fingers through his hair that had dried every which way. It made him feel more real and obtainable.

Not that she was looking to keep him in any regard, but it suited him.

His green eyes blinked open at her and he smiled. "Good morning."

He stretched, his long body rubbing against hers. Somehow the blankets had ended up on the floor and just a sheet covered them. They definitely made good use of last night, trying to burn through the attraction between them. Unfortunately, she still wanted more.

"We should get up." He sat up but didn't move to get out of bed. The sheet pooled around his lap revealing that maybe he still wanted more of her too.

"What, no breakfast in bed?" She shook her head at him. "Here I thought this was the whole fairy tale."

He glanced at the pillows scattered around the floor. "I don't think this bed could take breakfast. It barely survived dessert."

She laughed. "True. I'm surprised there aren't chocolate stains on the sheets."

He covered a yawn. "We should get our day started."

She glanced down his body, focusing on his erection. "What are you up for?"

"I'm always up for you, but I don't want you to think I'm using you for sex."

"Why not? I'm using you for sex."

Aiden rolled her onto her back and hovered over her. "In that case. . . ."

He nuzzled her neck, sending desire spiraling through her. His hand shifted down between her legs. She was already wet for him, for which he gave her an appreciative grunt. "Always so ready for me."

"But we will need breakfast," she said before moaning as he shifted down to latch his mouth on her breast. "Eventually."

"Once again, the hotel will provide." Aiden moved back up to her mouth as he leaned toward the nightstand for a condom.

She reached down to stroke him while he worked on getting the condom ready. Soft skin over hard steel. She could seriously just do this all day. Be with him. In the bed, in the shower, on the piano. Every surface of this hotel room had potential and she didn't want to waste a minute of it worrying about work on Monday. But the guy should seriously get his own place.

He eased inside her, not taking her fast and hard like he normally did, but slow and easy like mornings were supposed to be. Her breath quickened as he moved like they had all day to reach orgasm. No wonder she couldn't get enough of him. Just when she thought she knew all his moves, he surprised her with something new.

"We could skip the apartment hunting and stay here. Just like this," he said close enough to her ear his lips brushed her skin, sending a waves of desire crashing through her.

He hit a spot that made her moan.

He wanted her to think while he moved inside her? He had to be kidding. Her mind focused on the repetitive motion of his hips against hers. Like waves in the ocean getting bigger and bigger. Bringing her closer and closer to the edge.

She forgot what they'd been talking about and only focused on him. He was like her own personal Pied Piper. He could take her on the couch. He could take her on the bar. Fuck, she was even willing to try some public places if that's where he wanted to take her.

She wrapped her legs around him, trying to make him move faster, but he was relentless. His mouth found the spot on her neck that was directly linked to her pussy. Her breathing came in shallow pants as he gradually picked up speed.

"Phoebe?" His voice was strained against her ear.

"Mm-hmm?" She was so far beyond words at this moment.

"Stop trying to rush it. Enjoy the ride."

He was the devil, seriously, come to tempt her into giving him her soul just for a fucking orgasm. And she wanted it so fucking bad she was tempted to offer him anything for it.

The waves were getting closer and closer as he moved within her. Her body couldn't hold out any longer. He sucked on the spot on her neck and sparks skittered along her skin as she finally fell over the edge. Tingles coursed through her entire body.

"Fuck, Aiden!" She pulsed around his cock, feeling every

inch as he kept up his insane rhythm. The tingles continued everywhere as she came down.

He kissed her as he quickened his pace until he came. His beautiful face wrenched in ecstasy made her want to see it over and over again. That was her power over him. He collapsed on her and she savored the feel of their sweaty bodies pressed together. She didn't want him to get up. She could stay like this forever.

Her stomach growled. Loudly.

He lifted and smiled at her. "You weren't kidding about breakfast."

"I never kid about breakfast." She couldn't get the goofy grin off her face. Her stomach may be hungry, but her body was so relaxed.

He lifted off her. She made a disappointed sound and tried to pull him back down. He chuckled and headed for the bathroom. "If you want a shower, come on. I'll take you out to breakfast and then we can look for an apartment."

"Do I get to pick the apartments?" She swung her legs to the floor.

"Why not? You can be my personal real estate agent." He yelled over the sound of the shower.

She padded into the bathroom, completely naked and completely unashamed. She grabbed her toothbrush and toothpaste. "I hope you are as loaded as I think you are."

"I do okay." He grinned at her through the glass.

"Seriously?" She spit out the toothpaste and rinsed her mouth. "'I do okay?' You, my friend, are set for life it would seem."

He shrugged like it was no big deal. Maybe if she were as loaded as him, it would be no big deal to her either. Maybe. She joined him in the shower.

He grabbed some soap and rubbed it down over her

breasts. "I could probably still get a good apartment based off just my salary."

Her breasts were hard peaks as he rubbed them. She leaned into his palms, loving the feel of his fingertips. "Hate to tell you, but we're going for wealthy Aiden, not worker bee Aiden."

"You are my real estate guru." His eyes danced when they met hers. "I'll do whatever you want."

Oof, that got her in the warm and fuzzies. "You're paying for breakfast."

"Of course." He smoothed the soap over her hips.

"And not one of those fancy schmancy places you see your mafia friends at. I want pancakes and eggs." She soaped up his chest and sides, taking her time to get the suds everywhere. "IHOP or Denny's or something like that."

"Greasy spoon. Got it." His voice was strained as she soaped his hardened cock. He was always as ready to go as she was.

She ran her hands over him, loving the feel of his hard muscles twitching beneath her fingertips. Phoebe knew sex. She was comfortable with sex and sexual situations. But she'd never been with someone like Aiden before. He knew her body like it was his own. He touched her with familiarity and confidence. No hesitation, no "do you like that" bullshit. Everything he did she liked, and he made sure she got there before getting his. Some guys would rather she finish herself off if they couldn't get her there.

He lifted her chin and his eyes met hers. His lips pressed against hers as he gathered her into his wet body. The kiss was soft and exploratory, no urgency. When he lifted his head, she opened her eyes to see him watching her.

"Good morning," he said as he smiled. His green eyes sparkled in the bright bathroom.

Her heart thumped. He was going to be bad for her bad reputation.

~

"Okay, what's your price range?" Phoebe had her phone opened to an apartment app and shoveled eggs into her mouth at the same time.

Aiden smiled at her. Phoebe ate like she had sex, devouring it all with pleasure. Living expenses would barely put a dent in his trust fund and he liked being comfortable. "Doesn't matter."

Her fork clattered on her plate. When he looked up at her, she said, "Are you an international spy?"

He shook his head and gestured to her plate. "Eat your eggs before they get cold."

"Don't tell me it's something horribly uninteresting." She picked up a piece of bacon and chewed on it thoughtfully. "Because that would just be sad."

"Sorry to disappoint. Horribly uninteresting is accurate. Trust fund." Aiden leaned back with his cup of coffee and watched her over the rim.

"Well, that sucks." She finished the bacon and went back to attacking her eggs. "One or two bedroom?"

"Depends on if it has an office." He set his mug down and stole a bite of Phoebe's blueberry pancakes. She raised her eyebrow and smirked but didn't complain.

"Depends if it has an office, he says." She clicked a few things on the screen. "Close to work?"

"Of course."

She licked her lips, and he felt a pulse of heat go through him. Phoebe was fun to be around and even if he had other friends (which he didn't yet), he'd rather hang out with her.

Of course, his other friends probably wouldn't let him have sex with them the way Phoebe did.

"Do you have a minimum square footage?" She glanced at him, catching him staring at her. Her cheeks flushed pink. "What?"

"Nothing." He shook his head.

She set down her fork and gave him a look that said she knew it wasn't nothing, but she let it go. "I vote we go from highest rent to lowest rent. That way we can get the swanky places out of the way. I love looking at swanky places."

Aiden wore a pair of jeans and a nice T-shirt. Phoebe, on the other hand, wore a jean mini skirt with a blue halter top. She left her hair down and it teased her bare shoulders, which begged to be touched. Her earrings dangled the same length as her hair. Her makeup was barely there. Instead of her usual red lips, she had on a light gloss that made her lips shine. She looked so kissable he'd had difficulty leaving the hotel suite and even more difficulty resisting dragging her off to somewhere semi-private while waiting for a table.

"Earth to Aiden."

He lifted his gaze from her lips to her eyes. "Yeah?"

"Should we go look at apartments, or do you want to find some place to continue that dirty thought in your brain?" She raised her eyebrow and tilted her head. Damn, she was going to be the death of him.

He decided to focus on the task and not how her long legs ended in high heeled sandals that showed off her perfect pedicure. "Right, do we need to call ahead?"

"Nah, most of these places have offices and since your need is urgent, we'll only look at available apartments." She winked at him and stood.

"I wouldn't say urgent. . . ." Dropping some money on the bill, he followed her out of the restaurant, guided by her hips swaying back and forth between the tables. "More of an approaching urgency."

She tossed him a smile over her shoulder.

They took a cab to the first building, which from the outside was impressive. A doorman let them in and they asked for the rental office. They were seated in a small conference room to wait for the property manager. The woman who had shown them in offered them drinks, but they'd both declined.

Left alone in the room, Phoebe strolled around looking at the brochures and magazines laying around.

"I'm not sure which is more distracting." He rubbed the back of his neck.

"Hmm?" She met his gaze.

"Standing or sitting." He gestured toward her.

"Mr. Kingston, are you calling me a distraction?" Her smile was as cheeky as her cocked hip.

"You know you are. Come sit down." Aiden didn't think it would help much but at least he wouldn't be distracted by her long legs.

She shrugged and sat next to him. "Better?"

Lavender and spice wafted toward him. Nope. Not better as far as distracting him went, but before he could say anything, a woman walked in. She was young and attractive and perfectly outfitted for her job, but she didn't do anything for him. Not with Phoebe's heat directly next to him.

"I'm Hannah. I heard you're looking for an apartment." Her eyes drifted between him and Phoebe.

Standing, Aiden held out his hand. "I'm Aiden Kingston. This is my friend, Phoebe. I'm looking for an apartment."

He shook Hannah's hand and she turned to Phoebe, who did a small finger wave.

"That's great." Hannah straightened and clutched her

tablet close to her body. "We have a couple of apartments available currently. Do you have a price range?"

"I'm looking for something spacious with a view." Aiden offered a hand to Phoebe to help her up. "We'll look at whatever you have available to see if it is suitable."

Hannah nodded. Her judgmental eyes dropped to Phoebe's skirt before she opened the door. "Right this way."

Phoebe was quiet as they toured the facility. The gym, pool, roof top garden, etc. It was a nice setup. The first apartment Hannah showed them was on the tenth floor and had one bedroom.

"Your hotel suite is bigger than this apartment." Phoebe leaned against the counter in the kitchen of the smallish apartment. She gave Hannah a conspiratorial look. "He really needs a place for an office."

"You can put a desk in this corner." Hannah's eyes had grown big at the mention of suite. "But of course, our penthouse has much more space, but the rent is significantly higher."

"That's more like it." Phoebe headed to the door and turned to make sure they were following her. "Why waste your time with this, babe?"

He smiled at Phoebe, before saying to Hannah, "Honestly, I am used to having room to spread out. My family's house in the Hamptons is close enough to escape to on weekends, but work will keep me in town more often than not."

"Of course." Hannah led the way to the elevator and used a special key to get to the top floor. "Our penthouse offers the most security with the doorman and the security guard downstairs, plus the additional keys needed to access the level."

Aiden reached out and took Phoebe's hand as the elevator went up. Once again, she glanced at their hands like it was something foreign to her. It was hard to believe that a woman who liked hugs and holding hands like Phoebe did hadn't had relationships. He couldn't stop the crooked grin on his face that had been glued in place since she called him "babe." His ex-girlfriends had never called him nicknames before. He kind of liked it. Even if it wasn't real.

"Here we are." Hannah stepped out into the apartment. "This one is fully furnished, but we can move the furniture out if it doesn't suit."

Bypassing the furniture, Aiden walked with Phoebe over to the windows that wrapped around the corner.

Phoebe whistled. "Now that's a view."

They were high enough most of the city was visible from the windows. The furniture was leather in the living room with a large screen TV which doubled as a mirror when off. It opened to an actual full-sized kitchen with an island. A dining room sat off to the side. It was furnished but not decorated, which would actually suit him just fine.

"What do you think?" Phoebe asked as they walked into the master bedroom. A giant king size bed took up the bulk of the floor space, but there was still plenty of room.

"Don't forget to check out the walk-in closets." Hannah stayed in the other room, probably to give them time to "talk."

Phoebe sat on the bed and laid back. "You have to make sure it's comfortable."

Her long legs dangled off the edge of the bed and her skirt hinted at what lay beneath. He cleared his throat. "Is it comfortable?"

"Good enough." She leaned up on her elbows and his eyes dropped to the stretch of skin revealed between her shirt and skirt, so beautifully displayed. So much smooth, silky skin begging to be touched. She winked at him and held out her hands, wiggling her fingers toward him.

He took them and helped her stand. She looked up at him,

still holding his hands. "You should try everything before you plunk down a ludicrous amount of money for the apartment."

"Are you going to help me break everything in?"

She smiled up at him. "I'm always available for house warmings."

Phoebe dragged him over to the set of doors off to the side and opened one, revealing a walk-in closet. She tugged him in and pulled his head down to hers. He took her mouth and tried to listen for Hannah. He lifted his head and Phoebe gave him a naughty smile.

"What do you think of the closet, Aiden?" Phoebe fluttered her eyes at him.

"Spacious." He could barely think straight as Phoebe pulled him to the next door, which was an identical closet.

"For the little lady when you find a new one." She dismissed it quickly. She wiggled her eyebrows at him. "But the question we all need to know is, what about the bathroom?"

He let her lead him into the bathroom. It definitely had a large shower and a bathtub.

"I don't know," she said, dropping his hand. She stepped up to the bathtub. "It's not swim worthy. Do you think we'd both fit?"

He could definitely imagine Phoebe riding his cock in the tub. The water sloshing over the sides onto the expensive marble tile floor. Her breasts wet and glistening before his eyes.

"That's a naughty look," she said quietly and walked over to him. She placed her hand on his chest. "What are you thinking?"

"Definitely big enough."

She glanced over her shoulder at the tub. "We could make it work."

"How's it going in there?" Hannah yelled.

"Quite well." Phoebe pressed a finger against his lips and then walked around him. "But does it have an office? He's a workaholic so he needs somewhere he can really get down to business."

He drew in a deep breath, rearranged himself, and followed her out of the bedroom.

"Right through those doors." Hannah indicated a set of doors.

Phoebe opened them and turned to Aiden. "Nice."

She disappeared within, and he followed, smiling politely at Hannah, who was busy with her phone. The office wasn't huge, but it was big enough. A nice desk and chair, even room for a leather Chesterfield sofa. Phoebe sat in the chair behind the desk and propped her feet up on the desk. "What do you think?"

"It suits you nicely." He ran through the numbers in his head. It was well within the amount he allocated for living expenses. He liked the way Phoebe looked in this apartment and already had plans on how to make good use of the space.

"I could devise villainous plots nicely from behind this desk." Phoebe twirled a pretend mustache.

"Ah, yes, I shouldn't forget your evil plans." Aiden joined her behind the desk and offered her his hand. Would she plot against him if things went sour between them? Again? Would she turn everyone in the office against him? They weren't dating. They were just fucking. By the time he had this apartment, they might not even be together. Technically they weren't still fucking even. He assumed last night was supposed to be the last time.

She took his hand, and they joined Hannah in the dining room.

"What do you think?" Hannah asked.

He glanced at Phoebe, not that he needed her opinion.

After all, she would never be part of this apartment, at least not in the long run. She didn't do long runs, plus they worked together. Dating coworkers was always a bad idea.

"If you want the best. . . ." She gestured to the apartment.

"I do like the best." His eyes didn't leave Phoebe. Her eyes softened and her smile only had a little wickedness in it.

"If you want to start the paperwork. . . ." Hannah said.

"I would like to look at other places, but we can get the credit check out of the way."

Phoebe smirked at that, running her fingers across her lips, but she wandered over to the couch and made herself comfortable while he gave Hannah all the information she needed. He finished up and went over to collect Phoebe.

She looked up at him from her seat on the couch. He offered her his hand. She eyed it for a moment before slipping her hand into his.

"Where to next?" he asked.

Lifting her phone, she pressed a couple of buttons. "How about this one?"

He moved closer to look at her screen. It was another penthouse but unfurnished. "Let's do it."

CHAPTER 14

PHOEBE TAGGED along to the next few apartment viewings with Aiden and imagined what it would be like to have his kind of money. All the rents were definitely beyond her reach. The property managers gave her a disdainful once-over, noticing her non-labeled clothes and off the rack shoes. As soon as Aiden said the apartment was for him, they almost sagged in relief.

She didn't need to impress these people and hadn't really dressed to impress anyone except Aiden. She'd caught his gaze on her bare shoulders and legs multiple times.

Mission accomplished.

But then Aiden would look at her with a smile and reach for her hand. . . sigh. It was a double-edged sword. He included her and asked for her opinion, but she knew it wouldn't matter. She was temporary.

Some other woman would use that closet and have bathtub sex with Aiden. Meanwhile, Phoebe would be in her efficiency, hooking up with some random guy who would never be able to make her achieve the kind of orgasms Aiden gave her. But she'd be safe.

This particular saleswoman, Kimber, was being kind of a twat to Phoebe as she showed Aiden around the apartment. Phoebe jumped up to sit on the island while Kimber tried to make a play for Aiden. *Good luck, Kimber. He is out of both of our leagues.*

Phoebe stared out the windows overlooking the city. Her apartment view was of a brick wall. For her, the view didn't matter. It was what she could afford and she was content with it. Her best friend lived down the hall. When Morgan stayed there. And it was close to work. It was all she needed.

She couldn't afford to even furnish this current apartment. It was huge and cold. The high ceilings just made Kimber's heels clacking on the hardwood floors echo.

"And that's the bedroom. Definitely enough space for a king-sized bed." Kimber's high pitched voice assaulted Phoebe's ears.

"Could you give me a minute to talk to my friend?" Aiden asked. He'd called her that all day. His "friend." It was probably better than lover. Probably more acceptable than fuck buddy.

"Of course." Kimber's fake-ass smile could be heard in her words. "I'll just wait in the hallway."

The door opened and closed.

Aiden's footsteps got closer until she could feel the warmth of him. She put a smile on as he circled the island. He stepped between her legs and put his hands on the island next to her hips. Her breath caught in her throat.

"What do you think?" Aiden searched her eyes. She hated when he did that. It felt like he was trying to see who she really was. No one got that close to her.

"What do *you* think?" Phoebe threw back at him. "Was the bathtub big enough for two?"

"Unfortunately, no." Straightening, he moved his hands to

her hips, pulling her against the solidness of him. "I don't know about you, but I could use some lunch and a nap."

She traced her fingertip along his bottom lip. "Nap?"

"Laying horizontal on a bed for an amount of time. Preferably with you." He kissed each of her shoulders before taking her mouth. She leaned into the kiss, always wanting more from him.

Last night was supposed to get each other out of their systems but had it only created more longing?

She pulled back and immediately regretted the loss of his lips against hers. "Did you find something you want?"

"I want you." He kissed her and pulled her off the island to stand.

She straightened her skirt and noticed him watching her. "Like what you see?"

"Definitely." His words floated through her. Feeling desirable wasn't anything new, but this guy made her feel epically desirable. Like she was the only one in the world who could turn his head.

Unfortunately, she wasn't the only one on the prowl. "I bet if you asked Kimber, she'd give you her number."

Aiden glanced toward the door. "I don't want Kimber's number. I don't even have your number."

"You haven't exactly asked for my number either." Phoebe walked out of the kitchen and halfway to the door.

He caught her hand and pulled her against him. "Give me your number."

"Why?" She took her own turn searching his gorgeous green eyes. "We're just having fun here, right? Getting it out of our systems?"

He drew her hips against his. "What if we get separated and I need to tell you where I am?"

"Well, given we are adults and we know where each other lives and works, we'll be just fine if that happens." Phoebe didn't know what she wanted from him. Maybe an admission he would still want her after today, even if he didn't want to want her.

"Maybe I want to text you dirty messages." His lips captured hers, slowly destroying any resolve she might have had. "Or send you dirty pictures? Or have you send me dirty pictures?"

"Mr. Kingston," Phoebe chastised and then laughed. "You couldn't handle pics."

"Give me your number, Phoebe." His eyes were sincere and the joking was all gone.

Her heart leapt into her throat. "Fine, but if you send me a dick pic, it better have proper lighting and good angles. There's a real craft to truly capture the essence—"

He caught her lips again and pulled her up against him. She gave in to the kiss because she wanted to, not because she'd been excited about him asking for her number. Definitely not because she hoped he would ask her for more sex. He released her lips and drew her back to the counter.

"I will warn you, I'm a sharer on text," she said.

"I certainly hope so." He lifted her up on the counter and kissed her neck.

"I think Kimber might be getting worried."

"Fuck, Kimber." His mouth trailed down the side of her halter top. Her skirt rode up as he moved between her legs. His erection pressed against her, causing her pulse to race.

"We should probably go home for that nap." Not wasting any time, she tugged on his belt, undoing it, needing to feel his skin against hers.

"Probably." He slid his hand between her legs and pushed aside her underwear to feel her flesh. She caught her bottom lip in her teeth.

She undid his pants and stroked his cock. "I'd ask if you had—"

He reached into his pocket and handed her a condom and returned to kissing her neck.

She smiled and opened the package. "I like how you're always prepared."

"Hurry, Phoebe," he said as he thrust his fingers inside her, making her as desperate as he was. She caught her lip between her teeth to stop herself from moaning.

This guy could make her do things she never thought she'd do. Like getting off in the middle of a busy bar while her coworkers sat beside them. Or going down on him in the hallway of a bar. Or sex on a counter of a million-dollar apartment during a showing. She rolled the condom on him. He removed his fingers from her and grabbed her hips as he surged into her. She gasped.

"Watch the doorknob." He moved deep and quick within her. His lips stroked up and down her neck.

"Multitasking. Awesome." She held back a moan.

"I've been wanting to do this all day." His words were soft for her ears only. He latched onto that spot where her neck and shoulder met.

She stared at the doorknob as the pressure built within her. His hand found the center of her and stroked her as he increased his pace. Her orgasm flowed over her like plunging into warm water. Her mouth fell open and she sucked in air. His fingers dug into her hips as he found his own release.

He kissed her and straightened her panties before taking care of himself. She got down off the counter and straightened her clothing. He still had to get rid of the condom. There wasn't exactly a trash can in the empty apartment.

"Here." Phoebe opened her purse and pulled out a candy wrapper. She held it open to him, and he dropped the condom on it. As soon as they reached a trashcan, she would throw it away. She wrapped it up and shoved it in her purse just as the doorknob turned.

"Sorry I took so long," Kimber said. "I got a phone call."

Aiden walked over to the sink and washed his hands quickly.

Kimber spotted them and walked over. "So do you have any questions?"

Phoebe grinned at Kimber and then turned back to Aiden. "I don't have any. Do you, babe?"

"I think we're good here." Aiden gave her a small smile before directing Kimber out of the apartment. "Why don't we go discuss the rent?"

"Sure." Kimber looked over her shoulder at Phoebe who walked behind them. Phoebe must look like the cat that got the canary, but she felt so good she just couldn't care.

When they got on the elevator, Aiden took Phoebe's hand in his, and she let him because she wanted to, and why shouldn't she want to. What could holding hands with the guy who fucked her possibly hurt?

"I SHOULD GO HOME." Phoebe sat on the edge of the bed, completely naked. Just the way Aiden liked her. She was searching for her panties.

"It's late, just stay." Aiden leaned up with his head in his hand as he watched her. It was almost midnight. He didn't want her to go. "I like sleeping with you."

She looked over her shoulder at him with a half grin. "You like waking up and driving me fucking crazy with your morning wood."

"I wouldn't have morning wood if you didn't stay over." He dangled her panties between his fingers.

She glared at him and reached for her panties. Keeping them out of her reach, he grabbed her arm and pulled her to him.

"These panties will cost you." He tucked them out of reach and positioned Phoebe beneath him.

"Oh, yeah?" She lifted her eyebrow at him. "What exactly will they cost and seriously how do you have so much stamina?"

"Genetics."

She laughed. "What are your terms?"

"Stay the night with me." Aiden dropped his head to suck on her breast.

"I love having sex with you, but I seriously need a break." Phoebe pulled his face from her breast. "At least an hour or so."

Aiden rolled onto his side next to her. "We could watch a movie or play a game."

"I suppose." Phoebe settled into the bed a little more. "What is going on with you today? I thought we were only trying to get out of each other systems."

Aiden rolled onto his back and covered his eyes with his arm. "Besides the people at work, I don't know anyone else in this city. But I know you and you're fun to be around."

"The sex probably doesn't hurt either." Phoebe linked her hand with his as she stared up at the ceiling with him. "Aiden?"

"Yes."

"Are you telling me you're lonely?" She leaned up to look down at him.

"Maybe." Aiden reached out his hand and combed his fingers through her hair. Her hair was fantastic. "Would that be a bad thing?"

"No. People hook up for all sorts of reasons, but we can't have an actual relationship. I don't want that, and you said you weren't looking for one."

"I'm not looking." Aiden didn't know how to explain it. He pulled her down to rest her head on his chest, enjoying the skin-to-skin contact. "I like you as a person too. Not just as a sex object."

"Why, thank you." She laughed. "I like you as a person too. Except at work."

Earlier, they'd finally exchanged numbers, and he'd felt like he'd won a prize. Especially when instead of his name, Phoebe had entered him as Sex God. He caught her hand on his chest and covered it with his own. "I still want you."

"I think we've covered every surface of this suite and that counter in an apartment you aren't even going to rent. I'm beginning to think there might not be a way to get this out of our systems." She sighed, but her body was relaxed against his.

"So what do we do?" Aiden stroked his fingertip along her hand.

"I don't know. Make rules and figure it out? Just end it now and white knuckle it until we don't want to have sex with each other anymore? Keep fucking until we can't help but hate it?"

"Ah, the old fuck marathon strategy." Aiden chuckled and tightened his arm around her. "I'm not very good at white knuckling it."

"Me neither." She snuggled closer to his body.

"What kind of rules?"

Phoebe sighed. "Rules to stop us from becoming attached I guess."

"Like no kissing in public?" Aiden stroked his hand up and down Phoebe's smooth back. She snuggled in tighter to him. His heart pounded a little harder.

"Probably shouldn't hold hands in public either."

Aiden closed his hand over hers on his chest. "I like hand-holding."

"If you wouldn't do it with Drew in public, you probably shouldn't do it with me."

"Well, that sucks." Aiden sighed. "But you're saying if I hold hands with Drew, I can hold hands with you?"

Phoebe laughed. "If you want to hang out in public, that's a definite rule. Too many people who work with us play in this area too."

"So rule one is treat you like Drew in public. . . . What about public sex?"

She laughed and pushed up to look down at him. "Would you have sex with Drew in public?"

"No, but what if it's covert public sex?" Aiden smiled at her, remembering the bar and wondering if she remembered it as well.

"I'll allow it, but absolutely no getting caught, and you have to deal with the consequences if we do." Phoebe snuggled back next to him.

"This can't interfere with our work lives." Aiden trailed his hand along her spine. "We need to have some boundaries."

"And absolutely no sex at work." Phoebe leaned up again and looked at him with those brown eyes. "People will always figure out if you are boning at work."

"Got it." Aiden enjoyed the press of Phoebe's curves against his side. He would happily sleep like this. "I wouldn't have even thought about fucking in the office. Now I won't be able to get it out of my head."

"Well, stop thinking about it. It's off limits." Smiling, she traced a circle over his heart. "We probably shouldn't sleep together."

"What's the point then?"

"We can have sex, but I meant actual sleep."

"Except tonight."

"Except tonight. But that means after sex, no cuddling."

"I like cuddling." He pulled her in tighter.

"A little cuddling would probably be fine." She relented so easily.

"What if cuddling leads to sex?"

She laughed. He loved the sound of her laughter. It was rich and complex and hit him somewhere in his gut. She said, "Why are you even single?"

The light feeling in his gut twisted. "I work too much. The women I was with were in it for the wrong reasons."

She lifted her head and rested her chin on her hand to look up at him. "Did they just want you for your bathtub?"

"Only you are into me for my hotel's tub." He stroked his fingertip down her spine again as she continued to look at him. He sighed. "My family, while not mafia, have connections. We are one of the wealthiest families in Chicago. My mother works with a lot of charitable organizations while my father runs her family's business with the twins and me, when I was there. The women my mother vetted were all social climbers. Maybe they didn't want me for my money, but they wanted the prestige that went with the Kingston name. None of them were someone I could spend my life with."

"Do you want to spend your life with someone?" Her words were soft, drawing his attention to her.

"Someday. Definitely not this year or next. How can I concentrate on my career and ignore my children and wife? I've watched couples in my family try for years to strike a balance and it always ends in divorce, alimony, and child support. Only seeing the kids when it's convenient for your ex. That's not how I want to live."

"Better than being so in love with someone that when he does divorce you, you can't even love your own child. Even though he obviously doesn't really love anyone other than himself. If you can even call that love." Phoebe closed her eyes for a moment. When she opened them, the storm had cleared. "I'm glad you figured it out before making a family to tear apart."

A sharp pain struck him in the chest. One more piece of the puzzle of her slid into place. Phoebe had been a broken little girl when her parents split. She didn't feel loved as a child, so why would she expect it when she grew up? The temptation to try to help her deal with it was almost overwhelming. But even if he did fall in love with her, Phoebe wouldn't want his love.

So he dismissed that feeling, concentrating on just having fun with this amazing creature while it lasted. "Why don't we order some dinner and rent a movie?"

CHAPTER 15

"Definitely *John Wick*." Phoebe grabbed the remote from Aiden and scrolled down on the menu until *John Wick* was highlighted.

"I haven't seen it." Aiden lounged in the corner of the couch. He'd drawn Phoebe into him until they were cuddled for the movie. She'd managed to get her underwear back, but she put on one of his shirts instead of getting dressed. He wore a pair of pajama pants and that was it. She had to admit it was hard to keep her hands to herself with all those glorious muscles exposed.

"Then we are definitely watching it." She clicked on the movie and it started, all dark colors and shadows. And of course, Keanu. . . happy sigh.

Aiden's arms wrapped around her and she wondered how any woman would ever let him go. Sure, marriage was important to some people, but orgasms, man, the guy could sure deliver on those. About halfway through the movie, she turned to him. "Are you going to get one of the apartments we saw today?"

His fingertips traced a pattern on her upper arm. He

pulled his eyes from the movie and focused on her. "Hmmm?"

"Apartment?"

"What about it?" His eyes were drawn back to the action.

She hit pause on the remote. He sighed and looked at her.

"Are you one of those crazy people who talks during movies?" His eyebrow arched in suspicion.

"Not usually." She stretched her legs along his. "But I got curious."

"About apartments?" He tucked a strand of hair behind her ear.

Goosebumps skittered down her arms. "Yeah, did you pick from the ones we saw today or do you need to look at more?"

"I feel a solid connection to the last one we saw. The counters were amazing."

She laughed and heat flushed through her system, remembering him taking her on the island. The distraction of whether the property manager would walk in on them. "Maybe you just liked Kimber."

"Who?"

"Good answer." She trailed her fingers down his abs, following the dips and creases. "But it didn't have a good tub."

"And I'd have to buy furniture." He winced.

"That's the second time you've mentioned it. Is shopping that bad?"

"Worse." He captured her wandering hand and brought it to his lips. "The first one seemed nice."

"Perfect for when you have a girlfriend to move in with you." She tried not to sound bitter. She didn't really care if he had a future girlfriend. She sure as hell wasn't applying for the job. But she wasn't ready to stop having sex with him yet either.

"I'm not looking for a girlfriend and definitely not a live-in girlfriend." He kissed her hand again and stared at her with his "let's fuck" eyes.

"Some girl is going to walk up to you and sweep you off your feet." She didn't rub the ache in her chest at the thought. That was ridiculous. "You'll be shacked up in no time."

"Why don't you date?" He pressed his lips to the inside of her wrist and dragged his teeth against it.

"Are you asking?" She couldn't stop the tremor from her voice.

"I wouldn't dream of asking. I like my bits where they are. Besides, I heard you were a formidable opponent." His green eyes danced as he looked at her.

Her insides softened and she breathed out. "I've been known to be a little cranky on occasion."

"I'd take cranky any day." Aiden continued to kiss and lick her wrist and it was doing crazy things to her insides.

Phoebe shifted against him restlessly as he trapped both of her hands. "Aiden?"

"Yes?" He paid attention to the other wrist, making her squirm as shivers of want coursed through her veins.

"Stop teasing me." Her body was quickly heating up. She pressed her lips to his chest.

He dragged her up his chest until their mouths were aligned. His lips brushed hers in a whisper of a touch. "You like the tease."

"Mmhmm." She kissed him, tasting and teasing his lips and tongue. Losing herself in the unique taste that was Aiden. If she could stay like this, trapped in this moment with him, she'd be content.

Her phone rang. They both stopped and looked at it. The screen lit up with the name Doctor Cutie, Phoebe's on and off fuck buddy.

"Do you need to get that?" Aiden stiffened under her and not in a good way.

She grabbed her phone and sent the call to voicemail. Her pulse raced. She wasn't ready to stop whatever she and Aiden were doing together, but this might fuck things up. Her heart hurt as she turned back to Aiden. Now he'd want her to leave. The reminder that she wasn't his alone just blasted across them like a cold front.

She turned her phone off and set it on the coffee table.

"What are we doing?" Aiden sat up, taking his body heat from her, and she wanted it back. But she wouldn't be one of those girls who begged a man to keep them. That wasn't who she was.

Phoebe straightened. She'd been honest from the get-go. "Just sex, right? That's all you want from me."

"Yes, that's what I want." But he didn't look happy about it as he ran his hand through his hair. "We have rules, right?"

She nodded.

His green eyes captured hers. A fierceness resided in his as he said, "New rule. No one else but me."

"What?" Phoebe couldn't be hearing him correctly. No one had wanted Phoebe all to themselves. Ever. It wasn't part of the package deal. Not that she had a tribe of guys she rotated between or anything like that. But no one ever asked her to be exclusive.

"While you and I are doing whatever twisted fucking thing we are doing here. . . ." He moved in closer and took her chin in his hand, maintaining eye contact. Her body responded to his touch, craving more. "Just you and me. Otherwise this isn't going to work."

Ignoring her desire, she had to make sure she understood. Her heart ached. This was new. "You want me and you to be monogamous?"

"Yes."

"Like we're dating?"

"Yes."

Phoebe pursed her lips. "But we're not dating?"

"Exactly." His hand wasn't hurting her but it was tight on her chin.

"Do you honestly believe I would bounce from you and go get some strange?" Phoebe knew who she was. She didn't regret having sex with other people and she'd go back to it after Aiden didn't want her anymore. But she didn't usually mix guys up like that. She might rebound to a hookup, but she never spread herself that thin.

"I don't know how you work." He didn't sound disgusted or angry, just blunt and to the point. Like he didn't expect her to be pure and only his. At least that was decent of him not to slut-shame her. "If you want dick, I'm willing to give it to you. I just don't want to share."

She sighed and pulled her face from his hand, but then she looked him back in the eye because she needed him to hear this. "I don't generally bounce from guy to guy to guy. I don't have a rotating list of guys for every day of the week. If I'm interested in a guy, we might get together a few times, but then it's over."

"And that guy?" He gestured to the phone.

"Why does it matter?" She threw her hands up in the air. "Seriously, why? So what if I went from your hotel to his apartment? Or hooked up with him during lunch sometime this week? Why does it matter? We use protection. I always use protection. I've never not used protection. I get checked regularly. And I use birth control also."

"Fuck." Aiden rubbed the back of his neck, like he knew he was being unreasonable. She wanted to tell him she wouldn't have sex with someone else, but that would be giving in to his demands. This was too much. Was he just trying to fit her into the convenient boxes he always had in the past? But did that matter? She wanted him and wasn't planning on sleeping around. She could tell him that, but then she'd be giving in.

She searched his eyes for a second. Maybe she wanted to give in. Fuck. She needed a minute.

She stood. "I'm going to go use the bathroom. You figure out what you want and let me know."

~

AIDEN DIDN'T KNOW what he wanted or what was reasonable in this situation. He hated the idea of someone else touching Phoebe. Hated the guy who had called expecting her to be at his beck and call. Hated if she hadn't been with him tonight, she might have taken that call. If he hadn't given in to his longing Friday night, she could be in someone else's arms. Right now. The tight burning in his chest ached.

Fuck. What was he doing? The facts of the matter were simple. She didn't want a relationship. He didn't want a relationship. They couldn't even get along at work. But. . . .

He wanted her like he hadn't wanted anyone else. Originally, he thought it was the newness, but maybe it was the forbidden aspect of it. All he knew was he wanted to explore more of what was happening between them. He'd never been with someone so blatantly sexual before. Everything about Phoebe screamed sex. From her clothes, to her hot body, to her words and the looks she gave him.

He didn't want to share that with anyone else. Wanted to keep her all to himself. But what did that mean? Movement caught his attention.

Phoebe stood in the doorway to the bedroom, looking small in his oversized shirt. Her chin set stubbornly. "Should I get dressed?"

Standing, he went over to her until they were almost

close enough to touch, but he didn't. She fried his brain with every touch, and he needed to say this. Need her to hear him.

She just looked at him with her gorgeous lips cut in a thin line.

"I don't want to share you. I know it's not fair of me to ask. I know this might make you want to stop having sex with me, but I can barely concentrate around you on a normal day. I'm not asking for forever. Neither of us wants that."

Phoebe's lips softened. He reached out to take her hand and she let him link his fingers between hers. The tightness eased in his chest.

"There is something here between us. A physical attraction I've never had before. I want to explore it and you freely without worrying about who else might be with you. I'm not going to be with anyone else. I want you to myself. Not as my girlfriend, but as my lover."

Her eyes softened. "Why do you assume I want someone else when I have you?"

"At work, I have to pretend we're nothing more than coworkers." He drew her into his arms, hugging her to him as if that would make her understand. He couldn't be reasonable where she was concerned. "I'm going to see you at work and act like I don't want to pull you into a stairwell and ease the constant ache I have when I'm near you. I have to pretend during the day that I'm not dying to touch you. That you flirting with photographers doesn't drive me crazy. It will be agony, and if I thought there might be someone else. . . ."

The thought tore him apart inside.

Phoebe pulled back but kept her hands linked with his. She looked up at him. Her brown eyes ancient and wise. "I can be yours."

Those words sparked against his heart. "It's not fair—"

She held her finger against his lips. "I don't care about fair. I can be yours."

He kissed her fingertips and dipped his head to take her lips. She swayed into him and he lifted her. Her arms wrapped around his neck as her legs wrapped around his waist.

He started toward the bed, kissing down her neck.

"I don't want to be with anyone but you." She placed a kiss on his throat.

His chest filled. Those words spoke to something deep inside him that he didn't want to examine. "I don't want anyone but you."

He lowered her to the bed. Their bodies entangled. His mouth pressed to hers. His hands shook slightly as he unbuttoned her shirt slowly. The pressing urgency that usually accompanied being with Phoebe had been fulfilled many times today. Now he wanted to go slow and explore. He wanted to discover what it was about her that made him want to make exceptions.

Why he wanted her to make exceptions.

Her shirt parted and she lifted from the bed to ease it off, leaving only her panties on. Her soft skin rose beneath his touch like a flower tracks the sun. So responsive. Nothing was fake about Phoebe.

Her eyes fluttered closed as he cupped her breast, lowering his head to worship her nipple with his lips, tongue and teeth. Switching to her other breast, he could spend hours with her and not grow tired of touching her and kissing her.

"Aiden?" His name was soft on her lips.

He lifted his head and met her eyes. They sparkled in the dim light of the room. For a moment, she seemed vulnerable like she hadn't previously. He stroked his hand down her stomach as it quivered beneath his fingertips. "Phoebe?"

She wet her lips as his fingers traced the elastic of her panties. "I'm yours."

The words cracked something inside his chest, making warmth spread throughout him. He stripped her underwear down her legs, never breaking eye contact. He ran his hand up her thigh until he cupped the heat of her in his hand. "Mine."

Her hands wrapped behind his neck and she pressed herself into his hand. Her lips parted and her eyelids lowered but she didn't close them. Her eyes never left his. He slipped his fingers into her core, feeling the muscles pulse around him.

Phoebe arched up until she was sitting. He sat up with her and continued to move his fingers inside her. Her eyes were liquid pools of desire as she reached for his cock, still in his loose pajama bottoms. She stroked her hand over him and said, "Mine."

Fuck. He pulled her onto his lap, needing to feel her skin against his, and kissed her again. Her hands wrapped around the back of his neck, her breasts crushed against his chest, and her sweet pussy pressed down against his cock.

He lifted his lips from hers and met her eyes. "Condom?"

She nodded and rubbed herself over his clothed cock before reaching over to the nightstand to grab a condom. He pulled his pants down to free himself and sheathed his cock. She took hold of him and guided him to her entrance.

"I want to see your eyes when you come," he said as she lowered herself onto him. Every inch a fucking masterpiece of sensation. Her lips parted on a groan, but she kept her eyes open.

"OH MY—FUCK," Phoebe swore as she lowered herself on him, completely, filling her.

His green eyes held hers. "Okay?"

"Definitely okay." She lifted and lowered again. She wanted to close her eyes against the sensation to hold it in her mind, but she didn't. She wanted to watch his expression, how his lips parted. How his green eyes glowed with heat.

Their bodies moved together as one. Their breathing fell into sync as they climbed toward something, holding onto each other and maintaining eye contact. She could feel her body climbing to the peak when Aiden reached between them to press his thumb against her throbbing center.

She tightened around him as she fell into the sensations. She cried out his name, begging him to join her. No longer able to keep her eyes open or track him as the waves of her release crashed over her.

Holding her against him, he rolled her onto her back and took over. Finally, she opened her eyes and cradled his face with her hands, maintaining eye contact as he built to his own release. Everything about him wound around her as he moved within her, touching something inside her that had never been touched before.

His scent, that glorious combination, seeped under her skin. The scruff of his five o'clock shadow rasped against the palm of her hands. His breath caught and released as he moved. And his eyes. . . greens, golds, and browns mixed to perfection as he looked into the heart of her while he took her under him.

She lost track of time when she was in his arms. The world could end around them, but she'd stay here in his arms. She couldn't hold back as she climaxed again. This time she caught his satisfied smile before his own release overwhelmed him and his face froze in ecstasy above her.

He kissed her before collapsing half on her, still a part of her. His hand swept down her side and pressed her closer to him. She tangled her fingers in his hair.

"Wow," she said.

He propped himself up and looked into her eyes. She touched her hand to his heart, feeling the beat of it slowing. He moved to get up, but she held him to her. "Just a little longer."

He chuckled and nuzzled her neck, making desire pulse through her. "If we stay here much longer, I'm going to fall asleep."

"That wouldn't be so bad." She kissed his cheek. This wasn't so bad. Surprisingly. It wasn't like they were getting their emotions all tangled up in this. They could be exclusive and have sex for as long as they wanted.

He withdrew and took care of the condom before coming back to bed, lying beside her. Reaching out, he took her hand in his. Her heart clattered in her chest.

"One more rule," she said.

"How many does that make?" Aiden asked.

"Not sure, but it's important." She leaned up so she could see his face and eyes. "If either of us wants to end things, that's it. No backsliding, no mooning over the other person. Just done. Okay?"

He cupped her face with his hand. "What if neither of us wants to end it?"

Phoebe pressed her lips to his. To keep from saying what swirled around her brain: eventually he wouldn't want her anymore. She was nobody's keeper. It was inevitable.

"We found a brewery, looking for an advertising agency." Aiden had seamlessly inserted himself into the Monday meetings. "Noble Brewers."

Phoebe sipped on her coffee. He hadn't wanted her to leave on Sunday, and she'd been weak. She hadn't taken Morgan up on the Sunday morning run either. Morgan had sounded grateful, but wanted to make sure they could find another time to get together.

After picking up some more clothes, she'd spent last night in Aiden's arms. This morning, he'd woken her way too early, but in the best way possible, so she couldn't even be mad at him. But that didn't mean she couldn't give him a disgruntled look behind her sunglasses.

Logan edged forward. "I've been to their tap room. They do a lot of seasonal brews."

"Sounds like a good lead," Drew said.

Monday morning meeting, blech. She'd rather sleep in for a few more hours. Everyone sat around the conference table looking bright-eyed and bushy-tailed. Ready to conquer the week when all she wanted to do was curl back up in Aiden's bed.

Shit. She blinked and sat up straighter. *Her* bed, not Aiden's bed. He was definitely getting inside her head. She needed to find a way to back off but still have sex with him. Less talking more sex. Though how she could handle more sex, she had no idea. The man was a fucking machine. Literally.

She snickered out loud.

"Do you have something to add, Phoebe?" Morgan gave her a raised eyebrow.

Hell, Phoebe didn't even know what they were talking about. "Sorry, thought of this funny joke I heard."

Everyone else went back to discussing launch strategy for one of the businesses Phoebe had brought in. Everyone but Morgan. Her big blue eyes narrowed on Phoebe, and she had this look like she was trying to dissect Phoebe's brain. Phoebe made a kissy face at her and gave her a wink.

Morgan shook her head. Drew touched Morgan's arm, drawing her attention away from Phoebe. Phoebe let out a sigh of relief and downed the rest of her coffee. Morgan wouldn't approve of what Phoebe was doing with Aiden. Even if it was somewhat similar to Morgan and Drew's situation initially.

Nah, it wasn't even close. Those two had hated each other from the beginning. Sex just complicated their animosity. She and Aiden started with sex. Hot, wet panties, dirty sex. The animosity came when he tried to take over her job at work. They still hadn't figured out how to work together, but the sex was separate.

The sex was inevitable and undeniable. His knee brushed hers under the table. Tingles erupted from the contact and she pressed her lips together. If she didn't keep herself in check, she'd end up finding creative ways to have sex in this office without anyone being the wiser. With the exception of Aiden, of course.

The rest of the table left, bringing Phoebe back to the present. Morgan didn't stand but gave Phoebe an odd look. Phoebe just shrugged. It wasn't like she didn't space out these meetings normally.

"We should meet about our strategy for Noble Brewers." Aiden's soft, deep voice rippled through her like a caress. Fuck, but the man was potent.

"Your office or one of the conference rooms?" She turned and didn't miss the heat in his eyes before he banked it.

"My office." His gaze dropped to her lips for a moment.

Her lips curved into a smile and he swallowed. Who was it that decided to not have sex at the office? The thing about rules was Phoebe didn't like them. Rules were meant to be broken and right now she wanted to break them with Aiden, often.

"I'll be right in," she said.

He lifted his gaze to hers. The fire, swirling within, burned brighter. He gave her a curt nod before leaving the conference table. She watched that fine ass of his go for a moment.

Morgan cleared her throat.

Shit. Phoebe turned back to the conference table and it was just the two of them.

"I take it the apartment hunting went well?" Morgan tapped a pen on her notepad.

"Yup." Phoebe pushed back in her chair but didn't stand. "We're getting along a lot better now. Isn't that what you wanted?"

"I didn't mean for you to—" Morgan cut herself off, glanced toward Aiden's office, and then sighed. "I hope you know what you're doing."

"Of course." Phoebe had no clue what was happening

with her and Aiden. All she knew was she wanted to spend as much time as possible with him. No other guy seemed to do it for her right now.

"Phoebe?"

"What?"

"Do you know what you are doing?" Morgan stood and gathered her materials before looking once more at Phoebe. "He's not your usual type of guy. I just don't want you to get hurt."

Phoebe made a dismissive noise. She never let a guy get close enough to hurt her.

~

"Knock, knock."

"Come in." Aiden leaned back in his chair to appreciate Phoebe, standing in his open doorway. Her pencil skirt accentuated her hips and ass to perfection. Matched with heels and a flowing blouse and her hair pulled back in a bun, Phoebe looked like a pin-up model from the forties. She began to close the door.

He cleared his throat from the sudden lump in it. "Leave it open."

She smirked at him, but she left the door partially open. It wouldn't block out the sounds of the pool, but hopefully the rest of the office would be quiet because it was Monday. He couldn't risk closing the door and having Phoebe to himself. His control should be fine after having her all weekend, but something about her lit him up every time he saw her.

"Noble Brewers." Phoebe lowered herself into the chair across from his desk.

Aiden nodded and pulled his file closer. "Small brewery owned by brothers, Sean and Ethan Noble. This is their fifth year in business, and they've just struck a distribution deal to take them from a local brewery into a regional and hopefully a national brand."

Phoebe crossed her legs and bit her bottom lip. "So road trip?"

"We've got an appointment tomorrow at one." Aiden leaned back in his chair. "The brewery is about three hours from here, so we can leave first thing in the morning. Catch their eleven o'clock brewery tour and grab some lunch before meeting with the owners to discuss their advertising needs."

She nodded and made some notes on her tablet. "Should we take Logan with us?"

"No."

She glanced up at him.

"We need to get the lay of the land without someone pitching ideas." Aiden shook his head. "We'll get the details he needs for any campaign, and he may have to go down there eventually, but I think this time should just be me and you."

She nodded and returned her attention to her tablet. "Do you want me to rent a car?"

"I have one."

She smiled. "Of course you do. BMW or Lamborghini?"

"BMW for work. Porche for fun."

She rolled her eyes. "Must be nice."

She typed on her tablet for a moment. It still didn't make sense to him that she didn't want anything from him. Sure, they weren't dating, but every woman he'd been with had wanted something from him. Jewelry, flowers, expensive dinners. Yes, they had ordered room service, but Phoebe had suggested ordering a pizza before that.

Breakfast had been at a little diner that had cost him less than thirty dollars for both their meals. She didn't seem to want him for his money. Technically she only wanted him for his body.

"You should spend the night tonight," he said, quietly.

She looked up startled and opened her mouth, but before she could protest, he added, "Since we have an early start. That way I don't have to drive to get you."

Her eyes narrowed on him for his weak ass excuse, but a smile tugged at her lips. He knew he had her.

"We can discuss it later." She glanced at her tablet and stood. "I have a lot of things to finish if I'm going to miss tomorrow."

"It's been two weeks. We should really discuss how we are going to work together, but we can do that during the drive." Aiden leaned back in his chair as he watched her move toward the door.

She stopped in the doorway and glanced at him. She nodded. "Tomorrow."

MONDAY WOULD NEVER END. Phoebe stood in the copy room finalizing some proofs for the team. Driving to a brewery with Aiden sounded like heaven to weekend Phoebe, but hell to work Phoebe. It all depended on which Aiden showed up.

But none of that mattered if she couldn't get enough done that she could just sit back and relax while he drove. Work would happen tomorrow, but hopefully not the entire drive.

Most of the office was already gone for the day. It was a little past six, but both she and Aiden were still working. There hadn't been a lot of time to daydream or even think about spending the night with him tonight. Her body hadn't forgotten, but her mind had a million other things to conquer before that could happen.

At this point, she wasn't even sure if she would get to sleep tonight. So much to do.

The door to the copy room opened and Morgan stuck her head in. "Drew and I are heading out. You going to be okay?"

"Would you have asked me that three weeks ago?" Phoebe raised her eyebrow at Morgan. This sudden worry had everything to do with Aiden.

Morgan paused. "Probably. You don't normally work late and almost never on a Monday."

Phoebe shrugged. "A lot to do if I'm missing tomorrow."

Morgan looked over her shoulder before slipping through the doorway and letting the door close behind her.

Phoebe looked at her expectantly.

"You and Aiden seem to be getting along better. Is there anything you want to talk about?"

"Not really." Phoebe turned back to the proofs. "He's a nice enough guy once you get to know him. We should be able to sort out what we both want to do with the department without getting you and Drew involved again. We'll be discussing it on the drive tomorrow. So I'll make sure to update you Wednesday."

"Are you having sex with him?" Morgan's voice sounded a little strained like she didn't actually want to ask that question.

"If I was?" Phoebe looked up at the wall in front of her.

Morgan sighed. "Just be careful. I know you."

Phoebe turned around. "You haven't been around enough lately to know me."

"I'm still your best friend. I don't want you to get hurt." Morgan leaned against the door.

"Too late for that." Phoebe crossed her arms. "We used to chat almost every night. Now I'm lucky if I get a text from you. I came to this company so I could spend time with you. So I could help *you* build something new and exciting. I know I don't have a magical dick, but I'd still like some of my best friend's time."

Morgan's cheeks had flushed pink while Phoebe talked. "You and I are best friends and that will never change, but what I have with Drew is still new to me. I've never loved someone the way I love him. I do need to work on balancing him and you because I love you too. You've always been there for me, and I wouldn't know what I'd do if I lost you as my friend."

Phoebe's heart clutched at the thought of losing Morgan's friendship. She sighed and looked down at the floor. "I'm here. I'm not going anywhere. I'll always be your best friend and I love you too. Now let me get my work done so I can get the fuck out of this place."

Morgan stepped forward and gave Phoebe a hug. Phoebe wrapped her arms around her and gave her a pat.

"Though if I had a dick, you and I would have been a thing long before Ew Drew." Phoebe stepped away and gave Morgan a wink.

"I don't think you would have looked at me twice if you had a dick." Morgan laughed. "You'd be too busy."

"Probably." Phoebe shrugged and made a shooing motion with her hand. "Leave. I got work to do."

Morgan shook her head. "I'll call you later tonight."

Phoebe smiled and waved as Morgan left the room.

Phoebe wrapped up what she had to do and headed back to her desk. The office was eerily quiet. She glanced at Aiden's open door and he looked up at her. For a moment, their eyes locked and a rush of desire pooled inside her. He smiled and then went back to working on his computer.

She sighed and sank into her desk chair. Even if she spent the night in his hotel room, they weren't going to have much time to do anything. Time crept by as she worked on some emails that had to go out for scheduling. She was so preoccupied she didn't notice Aiden until his hands came down on her shoulders.

"Fuck!" She turned and his green eyes laughed down at her.

"You almost ready to go?" He raised an eyebrow and his hands squeezed her shoulders gently. His blond hair looked a little more ruffled than normal, like he'd been putting his hand through it.

She nodded. "One more email."

He grabbed a chair and pulled it over next to her. "We'll swing by your place first to grab your clothes. You still have all your other stuff at my hotel."

She'd been so tired this morning she hadn't thought about her toiletries still lined up on Aiden's spare sink. It made sense for her to sleep there. She slept better in his arms anyway. She didn't want to think too deeply on that though.

"Are you just going to watch me finish?" She quirked her eyebrow at him.

"I love watching you finish." His tone darkened, and her insides tumbled over themselves.

"Well, then, eat your heart out." She turned back to her laptop to work on the final email of the day.

Aiden's fingertip trailed over her arm, leaving sparks in its wake. She managed to get a sentence typed.

"This is going to take forever." Phoebe gave him a pointed look.

"You definitely need a break then." His smile was more playful than she'd ever seen at work.

"If I finish this, we can go." She couldn't wait to get him back to the hotel and tease the fuck out of him before they exhausted each other.

He cupped her cheek and leaned in until their mouths were a hair's breadth apart. She stayed still even when his breath fanned her lips. Heat pooled low and achy within her.

"Something to take the edge off?" His voice was low.

When his lips crashed against hers, she hadn't even taken her fingers off the keyboard. Kissing Aiden was like kissing a live wire. Everything in her body sparked to life and the rest of the world was forgotten.

A little sanity emerged, and she pulled away and opened her eyes to his darkened green gaze. She could lose herself in this man and not even care. She'd meant to laugh and tell him to wait literally five minutes for her to finish this email. Instead, she caved.

She turned in her chair. Standing, she hiked up her skirt and straddled his lap before taking his lips with hers again. He grabbed her ass and pulled her as close as they could get with their clothes on. He consumed her like a fine wine, tasting and savoring. She rocked her hips against his, loving his hard cock between her legs. Too many layers separated them.

She reached between them and scooted back on his lap so she could free his erection. He continued to explore her mouth as his hands worked on the buttons on her shirt. He was able to get his hands on her breasts before she had him free. His fingertips played over her nipples and her pussy throbbed in response.

Finally she had his cock in her hands. One of his hands slipped from her and she groaned in disappointment. He rustled in his pants before pressing a condom into her hand. She smiled against his lips and went to work on the package. He went to work on her breasts again. His lips kissed across her jaw and down her neck.

She tipped her head to give him better access as she rolled the condom onto his cock. They were in the middle of the office where anyone could walk in if it weren't after hours. Morgan always locked the doors at six, even if someone worked late.

Phoebe had always been in control when having sex. She controlled the where, the when, the how, and even the how long. But Aiden threw all her control out the window. She needed him like nothing she'd ever experienced before.

He dragged her panties to the side and lifted her to come down on him. Every inch of him brought her to greater heights as she lowered fully onto him. She opened her eyes and found him watching her.

"You are exquisite," he whispered before lifting her almost off him and bringing her back down. "I've spent all day hard as a rock, watching you work. It took everything I had not to drag you into my office and fuck you on my desk."

His words caused heat to flow through her. She gasped as he completely filled her again.

"You make me want to forget everything and just spend all day buried deep inside you." His hands squeezed her ass as he lifted her again. She found the wheels of his chair to give her some leverage to help. It felt good and pushed her closer to the edge, but he could be deeper. "Fuck work. Fuck my career. I only want you."

"Aiden," she brushed her lips over his. "Fuck me harder."

He lifted her off his cock and she almost cried out. Still holding her, he stood with her. She wrapped herself around him as he moved toward his office.

"Let go." He lowered her feet to the floor and kissed her hard. He spun her around and pressed her facedown onto his desk, her ass in the air. She heard his pants drop and then he lifted her skirt. She clenched in anticipation.

His fingers snagged the sides of her panties and dragged them down her legs. His hands grasped her hips and he thrust forward, burying his cock deep within her. She moaned at the feel of him filling her.

"I'm never going to be able to work at this desk without

thinking about you spread before me and my cock buried inside you." Aiden pulled back and thrust swiftly into her.

Phoebe stretched her arms out to hold onto the edge of the desk. She widened her stance more for him and he began to move quicker. His hands moved her hips back and forth on him. This position didn't give her much control so she had to follow his lead.

Control didn't matter though because everything he did pushed her closer and closer to the edge. He found a rhythm, and the only sound in the office was the slapping of their flesh against each other.

Just as she was going to tip over, he thrust in and held. She whimpered, but he leaned over her and kissed the back of her neck and left a trail of kisses to her ear.

"Not yet, Phoebe."

Her whole being pulsed, ready and willing to fall into oblivion.

He reached around and between her legs. His fingers destroyed any control she thought she had as he stroked over her clit and rocked against her slightly from behind. Her fingers tightened on the desk edge until she thought she might break it off.

"Come for me, Phoebe."

His words pushed her over the edge. Her insides burst into an orgasm that flooded her body with warmth. She went slack as the tension eased from her. She released her death grip on the desk and flexed her fingers.

"So fucking responsive." He kissed the back of her neck again and aftershocks rippled through her. He lifted and slowly pulled out and slid back in. Slowly the embers ignited into flames again as he stroked her.

"Harder, Aiden." She tried to push back against him, needing more, needing him to take her. Wanting another orgasm, knowing he could get her there.

He chuckled darkly before taking hold of her hips and giving her exactly what she wanted. A hard fuck against his desk. Her fingers tightened as her core clenched around him. Her next orgasm rolled over her like a runaway train and she cried out.

"Fuck," he yelled as he came. They hovered together, lingering in the afterglow. He lowered his body over hers and brushed her damp hair from her neck before kissing his favorite spot. "Exquisite."

She took a deep breath and laughed a little. "So much for not having sex at work."

Aiden withdrew before offering her a hand up. "What can I say? I'm a rule breaker."

"Sure." Laughing, she straightened her top.

He pulled his pants up and gave her a look. "I am."

Bending to pick up her panties, she gave him a look that said sure-I-believe-you as sarcastically as possible.

He fastened his belt and sat in his chair. "You don't believe me."

"Do you blame me?"

He grabbed her hips and brought her down to sit across his lap. "I'm a cheater."

She narrowed her eyes and braced to get up. That was the one thing guaranteed to send her packing. She couldn't tolerate being cheated on or being used to cheat on someone else. That was a no-go for her.

"At Monopoly." He tugged her back to him.

She relaxed. She wanted to believe he wouldn't cheat on her or someone else, but he was a man. "Everyone cheats at Monopoly."

"Fair enough." He crinkled his nose. "I'm not supposed to be with you."

She scoffed. "There's no rule against it. At least not really. If we had one of those rules here, everyone would be written up and fired. We wouldn't have any staff."

"Not because of work." Aiden grinned and stroked his thumb over her lower lip. "My family is very old school. My mom always vetted all my girlfriends. They had to come from good families and have their own money. Even if I had more money than theirs."

"But I'm not your girlfriend, so how is that breaking the rules?" Phoebe's heart raced. No one had been around to vet the guys she dated. Not that she dated. But would it have made a difference? Would she already be shacked up with some guy?

"I was supposed to be a one-night stand." He pressed his face into her shoulder.

"I'm the one breaking my rules with you." She shook her head. She sank her fingers into his messy blond hair. Right now he looked like the rule breaker he professed to be.

"I came here to start a new life. One that I could dictate. I would choose what I did and who I did it with." Aiden's lips found her neck and he dropped a brief kiss there before lifting his head to meet her eyes. "You are an unknown variable."

"Sounds about right." Phoebe needed to finish work so they could go, but she also didn't want to have a serious conversation with Aiden. It made all of this too real. She didn't do real. She did fantasy. "I need to finish my email and then we can go."

She shifted to stand but he didn't release her. His hand cupped her jaw and brought her face toward his. His green eyes weren't filled with heat, but a tenderness she couldn't quite describe.

His lips brushed against hers. Before she could deepen the kiss to make it something physical, he pulled back. He helped her stand and nodded at her. "Hurry up. We'll grab some dinner after we get your things."

She hesitated for a moment. Things were swinging in a direction she wasn't comfortable with. But Aiden made it feel normal and easy. And she wanted him. She shook her head and went to get her work done.

They'd have sex and she'd find her control. She didn't fit in his life. He'd practically said it. So she had nothing to worry about.

CHAPTER 17

THE STOP in Phoebe's apartment happened quicker than the first time they were here. Mostly because they didn't have sex. Aiden followed her into the bedroom this time though and sat on the bed while she grabbed a few things. He saw the pictures on top of her dresser.

Drawn to figuring out more about Phoebe, he walked over and inspected the pictures. A few were her and Morgan. One showed them after a run of some kind. Both of them sweaty and wearing a paper with a number on their chests. A couple were younger photos of Phoebe with friends. High school and maybe college.

Then there was one with Phoebe and an older woman smiling at the camera. Enough similarities existed to indicate that this was Phoebe's mom. Same red hair, though her mother's had faded. Same pert nose.

The picture was old by at least a decade. Phoebe looked carefree and happy. He wished he'd known that girl. Would she be the same vixen he knew? What had shaped her into this woman who fascinated him and made him risk everything just to be with her?

"Is this your mom?" He held out the picture.

She glanced over from where she was filling her bag. "Yeah."

She didn't say much about her mother, but she always talked about her in past tense. He wanted to know more. "Do you still talk to her?"

She stopped packing and stayed still for a moment. "She's dead."

Fuck. He wanted to go and put his arms around her, but he waited.

"It was years ago now, but when I was in high school, Mom got the big C." She sighed and closed her bag before tossing it on the bed. Her hands fell to her sides and her gaze was drawn to the floor.

"What type?" He didn't move, but he longed to hold her and take away some of the pain.

"Breast." Her eyes lifted and he could see the tears pooling in them.

Fuck it. His arms wrapped around her, pulling her against his chest. She released her breath and leaned into him.

"She got better. She did all the radiation and surgeries and she got better. For years she was good. She almost had a new outlook on life, and it seemed that she'd finally let the ghost of my dad's love stop haunting her."

His arms tightened. Her voice stayed even, as if she didn't want to betray herself by admitting it still hurt her to talk about it.

"It just happened. One day she woke up, said, 'I love you, honey. See you later.' And then she was gone. Car accident. Young, inexperienced driver not paying attention to the change in lights and smacked her car just right. They did all they could, but she was already gone."

"I'm so sorry, Phoebe." His arms squeezed her as if he could absorb the shock of the pain from all those years ago.

He wanted to hold her until everything was better, but this wasn't something he could fix. All the money in the world couldn't fix this.

"The cancer gave us the 'always say goodbye with your heart.' It never failed. If one of us was leaving, *I love you* would be the last words we said to each other." The words became muddied as tears streamed down Phoebe's face. "But beating the cancer also had given us hope of a future."

Aiden drew her over to the bed and sat. He held her in his lap while silent tears rolled down her cheeks. She seemed uncomfortable with him seeing this side of her, so he rested his chin on her head and just held her until the tears started to dry up.

"Gah, I don't know why I'm so emotional today." She swiped at her tears and pulled away from him to stand. Her gaze wouldn't meet his. "I'm going to wash up in the bathroom."

What could he say or do? He hadn't lost a parent. Not only a parent, but the only caregiver she had.

Aiden and Phoebe were having sex, not an emotional relationship. Instead of remaining physical, he'd had to trod his huge feet into a delicate subject for her.

After five minutes, she came out, her face washed and new makeup applied. As if nothing had happened, she smiled and held out her hand toward him. "What should we grab for dinner?"

He stared at her hand for a moment. He wanted to offer her comfort and understanding, but clearly she didn't want that from him. Standing, he took her hand and drew her against his side. He grabbed her overnight bag and moved toward the door.

"What are you in the mood for?"

She glanced up at him with a mischievous smile, and his heart melted for this woman. Like the final piece locked into place, he knew that some part of him was falling in love with her. Maybe all of him. But he knew her enough to know she wouldn't want his confession. So he went with his gut.

"Room service?"

~

"GET A MOVE ON IT, BUTLER," Aiden called from the living room.

Phoebe finished the last curl in her hair and walked out of the bedroom. "It takes time to look this perfect."

"You look perfect the second you wake up." Aiden grabbed a set of keys from his desk drawer.

"You must need glasses." She squinted up at him with a small smile on her red lips.

"We need to get to the brewery. But if you want to take a later tour. . . ." He closed the distance between them and leaned down to speak directly into her ear. "We could spend a little more time in bed instead."

She tapped on his chest for each time they had sex this morning. "Wake up, shower, after shower, second shower. I think we should be good for a while."

He kissed her briefly and stepped back. "Fine. But you'll stay again tonight? We'll probably get back late."

She should say no. She should stay at her own apartment and create space between them. But she didn't want to. So she shrugged. "Let's see if you can convince me."

He smirked at her and grabbed her hand to lead her out of the hotel room and into the elevator. The elevator slid past the lobby and ended up on a level or two below the hotel. Stepping out into the garage, Phoebe almost pulled him back when a sign read "For valet use only."

"I told you I'm a rule breaker." He pulled her forward until he stopped at a dark gray car. He opened the passenger side for her and closed it after she got in. This wasn't like her first and only car, a bucket of bolts held together by duct tape. From the leather seats to the perfect console, this car screamed luxury.

Aiden walked around the car in his nice label jeans and designer shirt. The brewery had insisted they come casual as they'd be touring the production floor. She sighed. This wasn't who she was. She was Levi's and two-for-twenty-dollars T-shirts. She could buy a full wardrobe with how much his "casual" outfit cost and still have some money left over.

He slid in and looked at her. "What?"

She shook her head and put on her seatbelt.

"Phoebe, what is it?" He caught her chin so she was forced to look into his gorgeous green eyes.

She sighed. "We don't fit."

"I disagree." He smirked. "You and I fit very well together. In the bed. In the shower. In the bath. I'm willing to show you how we can fit even in this car."

She held her finger over his lips. "I meant outside the bedroom. We can't even get along at work. The only thing we have between us is physical."

His smirk faded and he took a breath. "You don't want to date me, so is this a problem we have to talk about? Or is this something we ignore because it means nothing to what we are actually doing?"

She smiled a little. "You're right. I'm not applying to be Mrs. Aiden Kingston the third."

"I'm not a third." He gave her a confused look.

"But it sounds right." She shrugged.

"Fine. But just so you know, I bet my mother would love you if she met you." He started the car.

She almost put her hand over the ache in her heart at those words. It wasn't about his mother. He was wrong though. She doubted the woman that vetted his girlfriends would appreciate someone like Phoebe with her son. Even if they were just having sex. But the pain came from missing her own mother. She'd give almost anything for another day.

Aiden backed up and pulled out of the garage. "Let's get this show on the road."

"We should talk about work." Phoebe leaned back and closed her eyes. These were the plushest car seats she'd ever sat on in her entire life.

"You wanted me to sit back and observe before taking the reins." Aiden drove relaxed. "I think we've done that."

Phoebe cracked open an eye to look at Aiden's profile. "No, I wanted you to learn what we did before you made sweeping changes. We're a small company. We can't remain stable if you insist on growing us faster than we can grow ourselves."

"The company I started with was already huge when I walked in the door." Aiden took a turn and soon they were on the interstate heading to visit a brewery in the middle of nowhere. "There was no room for growth and that was stifling. Everything I did had to be within the constraints of what had been established. Coming to Taylor and King has been like shedding a straitjacket. I could finally explore all the things that were withheld from me previously."

Phoebe watched his profile as he talked with more animation than he usually did about work. She also couldn't help but wonder if being with a woman like her was one of the things that had been withheld from him in the past and the reason for his fascination with her.

"When Drew offered me the job, it was like the best present ever."

When she cleared her throat, he smiled and reached out to take her hand on the console.

"You are the best present, period." He squeezed her hand.

"But Drew was offering me a new lease on life. I didn't have to do what had been done for years before. I could come in and make the company something I could be proud to have built."

"But you weren't here from the beginning," Phoebe said softly. "We have been working on figuring out this business since we started months ago. When you walked in and spewed all your crazy talk about expansion. . . it was too much, too quickly. We'd just expanded from eight to ten people, and you were wanting to take us from our modest income to a multi-billion-dollar industry overnight."

"Not overnight," he objected.

"But it felt that way. I mean I get it. We can expand into different industries and get different clients and build that way. But we need to keep it organic and properly scaled. We need to stay a boutique company and not get so bogged down that we end up like the corporation we came from or the company you came from."

"I don't want that."

"Exactly," she said. "Neither do we. We have a fantastic opportunity to build something really awesome and not fuck it up like everyone else does."

"That would be great, but can we do it together without arguing?" He gave her a quick smile.

"As long as we are fucking, it seems like the arguments go away." She gave him a cocky grin. "All that sexual tension made us angry. Fucking you is awesome by the way. Have you ever tried it?"

He grinned. "If it's anything like fucking you, then I completely understand."

"Besides fucking, we do need to figure out how to work together without getting angry." She squeezed his hand.

"I haven't been angry with you. Just frustrated. It's hard to see you in your amazing dresses and not be able to touch you. Had we not spent the weekend together before meeting you that Monday. . . ." He stopped and shook his head.

"You still would have wanted me." Phoebe laughed.

"But I wouldn't have known what I was missing. I would have stuck to my no dipping my toes in the office pool. Done my job and still pissed you off."

"And I wouldn't have been so lenient because you gave me the most amazing orgasms of my life." She tilted her head slyly at him.

"Fuck, Phoebe," he said while squeezing her hand, "don't say things like that when I'm driving."

She laughed. "It's true, and trust me, sometimes a mediocre orgasm is all you get out of a guy. If you get one at all. Don't get me wrong. Sex still feels good even without the orgasms but when you deliver, you *deliver.*"

He released her hand. "If I keep touching you, we will never make it the whole two hours and twenty-three minutes left."

She shrugged and sat back into the car seat. "Okay, no more talk of fucking."

"Let's sort out the next five years for Taylor and King."

Phoebe groaned. "I'd rather talk about fucking."

Aiden laughed, but he hadn't been joking. They discussed where they were as a company and figured out how they wanted to expand the sales department. What it would take to expand the sales department. What it would take to expand the company. What thresholds they would have to meet to move to each new level. By the time they arrived at the brewery, Phoebe had typed up a plan they could tweak to share with Drew and Morgan.

Parking wasn't a huge issue at the brewery this early on a weekday. They were toward the outside of the lot under a huge tree. The brewery was literally in the middle of nowhere. Even Phoebe's cell phone didn't get a signal all the way out here.

"What do you think?" Aiden rounded the car to meet Phoebe beside the trunk.

She squinted up at the hand-painted, old Barn wood sign that read Noble Brewery. "It's quaint."

He slid his hand in hers and led her inside. The Noble brothers had converted an old barn into a pristine brewery. Before the barn stood a small building housing a gift shop and a tasting room. The tour should begin in the gift shop.

Aiden pulled Phoebe to a back wall and leaned against it with her leaning against him. The odd thing was it didn't feel wrong for him to loosely drape his arms around her and just be there. Phoebe felt relaxed and at ease. A spark always existed when they were close, but it wasn't the pressing need she'd had to hold back previously.

"The tour lasts about an hour and ends with a tasting of their most recent brews." Aiden's voice was near her ear. "After that, we'll meet with the owners to discuss what kind of advertising they're looking for."

Phoebe nodded and stepped out of his arms. Him talking about work reminded her. "We're at work, Aiden."

He gave her a grin. "Then I'll just have to start holding Drew's hand."

When the tour began, Aiden casually held her hand throughout. There were fifteen others on the tour. To everyone else, they must look like a couple. Normally that would make Phoebe pull away from a guy, but she didn't want to pull away from Aiden. Holding his hand filled her with warmth and a calm. She wasn't his girl-friend and they were here for work. It was confusing but also nice.

The tour took them all through the process of brewing beer and ended in the tap room. They were given a flight of five different beers to taste. Aiden led her to a table next to a window away from the rest of the tour group.

"I'd make this a game if we were by ourselves," Phoebe confided while looking at the flights in front of her. They were arranged from a pale ale to a dark lager.

"What kind of game?" Aiden picked up one of his and smelled it.

She gave him a Cheshire smile. "One that required nudity or at least partial nudity."

"You always have the best games." He lifted the glass toward her in a toast before downing it. "I will happily get naked with you later today."

She smiled as she took drinks from all the different beers, before settling on one that she liked.

Aiden's phone rang, and he looked at the face of it before hitting the decline button. Phoebe checked her own phone. She still couldn't get a signal.

"Rich people phones must have better reception." Phoebe drank all of the one she liked from her tray before snatching the same one on Aiden's tray.

Aiden shrugged and leaned against the wall. "If you need to call someone, you're welcome to my phone."

She shook her head. "Nope, just trying to remember our differences."

"Some differences are very good together." He drew her to stand between his legs until their different parts pressed against each other.

"Hmm." She stepped away from him and he let his arms drop. "We're still at work and about to meet with a new client. We should at least try to behave like professionals."

"Indeed." His eyebrow arched like he didn't want to be professional.

Aiden's phone rang again. He glanced at the screen with a furrow between his brows.

"You can take it." She held up her drink and took a sip.

He sighed and pressed a button on the phone. His eyes met hers. "Hello, Mother."

Phoebe set her drink down and found a stool nearby. Dragging it over, she took a seat. From what she remembered, phone calls with mothers lasted a while.

"No, I don't remember her." Aiden looked up at the ceiling. If he was looking for help, it probably wasn't up there. "Good for her."

Phoebe raised an eyebrow curiously, but Aiden turned away from her.

"No, I will not."

Another longer pause.

"Why would you give her my number?" He sounded exasperated.

Phoebe couldn't help being a little curious who the "her" was in the conversation. A newly vetted prospect for the Ms. Aiden Kingston position, perhaps.

He swung around to look at Phoebe. His gaze swept over her with almost a frustrated air, but then he sighed. "No, I'm not.

"Fine.

"If she texts me, I will text her back, but that's all I'm giving. I have a career here that takes up all my time."

A short pause.

"No, I don't have time for a charity function and definitely do not need you to find me a date."

He sighed again and looked up at the ceiling.

"I'm at work now, Mother. For future reference, call me in the evenings.

"Yes, I will take your calls.

"Love you too." Aiden ended the call and hung his head.

"That sounded like fun." Phoebe crossed her legs and settled against the wall.

"You are fun." Aiden held up his phone. "This was not."

Phoebe couldn't help wonder who they were talking about, but she'd agreed to a physical only relationship. She couldn't just ask him and he didn't seem willing to offer.

He rubbed the back of his neck before turning off his phone and sliding it into his pocket. "Oh look, now my phone doesn't get service here either. What were we talking about?"

"Behaving like professionals." Phoebe stood up and finished the last of her favored beer.

"Mmmm." Aiden stepped closer, taking the air away from her. He brushed a stray strand of hair behind her ear. He whispered against her ear, "Behaving is highly overrated."

Shivers raced along her spine.

Aiden finished his beer and took her hand. He led her down a hallway, and she couldn't help the little burst of excitement at the prospect of doing something naughty. But instead, he knocked on an office door. A twinge of disappointment burst inside her.

"Ethan texted to say they could meet early." He leaned next to her ear and whispered, "Later we'll make sure to wipe that disappointed look off your face. But now, let's try to stay professional."

She gave him a crooked smile and released his hand. "Later."

Aiden leaned back in his car seat and glanced over at Phoebe. They were still in the parking lot of the brewery. Apparently to get to know them better, the brothers decided they must try every kind of beer the brewery made. Including a few that weren't exactly perfected yet.

They'd also ordered in burgers and fries to help soak up

some of the alcohol, but both Aiden and Phoebe had a few too many to drink. It was only four in the afternoon, but they weren't going anywhere fast. They should already be halfway back to the city by now.

"We could just sleep in the back seat," Phoebe offered with a raised eyebrow.

"I'm sure I'll be able to drive after a little bit." Aiden glanced into the back seat. He'd never even been in his back seat. "I just need time to sober up."

"Time, huh?" Phoebe's eyes sparkled in the dashboard light. "Have you ever fucked in a car before, Aiden?"

He shook his head with a slight smile. "That wouldn't have been appropriate. Mother never would have approved."

God, his mother. She called to ask him to help out some woman who had transferred to the same city as him. This woman had the perfect pedigree along with an actual career. On Mom's scale, Rachel Sandburg ranked almost perfect. But Aiden bet Rachel wouldn't ask if he'd fucked someone in a car before.

He'd hoped moving away would squash his mother's matchmaking, but instead she got creative. He was sure Rachel was a lovely woman, but he wasn't interested in just any woman.

Phoebe laughed, slipped off her shoes, and climbed into the backseat. Her hip brushed against him as she went. She settled in and patted the leather beside her. "Come on. Let's take your car virginity."

Aiden laughed. He hadn't been a virgin in years. Instead of climbing over, he got out and entered through the car door, shutting them into the back together.

"Where did you lose your virginity?" he asked. He wanted to know more about her. Actually, he craved to know everything about her, but usually he kept a filter on his questions. The beer was definitely doing the talking today.

"Car or. . . ?" She cocked her eyebrow at him.

He lifted her off the seat and put her on his lap. "Your *first* first time."

"Oh, my God. Really?" Phoebe laughed. "Okay, I was almost nineteen—"

"Really?" He couldn't help but be shocked. This woman oozed sexuality.

"What, you thought I was an early bloomer?" Phoebe traced his lower lip with her finger, brushing slowly back and forth. "No, sir, I was a late bloomer. It was college. I had a roommate who was working her way through the entire football team. She went to all the games. She brought home a player or two every weekend."

"Ambitious."

"I know, right? So I wondered what the big deal was." Phoebe snickered. "He was one of my roommate's leftovers. He came to the door one day looking for her and found me. I have to admit I'd heard them going at it, and he made her make the most noise, so I figured he must be the best."

"Was he?" Aiden bit down on her teasing finger and held it in place. She chuckled.

"Compared to what? He was nineteen and I was an eighteen-year-old virgin. To me, he was fucking fantastic. We spent the whole day fucking. I wanted to try everything, and he was more than eager to help." She tugged her finger free.

"What happened to him?" Was this the asshole who ruined Phoebe for relationships?

She shrugged. "We hooked up a few more times during college, but we never dated. If that's what you want to know."

"Did you ever date someone?" He couldn't resist asking. He also couldn't resist leaning in to suck the spot on her neck that made her gasp.

"Is this an interrogation? Am I under duress?" Phoebe stopped when he hit that spot.

His hand slipped under her skirt. Fuck, he loved her body. But he wanted to keep her talking and if he kept up with what he was doing, they wouldn't be talking anymore.

"It's just a question to get to know you," Aiden said. He maneuvered her body until her head laid in his lap, faceup, and her body draped over the backseat. He put his hands behind his head to keep himself from touching her.

She smiled at him. "I didn't ever want to date any of those guys. I was curious, and besides a physical connection, I never really connected with anyone on an emotional level. Which seemed to be a requirement for dating or being someone's girlfriend. That and monogamy."

"Are you against monogamy?" Unable to resist, he trailed his hand down the front of her shirt between her breasts until he rested it on her lower abdomen, feeling the soft rise and fall of her breaths.

"Not particularly. I just never found someone I wanted to make all the other bitches back away from by proclaiming he was mine." Her dark eyes focused on him.

Was she remembering when she'd told him she was his? Or when she claimed him as hers? She'd called him babe in front of the apartment buildings' staff. Was that claiming him as hers?

He wanted to prove to her that she was his. That no man would ever compare to him.

"How many women have you been with?" Her voice was soft and in the darkened interior of his car, an intimacy wrapped around them. The windows were tinted and they were parked far enough away that no one would pass by. Most cars that were still here were parked closer to the building.

"Seven."

She sat up suddenly and straddled his lap. "For real?"

He nodded and cupped her cheek. "I told you about the

vetting process. Going against my family's wishes wasn't something I did. The twins, yes, but me, not so much. I tried to be the perfect son. That meant going out with women who they approved of. It also meant that sleeping around wasn't a good idea. According to my parents, every woman was out to trap me in a relationship."

"Do you still believe that?" Her eyebrows raised as she gazed at him.

"I don't know. Everyone I've been with before you was vetted." He shrugged. "You definitely aren't looking to trap me."

She grinned. "Nope."

Funny how the only woman he'd chosen for himself and actually liked enough to date didn't want a relationship. Phoebe wanted his body, and for now, that was enough for him. It wasn't just sex for him, though. The realization had been creeping up on him, but he knew he was falling deeper. It should terrify him, but it didn't. Maybe because she didn't want more from him.

Even if he was falling in love with her, he wouldn't push her for more. She didn't want love from him. She'd been clear from the beginning no emotional involvement only sex. If he admitted he was falling, she would cut off this thing between them.

And that would be the end.

"I know the follow-up to that question," Phoebe said. She leaned in and pressed her lips against his. She opened her mouth and they gently explored each other with their tongues and lips and teeth. It wasn't rushed, and even though he wanted her, he wanted to learn more.

When she pulled back, he felt almost dazed, but he managed to get out, "What's your number?"

"Much higher." She sat back a little on his lap, but she didn't leave. He would have pulled her back if she'd tried.

"I won't care, Phoebe. It could be one thousand and it won't change how I feel about you." He cupped her face and pressed his lips to each of her eyes, the tip of her nose and finally her lips. Honestly, it didn't matter. They were all in the past and didn't mean anything to her. Even if she didn't love him, she was still drawn to him. More than those other men.

"I don't even know if a thousand is humanly possible. I mean I've only been sexually active for ten years. That would mean one hundred guys a year. That's an awful lot of work." She shuddered. "I'm active but not that active. Two guys every week. I mean, it might be an aspirational goal."

He shook his head. "You don't have to tell me if you don't want to."

She sighed and pressed her hands on his chest. "It's second half double digits, but I haven't made it close to triple digits. I'm responsible and keep track. I get tested and take the necessary precautions."

"I'm not judging you." He rubbed his hands down her back. She had a past and so did he. He enjoyed the person she was now and she wouldn't be that person without her past.

She picked at something on his shirt and grinned. "I know you aren't. When I first started having sex, it was like unwrapping a new toy. I wanted to play all the time. Most of that number was during college and then the first few years of being young and exploring a huge city."

"You are like a new toy to me." He captured her lips. There was nothing tame or slow about this kiss. He put all the longing and heat he'd been feeling into it.

"You're like a new toy to me too." She combed her fingers through his hair, messing it up. She did that a lot and he loved that she did. "But isn't that the way sex feels with someone new? At first, you are all over each other and then it starts to fizzle and fade. Until one day, poof it's gone."

"I don't think this is going to fizzle and fade." Aiden shifted until she was spread out before him on the backseat. His hands dragged her skirt up her thighs until her pink panties were revealed. He moved his hands to those panties and tugged them down her legs before tossing them into the front seat. "I never get tired of playing with you."

"Everything fizzles and fades, Aiden." Phoebe let her legs fall open for him. Not a shy bone in her body.

This woman. Everything she did turned him on. "You tell me when it fades."

Before she could answer him, he lifted her lower half up, drawing her leg over his shoulder and pressing his lips against her wet heat. She braced her hands against the car door to stabilize herself while he lavished attention on the very center of her.

He could spend a lifetime between her thighs, licking, touching, sucking. Giving back what she always did when she went down on him. Her soft sounds and quickened breath made him even harder. The fact that if someone looked through the front windows of the car, they'd get a show somehow made it even hotter.

Of course, the tree in front of them provided a little more coverage. No cars were parked nearby. People were still inside the barn drinking beer and listening to music, while he was out here feasting on Phoebe. Her moans of pleasure filled the car, music to his ears.

She never held anything back from him when it came to sex.

Emotional stuff, yes. She was guarded and he didn't know why. But with sex, they were on the same page. No other woman had ever made him want her the way he wanted Phoebe. He wanted more from her, but he knew she'd never give it, so he would take what he could get. As long as he could get it.

And he would try to give her everything. She wanted nothing from him but an orgasm. But he would give her all of him if she asked.

Right now, he wanted to drive her wild with his mouth. Take her to the edge of oblivion time and time again until she begged for release. Until she pushed up and straddled him, sinking his cock into her wet heat and riding him until he couldn't think anymore. His cock twitched.

Her breath hitched as he brought her close. He lightened the strokes of his tongue and then sucked on her clit. Her breath came in pants as he thrust his fingers into her core. Her whole body arched hard as she cried out his name.

He didn't let her come down though. He kept up his sensual torture. In the backseat of his car, he made Phoebe come multiple times before she took him deep inside her, and he lost himself in the feel of her. Her nipples in his mouth. Her pussy greedily taking his cock. Her fingers running through his hair. It was the closest thing to heaven he'd found. As he came with her one final time, he wasn't sure he'd ever be willing to let her go.

CHAPTER 18

Phoebe slept most of the ride back into the city. As the city lights flickered behind her eyelids, she stretched and opened an eye to see Aiden's profile as he brought them back to his hotel.

"What time is it?" Phoebe yawned while she said the words.

Aiden smiled softly. "Almost eleven."

She smiled with satisfaction at him. "We probably could have been here an hour earlier if you hadn't spent so much time going down on me."

"Consider it my sobriety test." His mouth quirked into a cocky grin.

"Always willing to help out if the need should arise."

"The need always arises when you're near." Aiden turned into the parking garage.

"Lucky me." She practically purred as she stretched. Lucky her indeed. She could get used to him. At the moment, that thought didn't scare her. Maybe she was a bit dick-matized.

As they pulled into the garage, Phoebe's phone pinged.

"It's been doing that for a while." Aiden shrugged as he pulled into the parking spot for his suite.

Phoebe dug her phone out of her purse. "That's a lot of missed messages."

She had at least twenty messages, mostly from Morgan. A nervous ball settled low in her gut. The last time she'd gotten messages like this had been about her mother.

Time had stood still that day as the caller had told her that her mother had been in an accident and she needed to come to the hospital. For years, Phoebe had been Morgan's emergency contact. Her head started to spin out. What other reason would Morgan have for calling so much?

Her heart accelerated until she was certain it would burst out of her chest. Think. She had to think. Aiden was with her, but Morgan was not. She couldn't lose Morgan. Morgan was her family. The only family she had left.

But all her people in the office were becoming her family now too. Claire, Jonah, Lacy, Emily, Logan. Even Ben and Drew. She couldn't lose any of them either. By the time Aiden had shut the car off, Phoebe could only stare at her phone, unable to catch her breath. If she never called, she'd never know. They would all still be fine. Safe and sound.

Her car door opened and Aiden was there.

"Breathe, Phoebe." His hand went over her hair and the other hand grasped hers. "What is it?"

She held out her phone to him unable to say a word.

"Morgan called?"

She shook her head. How could she explain to him what a phone call could do to someone? What could be ended by a few words?

Holding her hand, Aiden squatted down next to her and tapped on the screen of her phone. He put the phone on speaker as it rang. Each ring was like a dagger into her heart. She wanted to close her eyes and turn off her ears.

"Phoebe?! Oh my God, Phoebe! Is that you?" Morgan's voice sounded like she'd been crying.

"Phoebe's here with me," Aiden said.

"Oh, thank God. I've been so worried. Where are you?" Morgan's voice said.

Aiden looked up at Phoebe like he expected her to answer. She shook her head, so he said, "We're at the Indigo Hotel."

Morgan exhaled. "We're coming to you."

"I'll leave a key at the front desk."

"We'll be there in fifteen minutes." The connection clicked off.

Aiden pocketed Phoebe's phone and reached out to brush her cheeks. The wetness on his thumb surprised her. She was crying?

"Hey. It's all right. Morgan is going to be here soon." He reached over her and unclicked her seatbelt. "Can you walk?"

"I can't lose anyone else." The words were on repeat in her head like a warning siren that wouldn't shut off.

"You won't. I've got you." His words echoed in her mind as he lifted her from the car and carried her to the elevator. She leaned her ear against his heart and listened to it, trying to find a center in the steady beat that would help stop the panic.

She didn't register if anyone else got on the elevator with them. Suddenly they were at the door to the suite. Then the bed came up to greet her as Aiden lowered her down. He sat beside her. At one point the phone was to his ear, but she didn't hear what he said. He brushed her hair out of her eyes as he watched her closely.

She reached up and took his hand. The fear and panic

were fading. Aiden was safe. Morgan was safe. It wouldn't be like last time. It couldn't be like last time.

"I'm right here." Aiden's voice drew her, and she focused on his green eyes. She drew in his ancient forest scent and inhaled again. He leaned in and pressed a light kiss against her forehead. "I'm not leaving."

She reached up and pressed her hand against his five o'clock shadow. "Thank you."

He smiled at her and helped her sit up. An edge of worry lingered in his eyes. "Are you okay?"

She nodded and looked at the door. "How long until they get here?"

"Five minutes maybe."

She could do this. She nodded and stood. Taking every step methodically, she went into the bathroom and turned on the water. She grabbed a washcloth and wet it before dragging it over her face. The last time she had a string of missed calls had been the worst day of her life.

There was a knock on the door. She set the washcloth down and looked in the mirror. Her face was pale and makeup free. Her eyes were lined in red from the tears. Aiden stood there watching her. His eyebrows drew together as he rubbed his hand on the side of his pants.

"I'm okay." She wasn't. She felt hollowed out and empty. Something she hadn't felt in ten years.

Aiden opened his arms, and she went into them without hesitation. He hugged her tightly and kissed the top of her head. The knocking began again.

She inhaled his scent, trying to calm herself.

"You ready?" he asked.

She nodded. He took her hand and led her into the living room and to the door. When he opened it, Morgan burst through it and snatched Phoebe into a tight hug.

"Oh thank God." She mumbled against Phoebe's shoulder.

Drew nodded to Aiden as Aiden closed the door. Phoebe hugged Morgan back. That fear was right on the edge of her mind that she'd lost someone she cared about again. She still didn't know what had happened.

"What's going on?" Aiden asked. Phoebe could have kissed Aiden for asking what she needed to know.

"Our apartment building caught on fire." Morgan leaned back and touched Phoebe's face tentatively as if Phoebe could vanish.

"What?" The words Morgan said didn't make any sense.

"It wasn't the whole building. They caught it in time, but our floor got hit the worst." Morgan clutched at Phoebe's shoulders. Tears started down Morgan's face. "I didn't know if you were there. I didn't know if you were in the fire and I couldn't find you after and you weren't answering your phone. I tried Aiden's phone and didn't get an answer and I was worried you were gone and I couldn't handle if you were gone. You're my best friend."

Big, fat tears rolled down Morgan's face. Tension slid from Phoebe's body. Everyone was fine.

Phoebe wrapped her best friend in her arms and tried her best to hug away that fear of loss. "I'm here."

"I turned my phone off earlier in the day and forgot to turn it back on." Aiden pulled it out and turned it on.

"Morgan's been going crazy. They haven't been able to make it into the apartments to search to see if there were any casualties. You were supposed to be back earlier." Drew was talking softly to Aiden, but loud enough Phoebe could hear. "Both of their apartments are going to be unlivable for a while. They are pretty certain the fire started at an apartment in between their two. They might just have smoke damage, but it could be worse."

It could have been much worse. If Morgan had been there, she would have lost her friend. She tightened her hold on Morgan. For once, Phoebe was thankful that Drew was boning her friend.

"You might want to stop trying to break each other," Drew said. His eyes went to Morgan, and Phoebe could see the love shining in them. For once, it didn't sicken her.

"Do you want a drink?" Aiden asked and gestured toward the bar.

Phoebe didn't care what the guys did or said. She was just grateful her best friend was here with her. Her apartment was filled with stuff and memories. Yes, some things would be irreplaceable. And she would mourn that stuff later. But the only thing she cared about in that apartment building was Morgan. And she was here and safe. That was all that mattered.

Once the guys moved to the living room, Phoebe and Morgan finally unclenched and moved to the couch. Still holding each other's hands like they could keep the other from harm by sheer will.

"She can stay with us," Drew was saying.

"What?" That brought Phoebe out of her happy daze. "No. Ew. No. Bad Drew."

She pointed her finger at Drew like he was a bad dog.

"You can't exactly go home, Phoebe," Drew said it as nicely as he could, but the reality of the situation was sinking in. She was homeless. Stuffless and clothesless. Oh, God, her shoes. She did a quick tally of how many were already at Aiden's because she'd been lazy about taking them home.

"You can take the couch tonight until we can get a blow-up mattress. Or figure something else out. But stay with us." Morgan brushed a tear from Phoebe's cheek.

"The couch where you two fuck?" Phoebe raised an

eyebrow. "I love you, but I can't listen to the two of you going at it like two wounded animals all night."

"You can stay with me."

Phoebe's gaze went to Aiden at his words.

"It's not like they don't know we're more than coworkers." Aiden shrugged. "I have the room, especially since my new apartment will be ready in a few days. You can stay with me as long as you need to."

Phoebe was speechless. Morgan and Drew offering her their couch was kind of expected. Not that she wanted to hear Ew Drew giving it to her best friend every night. But if she had no other choice, she'd be grateful even with the animal noises coming from the bedroom.

But Aiden. . . . That was unexpected. It did something to that piece of flesh inside her chest. Something warm and fuzzy she hadn't felt in years.

"I'll have to find another apartment anyway, so it won't be for long," she said, cautiously. She'd never lived with anyone else in a long time. Not since her dorm experience. Definitely not with a man she was banging.

"Take as long as you need. You won't be putting me out." His smile left an edge of heat in his eyes.

Yeah, they were banging now, but what about the fizzle and fade? Would it happen faster if she stayed with him twenty-four seven? He'd mentioned a girlfriend who attempted to move in with him before. He'd stopped it. How long before he decided she wasn't worth the effort? At least until that happened, she'd be comfortable at his apartment.

"Which apartment did you get?" Phoebe asked.

"The top floor of the first one. Fully furnished."

Amazing views. King size bed. His and hers closets. She didn't have anything to put in the closet. She had to call her insurance company. How long before she'd get anything from that? Did she remember to pay the premium? How long before she saved enough for the deposit on a new apartment? Quitting Hart Associates and starting at Taylor and King had wiped out a significant amount of her savings. The bonus they'd given her had replenished some of that, but she hadn't exactly been frugal with her money. Fuck.

"We're always here if you need us." Morgan placed her hand on her shoulder.

Staying with Aiden wasn't ideal, but it would work for now.

She turned to Aiden. "I guess everything I have is already here."

Morgan hugged Phoebe close and rocked back and forth. Phoebe could have lost more. She could have lost her best friend. Her eyes locked with Aiden. That weird swelling happened in her chest again.

His words from earlier echoed in her mind, centering her. *I've got you.*

WORK KEPT PHOEBE SANE, or at least that was what Aiden told himself. She acted like nothing had happened after Tuesday. Though that night, she'd lain in his arms and he'd held onto her, wiping away her quiet tears.

But after that, it was like that night had never happened. Physically she was all over him, but emotionally she had shut him out. He was supposed to be fine with that. After all, they were just supposed to be about sex.

"Meeting in fifteen." Phoebe paused in his doorway and flashed him a sexy smile.

Aiden nodded. Gone was the panic-stricken woman who had clung to him in the elevator. The past few nights had been amazing. They spent hours tangled up in each other before falling asleep together. Waking each other up had its benefits as well.

But it all felt off somehow.

Aiden shook his head and gathered his material for the meeting with Drew and Morgan. They wanted to review all the new businesses he and Phoebe were thinking about as well as go over the plan they put together on the drive to the brewery.

Something major had happened to Phoebe in the past that got triggered that night, but she wouldn't open up to him. He wondered if it had to do with her mom, but every time he tried to ask, they ended up having sex until they damn near forgot their own names.

At work, Phoebe was on top of everything. Schedules were made and deadlines were kept. They'd brought in a few more clients and things began to settle. Instead of working against each other, they were finally working together. Everything seemed perfect.

But something was missing.

Aiden joined Drew and Morgan in their office. He turned, expecting to see Phoebe following him in.

"She'll be right in. Had to stop at the Ladies'." Morgan gestured to the chair. "How is she doing?"

Aiden wished he knew the answer to that. "She says she's doing fine."

Morgan touched her perfectly coifed updo as if there was a stray hair. "Any issues with her staying with you?"

"None." And he meant that. He always wanted her in his bed and he finally had her there. Even under a less than ideal situation, she was still there.

"Good. I didn't realize it would make her panic to see all my phone calls." Morgan stared at the papers on her desk in front of her, but she wasn't seeing them. "I just wanted to make sure she was okay. I'm so glad she was with you."

Morgan looked up at him with tears swimming in her big blue eyes. She blinked the tears away as if they never existed.

"Ready to do this." Phoebe came into the office and closed the door behind her.

Morgan had turned away and when she turned back, she smiled at Phoebe, all professional in that moment. "Let's hear what you have."

The rest of the day went on like normal. Drew and Morgan loved what Phoebe and Aiden had put together. They had a few notes, but overall, they were now on the same page. It was Friday and everyone started to wind down around four o'clock.

Phoebe came to his doorway a little after. "I'm going for drinks with Morgan tonight."

"Half-price margaritas?" he asked.

She gave him a sexy smile. "You know it."

"You have your keycard?"

"Of course." Phoebe leaned against the doorway. "You gonna be okay?"

He smiled to reassure her. "The team was talking about going to happy hour. I might join them."

"That sounds great." Phoebe straightened and looked over her shoulder. "We'll see each other later then."

He wanted to call her back as she walked away. But he didn't know what good it would do. He'd want her to open up about what was going on, and she kept blocking him with either redirection or seduction. Whichever was handiest at the time.

He couldn't help worrying about her. When she'd shut down in his car, he almost had a panic attack of his own. Stark terror had been written across her face. He'd wanted to hold her until her usual spark burst back to life.

If anything, it made him realize that what he felt for Phoebe went way beyond lust. He'd fallen in love with her in a way he'd never loved anyone else before. He couldn't even tell her because she didn't want that from him.

His chest ached at that thought. He'd keep her as long as she'd let him.

But every morning when her guard was down, he made love to her to show her what he couldn't tell her. Because he was afraid if he told her, she'd leave him.

CHAPTER 19

Tomorrow would be the first time Phoebe could go into her apartment to see if she could salvage anything. It was also the day she would move with Aiden into his swanky new apartment. He'd been worried about her all week, but she just put on her brave face and went forward with life.

Phoebe glanced back at his office door as she waited for Morgan.

Aiden was being supportive and there for her. He'd seen her in her blind panic and now he was worried. Supportive, like a boyfriend. Her lips pressed into a thin line.

She didn't have boyfriends; she had fuck toys. And Aiden had crossed that line somewhere. He was no longer a fuck toy. If she were being honest with herself (which she really hated), he hadn't been since the beginning. He mattered to her. But he still wasn't her boyfriend. She needed to figure out how to reestablish boundaries, especially since they were together twenty-four seven now.

The weird thing was she didn't mind it. She liked being with him day and night. Most guys would drive her crazy, but not Aiden. Well, he did drive her crazy, but with sex, which was acceptable. She sighed. She was doomed.

"You ready?" Morgan's voice brought Phoebe back to the present.

"Yes, ma'am," Phoebe followed Morgan out of the office. Her eyes met Aiden's and he gave her a smile with a hint of heat for later.

It didn't take them long to get to the Indigo Hotel. They found a small table and had drinks in their hands quickly. The night was just gearing up, so the bar wasn't quite packed yet. Phoebe's gaze lingered on the bar stool that she'd sat in when she met Aiden.

"I'm sorry I haven't made time for us." Morgan placed her hand over Phoebe's.

Phoebe dropped her gaze to her margarita before lifting it to Morgan's blue eyes. "I understand it. I'm just glad we didn't run out of time."

Morgan nodded. "So, you and Aiden are back on then?"

"Nah, we use the whole bedsheet down the middle of the bed trick." Phoebe smirked at her friend.

Morgan just shook her head and laughed. "I'm sure there is a pillow fort involved too."

Phoebe chuckled lightly. "Ah, the games we play."

"Are you heading over to the apartment tomorrow?" Morgan lifted her margarita but didn't take a sip.

Phoebe nodded. "You?"

Morgan took a sip and set down her drink. "Planning on it. Did you contact your insurance?"

Phoebe swallowed, not looking forward to this discussion. "It lapsed."

"What?" Morgan leaned forward and said again, "What?"

Phoebe pressed her lips together. She lifted her margarita and took a long drink. She shrugged. "It was due last

Monday and the credit card on file had an old expiration date. Because I didn't notice it, they won't let me backdate it."

"What are you going to do?" Morgan asked as if it was the end of the world.

It wasn't as bad as when Morgan had been fired, but it was still pretty sucky.

"I have a little savings. I've been stashing away part of my paycheck to refresh my savings too. The bonus helped, so thanks for that. It might take me longer to get back on my feet than would be ideal, but I'll get there." Phoebe didn't want to think about it. Because then she would have to think about the situation between her and Aiden. She couldn't mooch off him forever.

"You can always stay with me if you need to. But Aiden might let you stay until you're back on your feet." Morgan took a sip again but didn't meet Phoebe's eyes.

Phoebe snorted. "We've been hooking up for what. . . three weeks? That's a fucking record for me. I'm already practically living with him. I can't ask him to house me for longer. What if things start to fizzle?"

"Ah, the fizzle and fade theory." Morgan leaned back in her chair. Her hands went to her blond hair tucked up in a bun. "I thought things would cool off with Drew, but they still haven't."

"That's different." Phoebe pursed her lips.

"Why?" Morgan leaned in again. "Why are you and Aiden any different from me and Drew?"

Phoebe threw her hands in the air. "Because I'm not you."

Morgan crossed her arms over her chest. "What's that supposed to mean?"

"You're loveable. You may work yourself to death, but you've always had a healthy approach to relationships." Phoebe took a quick sip. "I'm barely tolerable. I'm lucky you love me as much as you do. Maybe that's your flaw. Loving people who most people wouldn't."

"Phoebe." Morgan leaned forward and put her hand over Phoebe's. "You deserve love just as much as I do. If it isn't with Aiden, it isn't, but don't discount him yet. I've seen the way he looks at you."

"Lust is easy."

"It isn't lust." Morgan tapped hard on the table. "It might have started as lust, but something's softer now. The way he was looking at you on Tuesday, that wasn't lust or just respect. That was something deep."

Phoebe shook her head. "It doesn't matter because I'm not capable of loving someone. And even if I do, they leave me."

"You love me. I'm here and I'm not going anywhere," Morgan said, quietly. "You and I have been friends for years now. I have been party to some of your schemes, and you have always had my back. I think if you let Aiden in, he would surprise you."

Phoebe made a dismissive noise. "You saw his suite."

"Holy crap, did I." Morgan's eyes widened. "I had no idea he had money. I mean I noticed the nice suits and designer labels. But a lot of guys will drop some coin on a nice suit or two."

"He's so out of my league." Phoebe shrugged and tried to keep her shoulders from drooping. "Sure, I'm an excellent fuck, but beyond that. . . ."

"Beyond that, you're awesome."

"Beyond that, I'm nothing. I have no family. Now I have no home. I'm not the kind of woman a guy like Aiden settles down with, even if I was looking for that. Which I most definitely am not. Aiden and I are. . . ."

How did she put this into words to make Morgan understand? Aiden made her want to be that woman but she could never be that for him. She probably couldn't be that for anyone. She'd been broken since she was eight years old when she discovered even men in love don't stay.

"Physically, we fit." Phoebe set her hands on the table. "We are equals and a match when it comes to sex, but. . . . But let's be realistic. I'm not the woman you bring home to mother for a normal guy. Imagine some wealthy guy bringing me to his parents. The only thing they'll think is, who is this gold-digging piece of trash."

"But that's not you," Morgan defended her.

"But that's what they'll see." Phoebe shrugged as if she had already given up. "All the love in the world won't make up for the fact that I won't ever deserve him. My god, I've slept with more than eight times the number of people he's slept with. I'm new and exciting, but eventually he'll get bored of me."

"I think that's bullshit. I'm telling you right now that if you fall in love with that man, he would move heaven and earth for you because you are fucking Phoebe Butler." Morgan gave her the look that said *don't contradict me*. As much as she loved Morgan for standing up for her against herself, Phoebe knew better. She wasn't made for love. She got lucky with Morgan, but even then, her friend started to cut her out when she found a love that was better.

"You'll see, it won't be long before he has one foot out the door and is ready to move on to someone new and in his league." Phoebe straightened. "Until then I will take advantage of the man's many talents."

Morgan opened her mouth as if to contradict Phoebe, but she must have seen something in Phoebe's expression. She closed her mouth and took a drink of her margarita before she talked again.

"Ones you refuse to talk about." Morgan lifted an eyebrow and smiled a little. Calling a truce with her eyes.

"I don't ask about you and Ew Drew." Phoebe winked at

her. "By the way, what's your plan now that you're homeless?"

"My lease was coming up anyway, so Drew and I are going to be looking at places together. Save on rent and all that." Morgan's cheeks darkened slightly.

"The sex must be worth it." Phoebe shook her head.

"Just being with him is worth it." Morgan leaned forward. "You'll see, one of these days."

Phoebe scoffed. Not likely. She glanced back at the bar chairs where she'd met Aiden. She couldn't have known then what she would be going through now. Or that she'd be staying one last night in this fabulous hotel with Aiden Kingston.

Morgan thought Phoebe had a chance with Aiden, but Phoebe knew the truth, and to save herself from getting hurt, she needed to keep things strictly physical with him. Her heart squeezed, but she couldn't afford to fall and then watch him walk away. It would destroy her.

"You didn't have to come with me."

That was the fourth time Phoebe had mentioned that to Aiden.

"I'm beginning to think you don't want me here." Aiden placed his hand on the small of her back as they stepped out of the elevator.

She turned her head toward him. "I just don't want you to feel obligated."

"Phoebe, I care about you and want to be here with you. Can you just leave it at that?" Aiden rubbed his hand over the small of her back and felt the little shiver that went through her.

"Fine."

He brushed her sweet lips with his. They moved into the line of people waiting to get back into their apartments. Morgan and Drew wove their way over to them.

"Hey," Morgan said, taking Phoebe's hand.

Drew nodded to Aiden, and he nodded back.

"Remember, everyone," a woman shouted to be heard from the front, "hard hats are required. The structural engineers have been through and said it's safe to move around the floor. If there is tape in front of your door, please come back and see me. Axels Properties has provided plastic bags to carry out anything you want to keep. When the cleanup crew comes through, anything left behind that appears to be valuable or salvageable will be placed in a storage locker for you. Please let us know if you require any help."

A young man moved through the crowd handing out supplies: gloves, masks, helmets, and plastic bags.

Aiden leaned down to say to Phoebe, "I can make a list as we walk through for your insurance company."

"Did you get them to accept your payment?" Morgan said, excitedly.

Phoebe cleared her throat and gave Morgan a shut-up look before shifting her eyes to Aiden and back. Aiden took a deep breath.

"No insurance?" he asked in a non-judgmental tone.

Phoebe swallowed and met his gaze. Her expression was blank, but he could see a little strain at her eyes. "It lapsed and I would have paid it, but I missed the letter. Because there was an incident when it was lapsed, they won't cover it."

Fuck. He didn't say it out loud but he felt it in his gut. Insurance wouldn't have mattered to someone like him, but for Phoebe who was just scraping by, it meant everything.

"Okay, we'll sort through that later," Aiden said as the guy reached their group and handed them what they needed.

Morgan mouthed the word *sorry* to Phoebe before smiling warily at Aiden.

"You don't need to worry about it." Phoebe put on her hard hat. "It's my problem. I'll deal with it."

"Of course." Aiden gave her a smile while he knew he'd do something about it. But she seemed satisfied as they all walked down the hall.

The smell of smoke lingered in the air. Only some of the hallway had licks of charred marks. They stopped at Morgan's door.

Morgan and Phoebe hugged.

"Good luck," Phoebe said.

"You too." Morgan clasped Phoebe's hand and gave it a squeeze before opening her door. Besides the smoky smell, the apartment didn't look very damaged from where they stood.

Aiden took Phoebe's hand and let her lead him down the hallway. The smell and marks grew stronger until they passed three or four apartment doors with tape crossing them. The middle one's door hung open and he could see the damage. Everything was blackened, but there were still shapes of what used to be in the apartment there.

Phoebe tugged him along until they reached her door. She didn't hesitate and unlocked the door. It was almost as bad as the middle apartment. A heavy smoky scent hung in the air and her furniture was charred on the edges.

Straightening, Phoebe walked inside. She wore her short skirt and her halter top that he'd had laundered. The hard hat sat on top of her ginger hair. She hadn't had much at Aiden's apartment and she'd lost pretty much everything.

She moved with determination toward a spot on the wall. The shelf looked like a log from a fire, but on top of it was a perfect crystal dragon. She lifted it and rubbed at the char stains. He remembered her saying it was her mother's.

He went to the couch which didn't look very burned. The blanket on the back was still wet from the fire hose, but with the exception of a few sooty parts, it might be salvageable. Aiden lifted it and stuck it in the bag. When he finished, he didn't see Phoebe.

He set his bag down and headed into the bedroom. Phoebe sat on the bed. Tears streamed down her face as she stared at the top of her dresser. He winced as he remembered the pictures that had been there.

Sitting down next to her, he put his arm around her shoulder and drew her close. Her face pressed against his chest as she leaned into him. He wanted to make this right for her, but knew that all the money in the world couldn't replace the things she'd lost.

"Aiden?" she whispered after a moment.

"Hmmm?"

"What am I going to do?" Her voice cracked and it nearly broke his heart.

He lifted her onto his lap and wrapped his arms around her. Her forehead leaned against his neck as she curled into him. He wanted to make this all go away. He wanted so badly to fix this for her, but all he could do was hold her and be here for her.

"You'll stay with me as long as you need to get back on your feet." He kissed the top of her head.

She lifted her face to meet his eyes. "What if—"

"No matter what." He grabbed her chin and searched her watery brown eyes. "You and I are good. Even if we aren't having sex, you can stay with me. As long as it takes."

He brushed away her tears with his thumbs.

"My clothes are ruined. My shoes are ruined. Everything I owned is gone." Phoebe blinked up at him. If he could, he'd hold her forever to take the hurt away. "My mom's picture. . ."

"Is there a digital copy?" Aiden stroked his hand up and down her back.

She sighed. "I hope so. Of course my laptop was here too."

"We can take it with us. Maybe some of the hard drive can be restored."

She nodded and began to get up, but he pulled her tight against him.

"I'm really sorry this happened to you, Phoebe."

She met his gaze and he brushed his lips over hers.

"I want to help you in any way I can."

Her hand came up and cupped his cheek. She searched his eyes for a moment. "I'll get back on my feet. That's what us Butler women have to do. Life knocks us down, but we keep getting back up."

She moved off him and went over to her nightstand. Her laptop sat there. She put it in the plastic bag. As she went around her room picking up pieces of her life, Aiden could only sit and watch her. She drifted from object to object, occasionally finding a treasure. Most of her jewelry had made it. Anything that seemed sentimental, she added to the bag.

They would need to drop them off at place Aiden found that repaired damaged items. Aiden held Phoebe's arm and the bags while Phoebe carried out the crystal dragon. He could only hope that he had eased her worries. If only a little. She had to know that he'd never turn her out.

Even if she couldn't love him back.

CHAPTER 20

THE ELEVATOR OPENED into the penthouse apartment. Phoebe stepped out and turned to help Aiden bring in the few bags she had. Phoebe's mind raced with everything she'd have to do today. The few outfits and shoes she had at Aiden's wouldn't be enough clothes to get her through the week.

She needed to go shopping, which meant loading up her credit cards. Her shoulders sagged. It was all too much. She really just wanted a nap.

"Come on. There's a freshly made bed calling your name." Aiden flashed a smile at her.

"I should really go shopping." She did mental calculations to decide how much she could spend and how much she needed to save to be able to rent a new place. It wasn't just clothing she needed, but a new laptop, and when she finally had an apartment of her own, dishes and pots and pans, though she might get some of those back when the property managers had the crews come through.

Not much had made it between the smoke and fire damage. Even her poor vibrators hadn't survived. Not that she needed them with Aiden around, but eventually he wouldn't be around.

She sighed heavily. She couldn't muster full Phoebe mode today. Not after seeing the ruins of her life. But she couldn't damage this last thing she had with Aiden. So she sucked it up.

"Shopping can wait. Why don't we unpack and then take a nap." Aiden brushed past her on his way into the bedroom. He did make it easy to forget all the crap going on.

"When you say nap, do you mean sleep?" She smiled at him as she followed him into the bedroom. The king bed had new coverings on it and a lot more pillows.

After the smoky smell of her apartment, his new apartment smelled fresh and clean. The bed looked so tempting.

Aiden set his luggage down and took hers to place next to it. Then he closed in on her until she had to tip her chin up to look at him. She breathed in his scent and let it curl around her like a blanket along with the heat of his body.

"I'm sure we'll sleep. Eventually." His green eyes darkened and his arms snaked around her waist, pulling her tight against him. "You did say you were available for house-warmings."

"Do you know what a housewarming is?" She raised an eyebrow at him and some of the tension eased out of her. She was worried he'd handle her with kid gloves because she'd cried in her apartment.

He bent down and lifted her up against him.

She squeaked in surprise. "What are you doing?"

His eyes twinkled as they met hers. "I don't know about you, but rummaging around in ashes made me feel dirty." He wiggled his eyebrows at her on the word "dirty" and she almost snickered. "I think we should shower."

Wrapping her arms around his neck, she leaned back. "All of our toiletries are still in our bags."

"Good thing this apartment came with a magic phone." He grinned at her as he strolled into the bathroom. "I called concierge service and had them clean and stock everything."

The bathroom was as gorgeous as she remembered, and that tub. . . . She and Aiden could do a lot of dirty things in that tub. Aiden lowered her feet to the floor and kissed the tip of her nose.

"Don't go anywhere." He went over to the shower. As he turned the handles, the sound of water hitting the tiles filled the room.

She sat on the edge of the tub to take off her wedges. "So, how magic is the phone here?"

"Pretty fucking magical." His smile made her heart melt. "Fresh linens, fresh towels. Maid service once a week. Anything you want. Day or night."

When he winked at her, she swore she felt giddy. At least her time with Aiden wouldn't be dull.

"Did they sprinkle condoms everywhere too?" She smirked at him.

Taking off his shirt as he walked, he came back over to her. His shirt dropped to the floor, followed by his pants and underwear. Aiden stood before her completely naked.

She didn't think she'd ever grow bored of seeing Aiden naked. His usually perfectly coifed, blond hair was ruffled from taking off his shirt. Everything about the man was solid muscle and perfectly formed, including his hard cock.

He lifted her to standing and she placed her hands on his warm, smooth chest. Tingles flowed across her fingertips as she followed the sculpted lines of his chest and abs. Anticipation welled inside her stomach. She couldn't seem to get enough of this man.

He made quick work of her shirt and skirt. Her bra and panties joined the rest of the clothes on the floor.

"I made sure condoms were available wherever we need

them." He dipped his head and captured her lips, taking her breath with him. She'd always loved kissing, but kissing with Aiden was next level shit. She melted into him as he deepened the kiss. Her naked skin pressed against his and all she could think about was him deep inside her, giving her everything she needed. Her knees weakened.

His hands followed the curve of her back down to her ass, and he lifted her against him. She gasped in surprise and pulled back from his lips. His knowing smile made her flush with heat. He knew what he did to her and it excited him almost as much as it excited her.

She wrapped herself around him as he carried them into the hot steamy shower. His warmth seeped into her even as the shower created a cocoon around them.

"What do you need, Phoebe?" He cocked up one side of his lips into a smile as he pressed her back against the shower tile. His hips rocked against hers.

She leaned her head on the tile and searched his eyes. She couldn't seem to help herself, looking for something she wouldn't recognize even if she saw it. Fuck, she wanted this man, more than just his body. This craving wasn't fading at all. If anything, the need was growing stronger.

It would fucking hurt when he didn't want her anymore.

But for now, he was hers.

"You," she said.

Her legs slid down and she pressed him back until he stood under the rain showerhead. Reaching up around his neck, she pulled his mouth down to hers. She wanted all of him. Their bodies slid against one another as they kissed like it was the last time or maybe the first.

His hands followed the water as it caressed her skin. He stopped on her breasts, devoting time to worshipping her breasts and nipples. His lips moved away from hers down her neck until he captured her nipple in his mouth.

She tipped her head back, losing herself in his touch. Of all the guys she'd been with, Aiden was the only one she hadn't stopped wanting. He lifted his head and gave her a cocky smile that had her insides pulsing.

Pressing her hand against his chest, she pushed him back until he sat on the tiled seat in the shower. He drew her with him until she straddled him. She stayed up on her knees, hovering above his cock, teasing both of them. His hands held her against him as he lavished attention on her other breast.

Her fingers tangled in his hair as wave after wave of pleasure rolled through her. His hand slipped down her trembling belly and found the center of her, his touch teasing, tormenting her.

"Do you have any idea how incredible you are?" His tone was worshipful.

She tilted her head to meet his eyes. Her forehead rested against his as she breathed him in. A wide crack formed in the wall around her heart. Next to all the other cracks that had started forming when she met Aiden. It would be easy to forget that this was temporary and that playing house wouldn't last forever. That this thing between them was only supposed to be about sex.

She hovered over him, looking into his green eyes darkened by lust. Her heart filled her chest, pounding out a rhythm only he could cause.

Because she wanted to believe that this could last. She wanted to believe that he wouldn't leave her. That he wouldn't stop wanting her. That they could fit in real life as well as they did when they had sex.

"Phoebe." His voice was soft and she felt it all the way into her soul.

Fuck. The realization struck her hard and she almost gasped. She loved him.

Almost weak with her revelation, she kissed him, not wanting him to see it written on her face. All of him pressed against all of her and she longed to feel that completion. She wanted the fucking fairy tale and knew that it would never be hers.

She felt him shifting beneath her as he put on a condom while they kissed. After a moment, he grabbed her hips and lowered her slowly, achingly onto his cock, until she took him fully into her. She broke off the kiss to throw her head back, needing air.

"Fuck, Phoebe." Aiden pressed his mouth against her throat and bit and sucked on her. "You don't know what you do to me."

She rested her forehead on his. Needing the connection. This man, he'd captured her body and soul from their very first meeting.

"You do the same to me." She lifted on him and lowered herself back down.

"I can't get enough of you," he whispered like they were sharing secrets as she rocked over him. Maybe they were.

"Aiden?"

His eyes never left hers. It felt too intimate, like that first time. She couldn't find her rhythm. She loved the feel of him and what they were doing, but she needed more. She needed him to take control.

"Phoebe."

"Please," she whimpered as she ground herself against him.

"Only you." He kissed her briefly and stood with her. She wrapped her legs around his waist. He pressed her against the tile and full seated himself within her. "Open your eyes, Phoebe."

His words were still soft, but the command was irresistible. His forehead pressed against hers and she opened her eyes.

His smile widened and he winked at her. "Hold on."

His hands anchored her hips against the tile while he did all the work. All she could do was hold onto his face and stare into his soft green eyes. Even though she'd been naked in front of Aiden more often than not, this was the first time she felt stripped of the wall she'd always kept between them.

Her heart pounded until it seemed like it would jump out of her chest. Her climax built in her whole body. Sparks raced along her nerve endings.

Through it all she was connected, not just physically, but emotionally to Aiden. Maybe she always had been. He shifted slightly and took her breath away.

She couldn't take her eyes from his as she toppled over the edge into ecstasy. He kept going, still maintaining that eye contact and keeping her right there with him until he found his own release.

Their heavy breathing combined with the water falling from the shower. Neither of them moved but kept their eyes locked. She never wanted to leave this moment.

She loved Aiden. The words wanted to burst from her throat.

His eyes held secrets that she didn't know if she was ready to see. From the beginning she'd told him she didn't want more. That she wouldn't want more. That she wasn't created for love. Just a good time.

He kissed her long and hard before withdrawing to take care of the condom. She stood in the warm shower and let the water pour over her. He captured her against him when he returned.

His green eyes melted her as he studied her face. His thumbs brushed her hair off her face. She couldn't imagine not wanting him.

"You and I," he said, pausing to take a breath, "aren't going to end anytime soon. Every time I have you, I just want you more."

She held her breath as he took in a deep breath. His hands cupped her face.

"Would you—" His eyes cleared and he stared into her soul. "Would you consider more?"

"More?" The word barely squeaked out of her throat. Her whole being longed to hear what he would say next.

"Be more. I'm not saying you have to be my girlfriend or anything like that. We obviously fit physically, but there's more to us. More than sex. If you don't feel it, it's fine. I'm happy with what we are doing."

She couldn't help the soft smile on her lips. She brushed her thumb over his soft lower lip. What she wouldn't give. . . .

"I—" The words stuck in her throat. She cleared the lump and just nodded.

"Yes?" Aiden's body tensed against hers even as his grin grew.

She could try. What would it hurt? "Yes."

AIDEN COULDN'T WIPE the grin from his face as they actually showered. Phoebe washed him while he washed her. By the time they finished the shower, both of them were turning into prunes.

"I still need to go get clothes today," Phoebe said as she dried him with a towel. Her laughter sounded more relaxed and free as they kept getting tangled while he tried to dry her at the same time.

He could live a lifetime and not hear enough of Phoebe's laugh. "Maybe we should put away what we already have first."

"Doesn't your magic phone take care of that?"

"The magic phone doesn't do everything." He wrapped the towel around Phoebe and pulled her into him for a kiss. He'd meant for it to be brief, but when her tongue slid against his, he groaned and gathered her closer. Her naked body was still warm from the shower.

She broke away and pressed her finger to his lips. "Okay, put that on pause. I need to get to the stores before they close for the day."

"Sure." He grinned at her, not wanting to give away his surprise, but it was hard to keep it a secret.

He wrapped the towel around his waist as she tucked hers around herself. They walked into the bedroom and he picked up her bags.

"I can do that." She reached for them, but he backed toward one of the closets.

"You can open the door for me." He nodded toward the door, trying to suppress his grin.

She scoffed as she followed him. "I don't need a whole closet for my few outfits."

"Humor me." He backed up against the wall next to the door and nodded toward the door handle.

She gave him a weird look before she opened the door. The closet light was already on. Aiden had to admit it was pretty spectacular. He'd had Morgan call a few shops to get Phoebe clothes and shoes so she wouldn't have to bother. Definitely wrap dresses too. It had all been delivered to the apartment building this morning.

Her eyes widened as she walked into the closet. "What did you do?"

Her fingers trailed along skirts, shirts, and dresses. The shoe rack was filled to the brim with the high heels. He couldn't wait to see her in them.

"This is too much, Aiden." Phoebe turned. Her lips drawn down.

For a second his heart dropped. He closed the distance between them. "You needed clothes. I have a magic phone that will bring me what I want. Therefore, you have more time with me."

She shook her head like a mother does to a child who's been naughty. Like he picked the neighbor's flowers to give to her. "This was really sweet."

"But?"

She sighed and tapped her fingers on his chest before she lifted her gaze to him.

"I may fantasize about *Pretty Woman*, but I don't actually want to be a prostitute." Her lips set in a thin line, but her hand reached out to feel the fabric of one of the dresses.

"Whoa, who said you were a prostitute?" Aiden held his hands up in front of her.

Her lips quirked into a side smile while her eyes narrowed at him.

"From the beginning of this" —her hand went back and forth between the two of them— "we've been about sex. That way we both have power. Because let's be honest, this closet is almost half the size of my bedroom in my apartment. Money equals power normally, but you and I are equals when it comes to sex. Yes, I liked it when you could get me bubble bath and champagne and croissants, but this is a whole new level, Aiden."

She turned and her fingers ran along the toes of the shoes. "I don't want to feel obligated to have sex with you."

Aiden stepped behind her and put an arm around her shoulders to draw her back against him. He kissed the top of her head. "I'm not trying to pay you for having sex with me. I'm trying to help my. . . friend. I . . . care about you and know that you've suffered a blow financially. I want to help you."

Phoebe opened a drawer and pulled out some silky panties. "You buy your friends underwear like this?"

He could hear the smile in her voice and the weight lifted from him. He brushed his lips against her earlobe. "If they're willing to let me see them try them on."

"I can't possibly repay you for this." Phoebe sighed and set the panties back in the drawer. "I'm going to feel like I owe you big time. First you take me in when I'm homeless. Then you clothe me. What can I offer you in return?"

Your love. The words sat on the tip of his tongue, but he couldn't say them. It was all he wanted from her. She didn't want him to pay for her body. She most definitely wouldn't want him to try to buy her love.

"I'd say the pleasure of your company, but I'm pretty sure you'll accuse me of trying to solicit you again." He squeezed her shoulders.

She turned and he let his arm drop. She placed both her hands on his bare chest. "Thank you for doing this. All these clothes are lovely and I'm sure they'll all fit me perfectly. But I'm still not certain I can accept them."

Aiden scratched his chin. "I don't think they'll fit me."

She laughed and it went straight to his heart.

"How about this?" He put his hands on her hips and drew her close to him. "You use these clothes until you're able to buy your own without making yourself go further in debt."

She opened her mouth, but he kissed her to stop her from saying anything. When she leaned into the kiss, he pulled away.

"You can replace the clothes or pay me back if you want to keep them. We'll donate the rest to a women's shelter."

Phoebe's eyes welled up with tears and she smiled up at him. "I like that idea."

One tear escaped and he used his thumb to capture it and bring it to his lips. She wrapped her arms around him and hugged him. Unable to resist, he returned the hug and snuggled her against his chest.

"Now that you are keeping them," he said against her wet hair, "do you want to model them for me? I'd particularly like to see those panties you were holding, and I'm pretty sure there is a whole drawer of lingerie in here."

He could feel her smile against his chest.

"You mean like the shopping scene from *Pretty Woman*?"

He chuckled and pulled her tighter against him, like he could fuse them into one so she'd never leave him. "Exactly. Then we can actually watch the movie so I know what the hell you are talking about all the time."

She laughed and pulled away. Her brown eyes sparkled as she looked up at him. There was something soft and tender lurking in her eyes. "I—I—like you, Aiden."

When she stumbled over the word, his heart stopped. He wanted her love more than he wanted his next breath, but he'd settle to have her in his arms for now.

"I like you, too." He kissed her briefly, then turned toward the drawers, rubbing his hands together. "Let's find that lingerie drawer."

CHAPTER 21

"How's living with Aiden going?" Morgan entered the breakroom while Phoebe was sipping her coffee staring into space, daydreaming about the weekend. Monday had come too soon, but the workday was almost over.

"It's going well." Phoebe's lips betrayed her and pulled into a soft smile. God, that man and what he could do to her. They'd spent all of Sunday "breaking in" his apartment. If there was a surface they could have sex on, they did. Even against the windows, staring out into the city skyline.

"Is this one of the dresses he bought you?" Morgan gestured toward her dress as she took down a coffee mug.

"Of course you would have been involved with that." Phoebe rolled her eyes but gave Morgan a twirl of the wrap dress. "He didn't go cheap on anything."

She held up her foot with Louboutins that cost as much as she made in a week.

"Nice." Morgan admired the heels.

"I'm going to be sad when I have to go back to what I can afford." She turned her ankle with a frown.

"What do you mean?"

"I can't keep all this." Phoebe pursed her lips. "He spent way too much. It would shift the power dynamic and I would feel like I owed him. I already feel like I owe him."

Morgan shook her head. Her lips flattened. "That's not why he did it."

Phoebe's stomach clenched. The moments of tenderness and connection seemed to increase the longer they were together. But there was still this cracked wall between them. She needed it to stay sane.

"I know, but I can't help the way I feel. Besides when I replace things, we are going to donate the clothes so they won't go to waste."

"Why are you obsessing about 'power dynamics' anyway?" Morgan poured her coffee and took a sip.

Phoebe looked away from Morgan because she didn't want Morgan to see the fear that probably lingered in her eyes. "Right now, we're equals. I don't want to have to owe him."

"I don't think he feels that way."

Phoebe knew Morgan was right, but that didn't stop the churning in her gut whenever she thought about it. "He's way out of my league."

Morgan scoffed. "You are in a league of your own, Phoebe. No one is out of your league. Not even Aiden."

The door opened before Phoebe could respond. If anyone was in a league of their own, it was Aiden. She'd never met anyone quite like him. Emily came in looking harried.

"Morgan." Emily took a breath. "I have to go. Grandma fell and a neighbor took her to the hospital."

Phoebe stepped forward and hugged Emily briefly. "You go and I'll take care of the phones."

Emily nodded and looked at Morgan.

Morgan didn't hesitate. "Yes, go be with your grandma."

The door to the breakroom opened and Ben walked in,

looking down at his phone. Emily had her back to the door and didn't notice him coming in.

"I have to call an Uber to get to the hospital and the cost will be a lot, but I have to get there." Emily pulled up her phone.

"I have a car here." Ben's voice surprised them all. As one they all turned to him. His dark blue eyes lifted to Morgan. "If you don't mind, Morgan, I can take Emily. I'm pretty much done for today."

Phoebe smiled at the look of relief on Emily's face, followed by a blush.

"Of course," Morgan said with a smile. "Take care of your family, Emily."

"Thank you," Emily said to Morgan before she glanced up at Ben with her cornflower blue eyes and a shy smile. "I'd appreciate a ride."

Ben slipped his phone in his pocket, but he didn't crack a smile. "No problem."

Emily gave Phoebe and Morgan a small finger wave before she and Ben headed out of the breakroom.

"Think she'll be able to breathe enough to give him directions?" Phoebe smirked.

Morgan laughed. "I'd love to be a fly in that car."

"I need to get out to the desk apparently." Phoebe set her mug in the sink and walked toward the door.

"Let me know if you need someone to relieve you."

"I will." Phoebe went to her desk and grabbed a few things to work on before heading to the receptionist desk. The phones stayed quiet for a while, so Phoebe got into her groove of working on some of her project planning. Jason was supposed to have the first proofs to her next Monday.

The exterior door opened and Phoebe glanced up, expecting someone coming back from lunch or something. A woman stood there looking around. She had blond hair that was perfectly straight and perfectly highlighted. Her blue eyes took in the entire office before settling on Phoebe. She had a model's face and body, tall, slender, with curves in all the right places. Her clothes and jewelry dripped with wealth and privilege.

Maybe this woman had gotten turned around and wanted the law office that was on this floor. It was the only scenario that made sense to Phoebe.

"May I help you?" Phoebe asked, ready to give directions.

"Yes." Even her accent spoke of wealth. "I'm here to see Aiden Kingston. Our parents are old friends."

The woman smiled, showing off perfect white teeth. Maybe it was the way she'd said "old friends," but suddenly Phoebe want to punch this perfect creature in those teeth, so she wouldn't be perfect anymore.

"Who may I say is here?" Phoebe picked up the phone like she was going to dial Aiden's number.

"Rachel Sandburg." Rachel leaned in as if they were going to be coconspirators. Good luck with that, lady. "He probably isn't expecting me though. His mother thought dropping by might be the best way to reach him."

"Give me a second and I'll let him know you are here." Phoebe stood and put the phone down. The woman had a few inches on her, but Phoebe was certain if it came down to a fight, she could take Rachel.

Phoebe straightened and smoothed down her dress while Rachel waited. She turned and headed to Aiden's office door. Not bothering to knock, she slipped in and closed the door behind her so Rachel couldn't hear what they said.

"Phoebe." His soft voice filled with pleasure went through her, warming her. His eyes lit up and she wanted to just stand and bask in his warmth. She almost forgot why she came in.

"You have a visitor."

Aiden stood and walked around his desk, closing the distance between them until she could barely breathe as he towered over her. "A visitor?"

His fingers reached out. She sucked in a breath, preparing for his touch, but his fingers just lingered on the strings of the wrap dress. Her focus dropped to his lips.

"Keep looking at me like that and I'll have you on my desk." His lips curved up in a smile. "Again."

She groaned and lifted her gaze to his eyes. "You have a visitor. Rachel Sandburg."

"Fuck." Aiden closed his eyes. "Did she say what she wanted?"

"From the way she looks, I would guess she wants you." She let her fingers walk up his chest and then slid them down his tie. "I'd kiss you, but I don't want to be one of those women who marks their territory."

He raised an eyebrow and dipped his head until their mouths were a hair's breadth apart. "You can mark me."

She chuckled and stepped back. His fingers dropped from her dress tie. "You should see to your visitor."

"Only if you promise we'll revisit this later." Heat burned in his green eyes and she swore she smoldered for him.

She pressed her thighs together from the ache between them and smiled up at him. "Definitely."

A FEW MINUTES after Phoebe slipped back out, a discreet knock came from his door as Aiden circled his desk to be on the other side. If this woman was anything like the other women his mother tried to set him up with, she'd be a cheek kisser.

He didn't care if this woman was a veritable angel. He only had eyes for his own personal devil.

Phoebe opened the door. Speak of the devil.

As Rachel stepped into the office, her cloying perfume overwhelmed the space and he had to breathe through his mouth.

"Aiden, darling. I've heard so much about you." She stepped forward and paused when he didn't come around the desk to greet her but stuck out his hand over the desk. Her smile didn't falter as she took his hand. "Your mother said I must meet you."

"My mother said you're in town for a new job." Aiden shook her hand briefly and gestured toward the seat across from him as he sat.

Rachel took the chair. Phoebe left the door wide open and winked at him before leaving him alone with this potential lioness. He wanted to give this woman the benefit of the doubt, but so many of the women his mother "vetted" were cut from the same cloth. His mother hadn't said much about Rachel, but the fact his mom wanted him to call Rachel and maybe take her to lunch or preferably dinner meant set up.

"Yes, I decided a career would be a nice change of pace for me. And to work somewhere that does so much good in the city and pulls together so many of our equals to support such a great cause, it really makes me feel accomplished." Rachel pressed her hands over her heart before she straightened her skirts to perfectly cover her knees while crossing her ankles to one side of the chair. "My job is actually why I came to see you."

Aiden raised an eyebrow. "How so?"

Rachel smiled as if she had him on her hook. "I've been hired to help the Home Again Foundation. We raise money to help homeless children in the city. Our current advertising firm is botching the job something horrible. Our annual gala is on Friday this week and we still have available tables. We need something new and exciting for next year and that's where you come in."

Her thousand-watt smile was almost blinding, but Aiden was used to that smile and it didn't blind him. Not when he had Phoebe's smiles.

"We've been looking at getting involved with a charity of some sort to diversify our portfolio." Aiden lifted his cell phone and texted Phoebe to come in. "I need to bring my partner in so we can discuss business."

He emphasized the word partner, hoping she would take the hint when Phoebe joined them. His mother had asked at the Brewery if he was seeing someone and at that point, Phoebe and him hadn't decided to try to be more. But he also couldn't tell Rachel, his coworker was also his live-in relationship of some sort. The likelihood of Phoebe calling him *babe* at work was probably too low.

Rachel frowned. "I was hoping to work with just you. After all, you are the boss."

"I'm only part of a team." He picked up a pen and fiddled with it while he waited. "We do things a little differently here than in Chicago. But I'm sure we can be helpful to each other."

"I certainly hope so." Rachel's flirty smile returned. "My parents and yours are like two peas in a pod. It would make sense that we could be. . . friendly with each other. We're so similar. You wanted to branch out on your own and start a new life here, which is exactly what I'm trying to do too."

Aiden pressed his lips into a thin line. His mother was trying a new tactic with Rachel, which while amusing, he still didn't want a trophy wife.

"I haven't had the chance to really go out much since I moved here." Her gaze stopped on his cufflinks and she smiled. "So many different restaurants to try. Don't you agree?"

He hoped having Phoebe in here would keep Rachel from flat out asking him out. Phoebe oozed sexuality. She'd be the perfect foil to this woman's flirting.

"I don't go out much myself," Aiden said. "I prefer to stay at home." With Phoebe.

If Phoebe ever joined them. . . .

"Sorry, I had to get Lacy to watch the phones." Phoebe strolled in and he released the breath he'd been holding. "Hi, I'm Phoebe Butler."

She held out her hand to Rachel.

"Oh, I thought you were the receptionist." Rachel took Phoebe's hand for a brief second before releasing it.

"Our receptionist had an emergency, so I was helping out." Phoebe sank into the chair next to Rachel. "So, what's happening?"

Aiden cleared his throat and Phoebe focused on him with a slight smirk. "Rachel works for Home Again Foundation and they're looking for a new advertising firm, which is why she is here."

Phoebe's eyebrows raised in surprise. "That's great. I have a few friends who volunteer for the organization's annual gala."

"Yes, it's coming up this weekend." Rachel's voice held just a hint of disdain. She probably believed Phoebe was beneath her. Phoebe was worth at least ten Rachels.

"We would love to be able to figure out how we can help each other." Aiden leaned back in his chair. "So, let's talk logistics."

Obviously Rachel wasn't quite prepared for all this. Maybe she'd hoped she'd walk into Aiden's office and he'd take one look at her model-like features and sweep her off her feet. He was sure his mother had told her he was single and needed a wife.

Rachel only stumbled over a few words before getting

into the flow of what they were looking for in an ad agency. They discussed the scope of the project along with how much they were looking to spend budget wise.

"Of course, any cost savings would go directly to help the children." She laughed a little when she said that, but her smile was soft like she was only doing all this for the children and not to look good for potential husbands. A husband was her number one goal, otherwise his mother would have never mentioned her.

She continued to talk and Phoebe asked a few questions, but Aiden just sat back and watched the dynamics. Phoebe took control of the conversation easily from Rachel. He knew from working with her that even though she didn't write a thing down, Phoebe was taking notes in her head. She'd remember everything about this conversation and would have an advertising profile entered before the day was out.

Phoebe amazed him.

"I think we could be able to draw up a fairly good plan for you." Phoebe leaned back in the chair. "If you don't mind, I need to go relieve Lacy. She's one of our creatives who will most likely be working on your ads."

"It was a pleasure meeting you," Rachel said, with the most plastic smile Aiden had ever seen.

Phoebe just nodded and gave him a quick look before heading out of the office. Again, she left the door open.

"Thank you for stopping by, Rachel. We'll be in touch once we draft a proposal." Aiden started to rise but stopped when Rachel settled more into her chair.

"The Gala is this Friday, and I was hoping that you would come to it." Rachel's face brightened with a hint of pink on her cheeks. "I know it's last minute."

"I don't think that's a good idea." Aiden straightened his tie. "I'm not really looking to get involved with anyone—"

Rachel laughed and held up her hands. "I wasn't asking for you to go with me." Sure she wasn't. "I meant you should come and see how it's done. Get a feel for our organization. There are plenty of seats left."

Drew stopped in the doorway. "Excuse me, Aiden. We have a meeting in a few minutes. I just wanted to remind you."

Aiden stood, grateful for the interruption. "Drew King, this is Rachel Sandburg. Rachel is overseeing the fundraising for the Home Again Foundation and they are considering a new advertising firm. Rachel, this is Drew, one of the owners of Taylor and King."

Rachel flushed as she stood and shook Drew's hand. "It's a pleasure to meet you."

"Hopefully we can work something out. I'd love to help the Home Again Foundation. I've heard nothing but good things." Drew released her hand and stepped back. "Your annual gala is coming up, isn't it?"

Rachel smiled. "It is. We don't have quite as many donors as last year. We even have a few tables open."

"We can't have that." Drew glanced at Aiden before saying. "I'm sure I could get the team to come. Why don't I buy a table? That way we can see how things are being done this year."

"That would be amazing." Rachel's eyes brightened and Aiden could almost see the dollar signs spinning about her head. "Tables are for eight."

Her eyes landed back on Aiden, and he had the urge to loosen his collar. Aiden pressed his lips together, refusing to give Rachel any encouragement besides work-related.

"Great. Our whole team can come. Right, Aiden?" Drew's gaze landed on Aiden.

"Of course. We can make it an office outing instead of happy hour. It'd be nice to see everyone dolled up." Aiden didn't have to force his smile when he thought of the dress he wanted Phoebe to wear.

"Fantastic." Rachel clapped her hands together.

"Why don't you come with me and I'll get you a check for the donation and table?" Drew held his arm out to usher Rachel out of Aiden's office.

Rachel turned back toward Aiden. Her smile was huge. "I have your number. I'll text you some details. I can't wait to see you on Friday."

Aiden just smiled tightly and nodded. If she was anything like the other women his mother had chosen for him, she'd already be planning a fucking wedding for them a year from now.

Phoebe stopped as she was walking back to her desk. Her eyes met his.

Her smile widened as she stepped toward him. "Do you need something, Mr. Kingston?"

Fuck, did he. He needed her all the fucking time and to know she didn't already have one foot out the door. "I've got everything I need."

CHAPTER 22

EVERYONE TOOK off early Friday afternoon to get ready for the Gala. Thankfully Emily's grandma was fine, just a small fall and they weren't worried about it.

Phoebe almost refused Aiden's gift of a dress until she saw the dress he'd picked. It wasn't an exact replica of the red dress that Julia Roberts wore in *Pretty Woman*, but it was a modern version of it.

Aiden had left her to dress while he took a shower and changed into his tux, of which, of course, he owned several. She didn't want to turn her nose up at him, but seriously, who needed several tuxedos if they weren't James Bond.

When he stepped out of the bathroom, though, her breath caught. The towel wrapped around his waist looked like it could drop any moment. Maybe they should skip the gala and stay in bed all night.

"Stop it," he said, playfully. "If you keep looking at me while you stand there in sexy underwear, we'll never get ready."

"Maybe that's my evil plan." Phoebe cocked her hip and gave him a sassy smile.

"Remember, we're doing this for the company." He disappeared into his closet.

"And not for Rachel." Little miss perfect had had the audacity to text Aiden a few times this week. Nothing overtly flirtatious, but Phoebe didn't know how the other half flirted. Maybe her texts were the equivalent to a boob selfie.

"I want to see you all dressed up." Aiden's voice was only slightly muffled by the closet. "I may regret seeing your 'before' look in those panties, though, because I'm going to be hard all night every time I look at you."

Heat flushed through Phoebe's system as she applied her makeup. "At least you don't have to worry if I'm coming home with you tonight. It's not like I have anywhere else to go."

Her apartment manager had left a message this week saying that the apartments would take a few months to renovate. During that time, she wouldn't owe rent (how nice of them). Once the apartment was ready, she would be able to finish out her lease. The problem was she didn't know how to talk to Aiden about spending months here.

Sure, he said he wanted her here for as long as needed, but two months was a long time. Even if they were still going strong, she would imagine he would want his space back. Didn't he say something about a girlfriend who tried to move in with him? Phoebe wasn't even his girlfriend.

"You are always welcome here." His voice drew her attention. At first, she thought she'd accidentally said all that out loud, but then she realized she'd mentioned not having anywhere else to go. She looked at him in the mirror. If she thought Aiden was hot in a suit, Aiden in a tuxedo was smoking, panty-melting hot.

She spun around and leaned back against the dresser. "Remind me never to think you have too many tuxedos."

He smirked at her as he straightened his cuffs. "I've been told they look good on me."

"Whoever said that was lying." She bit her lip and let her gaze take in the perfectly draped tuxedo on his hard body.

"Are you saying I don't look good?" He walked across the space until his heady scent surrounded her.

"I'm saying you'll be lucky to survive the mob of women who will want to be with you." Phoebe swallowed the bitterness that filled her mouth. He did say he met women at events. The women at this event would be the type of woman his mother vetted for him. Meaning they would be in his league.

"You won't fight them off for me?" His smile filled her heart as his hands touched her bare waist to draw her closer.

"I suppose I could rub all over you so they'll know I've claimed you." Her heart leapt into her throat at the heat in his green eyes.

"I would gladly let you rub all over me, but we're on a schedule. I'm fairly certain that would take more time than we have, but I will be taking you up on that later." He kissed her with such promise that she clung to him helplessly.

When he lifted his lips, he brushed a strand of hair from her face and stared into her eyes. She loved him so damned much.

"I can't wait to see you in your dress," he murmured. His gaze fell to her lips again. A pulse of heat settled low in her belly.

"You better go wait in the living room or I won't be able to put on my dress." She pressed her lips to his chin. Her thumb came up to rub her lipstick from him. "But first, I think you are wearing more lipstick than I am at this point."

He grinned at her and moved away. "Put that dress on before I take you up on that offer in your eyes."

She sighed as she watched him walk to the bathroom. His

ass was hella fine too. She shook her head and went back to applying her makeup and fixing the damage Aiden had done.

As he passed by her on his way to the living room, he stopped to press a kiss to the nape of her neck. "Soon."

Shivers rippled down her spine. Her brain tried to come up with places they could get away with sex in the museum. Maybe she should go commando. She nixed that thought when she pulled out the silky dress.

It fit like a glove and showcased her small waist and decent sized breasts. It was probably the most expensive thing she'd ever worn, but it was gorgeous beyond words. She tucked a few strands of hair into her updo and slipped on her heels.

When she looked in the mirror, she felt how Vivian must have felt. The woman in the mirror didn't look like her at all. She looked sophisticated with a hint of fun. She almost looked like she could belong in Aiden's world.

With one last glance and a deep breath, she turned and headed toward the living room. Aiden sat at the kitchen bar, but as her heels clicked on the wood floor, he stood and turned to look at her.

His mouth curved into a smile and his eyes seemed to light from within. "You look gorgeous."

She could feel the heat in her cheeks at his frank appraisal. Somehow, she felt more vulnerable in these clothes than she did fully naked in front of him.

"It's missing something though."

"What?" She glanced down at her dress and shoes. Nothing was out of place. When she looked up, he held out a flat box like the one in *Pretty Woman*.

"Aiden," she chastised.

"You deserve the whole fairy tale, Phoebe." He opened the box to reveal a diamond necklace and two diamond encrusted earrings.

What she wouldn't give for a fairy tale ending. She leaned forward, knowing this jewelry probably cost more than her annual salary five times over.

"Come on. Don't you want to touch them?" He raised an eyebrow at her.

She narrowed her eyes even as she smiled. "You know he wasn't supposed to close the box on her, but her laugh was so genuine they left it in."

He set the box down and took out the necklace. "Turn around."

Fuck it. Why not live the fantasy just this one time? She turned and the cold diamond draped over her neck. She reached up and touched the necklace. Aiden's fingers brushed the nape of her neck as he fastened it.

His lips replaced his fingers for a second and she swore the room got hotter.

His hands settled on her hips and turned her toward him. "They look perfect on you."

When his eyes landed on her lips, his eyes darkened further. She pressed her fingers against his lips. "Trust me, the lipstick looks better on me than on you."

"If I can't kiss you with it on, I'd rather it be off." He growled lightly and kissed the tip of her nose.

"Behave." She didn't mean it. She liked it when Aiden was naughty. She moved to the counter and took the earrings out to put on. "When do you think we'll get home?"

"Before the stroke of midnight."

She glared up at him as he chuckled.

"I love that you call it home." He gripped her again and pulled her hips into his.

Heat raced to her cheeks. She hadn't realized she'd called it that. She turned to face him. "I didn't mean—"

"Phoebe, it's okay. I want my home to be your home. Hell,

it's more of a home with you in it." His soft smile went straight to her heart and gave it a jolt.

His phone buzzed and Phoebe hoped it wasn't Rachel. Every time she texted this week, he'd get this stony look on his face.

"Limo is here."

AIDEN WAS on cloud nine as he walked into the gala with the most beautiful woman on his arm. Phoebe was radiant in red. As other men gazed longingly at what was his, his chest puffed out. If he could make it official, he wouldn't waste any time in locking Phoebe down.

The limo had picked up the rest of the group. Logan and Claire being the odd ones out as they weren't dating. But being best friends, they probably would still have a good time. Jonah held Lacy close to him, while Drew and Morgan stood close enough to touch but were not quite as possessive of each other.

When they first arrived in the museum, a small table was set up to show which table was theirs. Phoebe's eyes swept through the marble hall they stood in. Soft music played from hidden speakers and a general murmur of conversation provided a low undertone. Men in tuxedos mingled with women in every color dress imaginable.

"This is lovely," Phoebe whispered to him in awe.

"You're lovely."

"Aiden," Rachel's voice hurtled toward them as her heels clicked and echoed. "I was beginning to wonder if you would make it."

Her eyes shined up at him like he was here especially for her.

"Good to see you, Rachel," he said without inflection. He didn't want to encourage her.

Rachel's smile tightened as she noticed Phoebe on his arm. "You brought your assistant, Phyllis, was it?"

"She's not my assistant." Aiden spoke before Phoebe could interject. "This is Phoebe, my partner."

Again he emphasized partner. Even if everyone else thought it was work only, he knew it was more and he wanted to convey that to Rachel.

Rachel smiled and added, "You'll have to save me a dance later, Aiden. I'll let you find your table. I have to get back."

Before anyone else could speak, she wandered away.

Aiden squeezed Phoebe's elbow. "Shall we?"

They found their table toward the back, which wasn't surprising given how late they'd purchased it. Plenty of room surrounded their table for at least a half dozen more tables. Most galas Aiden had attended in Chicago had always been filled to the brim. He wasn't sure what they were doing wrong here, but he was sure Taylor and King could help fix it. At least help get the word out about the organization.

"Aiden and I will go get some drinks." Drew patted Aiden on the back as he held out Phoebe's chair for her. After she sat, he followed Drew. The other two guys had beat them to the bar and were a few people ahead of them.

"How's it going with the hellcat?" Drew asked.

"Good." Aiden straightened his cuffs. "I haven't pissed her off yet, so. . . ."

"Yeah, that's when the shit really hits the fan." Drew smiled and looked over his shoulder at their table.

Morgan and Phoebe had their heads together talking about something. Probably world domination.

Before Aiden could add anything, a guy walking by stopped and said, "Drew King?"

"Kyle Morris?" Drew grinned as he stepped toward the guy and shook his hand while bumping shoulders and clapping each other on the back. Kyle was a little shorter than Drew with a classic style tux. His hair was dark and so were his eyes.

"It's been since graduation, right?" Kyle still had a smile on his face.

"Did you go to the fraternity reunion last year?"

"Nah, man. I was out of town for work."

The line had moved, but Drew and Kyle seemed too focused to realize. Aiden cleared his throat and Drew moved up in the line.

"Aiden, this is Kyle Morris. We were at the same frat during college." Drew finally introduced him. "Kyle went to work in the financial district. You still with Steward Reed?"

"Yes." Kyle held his hand out to Aiden and they shook. He turned back to Drew. "Weren't you at a marketing firm downtown?"

"Two jobs ago." Drew smiled. "Started my own firm this year. Aiden is our account executive."

"Sweet." Kyle looked over his shoulder. "I don't know about you guys, but this is the best place to pick up chicks. I think it's the tux."

"I'm already taken." Drew glanced toward the table. "Happily."

"Harsh, dude. You were my best wingman in college." Kyle turned to Aiden and gave him an accessing look. "If you're looking for a little strange tonight, I could use a wingman for my hunt."

"I came here with someone." Aiden wanted to say he was taken, but that wasn't what he and Phoebe had. They had an understanding and he'd told her he wanted more, but they never defined what they were to each other.

"Our company has a table." Kyle pointed back to a group

of guys. "It's a total sausage fest. But I have hopes because there are some pretty birds here tonight."

The line moved again. Kyle and Drew talked a little longer before Kyle finally headed off.

They got drinks for themselves and their ladies and headed back toward the table. The path was a little more crowded now. They were only a few feet away. Phoebe lifted her eyes and met his gaze.

"Aiden?" A feminine voice carried through the air.

Aiden turned toward the source and tensed. Standing five feet away was Tate Gray, looking every bit as beautiful as she had been a year ago when he'd left her.

CHAPTER 23

Phoebe had tried to focus on the conversation with Morgan, but her attention had kept drifting to Aiden at the bar. Everything about him drew her eye, but when his eyes met hers, it was like sparks ignited within her.

"Are you going to tell me about the diamonds?" Morgan reached out and touched the necklace. "Please tell me they are fake and you don't need a security detail to keep you from being stolen."

Phoebe smiled and touched the dangling earrings. "I have no idea if they are real or fake. I don't think I want to know."

That was the truth. This whole night just showed how far out of her league Aiden was. Everything on her he had bought and all of it was out of her price range. But she couldn't resist living the fantasy for one night. Try it on and see how it fit, to find out if she could realistically fit into Aiden's life.

His eyes locked on hers as he and Drew made their way through the crowd with the drinks. Warmth flooded her chest and butterflies scrambled to fly in her stomach. His slight smile at finding her looking at him made her heart race. For a moment, she felt like they were the only ones in this room.

He had almost reached her, when a woman called out his name

Aiden stopped and looked, so Phoebe followed his line of sight to a woman. The woman wove her way through the tables to get to Aiden. Tall and thin with blond hair flowing in gentle curls down her back, she wore a gorgeous gold dress clinging to her Victoria Secret curves. Her heels and jewelry sparkled with diamonds.

The smile on her face spoke of familiarity as she closed in on him.

Something caught in Phoebe's heart, stopping its beat, and the butterflies crumbled in her stomach like a lump. Phoebe stood and walked over to Aiden. His face was a blank mask as he stared at the woman. Phoebe couldn't tell if he was happy to see the woman or not. She reached him at the same time the blonde did.

Drew had continued onto the table, so it was just the three of them.

The blonde glanced at Phoebe for a second before looking down at Aiden's full hands. Her smile was soft and reprimanding. She tipped her head like you would to a small child who disappointed you for not hugging you.

"Aren't you going to say hello?" the woman said.

"Tate," he acknowledged before turning to Phoebe and handing her a glass of wine. His fingers lingered against hers for a moment, and his green eyes were apologetic. He turned back to the woman.

"That's not how we say hello," Tate chastised. Grabbing his arms above his elbows, she leaned in to air kiss beside both of Aiden's cheeks. When she pulled back, she kept her hands on his arms, standing almost against Aiden's hands, which held his scotch in front of him. "How long has it been?"

Tate needed to back off from Phoebe's man before Phoebe started an all-out drag-down catfight with this woman for touching Aiden like she owned him.

"Almost a year." Aiden's voice lacked inflection or emotion, which brought Phoebe's attention to him instead. He was downright frigid to this woman. The iciness left a chill running down Phoebe's back.

Tate squeezed his arms. "You never told me you were moving here. I'm on a shopping trip with friends. If I'd known you were in town, I would have called to go out for dinner. We could catch up."

Her eyes twinkled when she said *catch up*. Was this really the way these people flirted? No wonder Aiden hadn't known how to pick Phoebe up in the bar.

Aiden stepped back and Tate's hands fell from his arms. The three of them stood there awkwardly, waiting for someone to mention the elephant in the room. Or at least acknowledge it.

Both of them waited for Aiden to introduce them to each other and tell them what the other woman meant to him. But so far, Aiden seemed content to just let both women flick their gaze from him to the other woman.

Maybe he was embarrassed of Phoebe and didn't want to introduce her to this woman that she guessed he had history with of some sort. Especially from the way Tate's eyes devoured every inch of Aiden in his tuxedo.

"It was good to—" Aiden began as his hand went to Phoebe's elbow. At his touch, Phoebe relaxed.

"Oh, who is this?" Tate's blue eyes stopped on Phoebe's. Her gaze dropped to the jewelry and the designer gown and shoes. When she lifted her gaze back to Phoebe's, a hint of jealousy lingered in her eyes.

Of course, tonight Phoebe looked just like one of them. Cleaned up and jeweled, she could be some wealthy heiress for all Tate knew.

Straightening her spine a little more, Phoebe smiled politely and held out her hand. "Phoebe Butler."

"Tate Gray." Tate took her hand for a brief second before pulling back and taking in a breath before turning her fake polite smile into a sweet one as she faced Aiden. "How do you know my Aiden?"

My Aiden, trying to lay a claim. Oh, that was a low blow, but Phoebe didn't scare easily. She stepped closer to Aiden and put her hand on his arm. She smirked at Tate before smiling up at Aiden. His green eyes softened as he looked down at her, making her jealousy lessen. A little.

"Are you *old* friends? Funny, Aiden never mentioned you." Phoebe looked at Tate with fake concern. She wanted to knock this woman off her goddamned high horse, but what could she say? They weren't exactly public with their relationship and weren't exactly boyfriend and girlfriend.

"Phoebe lives with me." Aiden's fingers wrapped around Phoebe's on his arm. Warmth slipped back into his voice and flowed directly to her heart.

For an unguarded second, Phoebe swore she saw fury and an edge of hurt in Tate's eyes, before Tate slipped back on her public mask. If she hadn't been looking at Tate, she would have missed it.

"How long have you two been dating?" Tate asked and glanced over her shoulder, probably looking for reinforcements. Her posse of shopping buddies to help protect her from this unknown factor.

Phoebe laughed, bright and fake. "Oh, we're not dating. We're just fucking."

Tate gasped and brought her hand to her chest. "What?"

"It was pleasant running into you, Tate, but we need to

get back to our friends." Aiden's hand tightened slightly over her fingers.

But Phoebe was way too pleased with herself for making this woman gape like a fish starving for water. "Definitely a pleasure to meet you. Don't be a stranger."

Okay, maybe that wasn't the nicest thing to say, but Tate had tried to claim Aiden. Phoebe wasn't cool with that. Jealousy had never been Phoebe's thing, but Aiden was clearly hers, not Tate's.

As they approached the table, Aiden laughed softly under his breath. Phoebe stopped beside him and looked up since he still towered over her even in her heels.

"You are something else." Aiden wrapped his arms around her waist and pulled her into him in an all-consuming hug. His warmth spread through her like a warm cup of coffee.

She inhaled his earthy scent and sighed as she pressed her cheek against his chest. She belonged here. He kissed the top of her head.

She lifted her head to look at him. "Who was she?"

He kept her close. His green eyes danced. "My recent ex. The one who tried to move in her stuff without me realizing it after two years of dating."

Phoebe was dumbfounded. He'd told Tate he and Phoebe were living together. She had to know they hadn't been together long. Sure, they had extenuating circumstances, but Tate didn't know that. Aiden's coldness made sense a little if he hadn't been as into her, but then why date for two years?

"You look baffled." Aiden stepped back a little and Phoebe missed his warmth.

Trying to gather her thoughts, she reached out and fixed his lapel that wasn't out of place. "What happened?"

"Between me and her?" Aiden caught Phoebe's hand and brought her knuckles to his lips to brush a kiss against them.

"We were at different stages of life, I guess. She was looking to settle down and raise a family."

"And you?"

"I was looking to get away from mine." Aiden shrugged. "Honestly, the only reason we dated so long was so I wouldn't have to find someone else to date. Her moving in was the last straw."

Phoebe didn't understand how dating worked in Aiden's world, but after two years of being with someone, even she would wonder why they hadn't moved in together. Or at least advanced the relationship in some way. But maybe it was just a lack of communication on both their parts. They obviously wanted different things.

"Hey." His voice was only loud enough for her to hear. He tipped her chin up until she met his eyes. "She was convenient. At the time, we had similar goals and needed someone to attend functions with. I didn't think feelings were involved until it was too late. I didn't want to hurt her, but I knew forcing a relationship out of what we had would do neither of us good."

Was that what was happening between her and Aiden? Had she fallen in love with him while he was just having fun? Sure, the sex was phenomenal, but what happened when he wanted someone he could take home to his family? What happened when he wanted someone like Tate? Someone who could attend functions without telling everyone they were fucking?

Something hardened in Phoebe's heart. She had to protect herself for that day, because she had no doubt it would come.

"Phoebe. . . ." Aiden's thumb stroked her jaw. His eyes were concerned, but he still had that soft smile that made her heart race.

"Phoebe?"

They both turned their heads to one of the staff members. Phoebe recognized him right away. Brandon was still built like a football player even if he never went pro like he'd hoped.

"Hey, Brandon."

Aiden's hand dropped from her face and slid into her grasp.

"It's been forever." Brandon trailed his eyes over her, noting her hand locked with Aiden's before lifting. "You haven't changed a bit."

"You know me. I like to keep it tight." She grinned and turned to Aiden. "Aiden, this is my friend Brandon. Brandon, Aiden."

"Me and Phoebe go way back." Brandon's brown eyes lit up and he winked at her. "All the way to college."

"I heard you volunteered at this gala. One of my other friends works it as well and knew you." Phoebe gave Aiden a quick glance to see how he was handling this. Did he feel the same jealousy she'd felt with Tate?

"You still have my number. Right, Bee?" Brandon lifted an eyebrow at her. "I'm between girlfriends right now."

Aiden's hand tightened on hers, but before he could say anything, Phoebe just smiled and said, "Maybe, maybe not. I'm kind of on a date right now though."

Brandon actually looked surprised as he looked over Aiden. "Oh, yeah man. Sorry about that."

"No problem." Aiden's voice was tight.

Phoebe wasn't sure if he was jealous or mad at her. "It was great running into you, Brandon. If you see Mark, tell him I said hi."

"Sure thing." Brandon backed away. "I'll catch you later, Bee."

She smiled and waved a little. God, who knew a charity event would be a minefield of exes. When they were alone again, Phoebe risked a peek up at Aiden. He looked deep in thought. She wondered what he was going to say to her before Brandon walked up.

Before she could ask, he smiled at her. "Shall we join the others?"

Phoebe swallowed and nodded her head. Obviously they weren't going to talk about it now. Which was good for her. Because what could she say about the guy who took her virginity years ago that would make Aiden. . . what? Feel better? Be as jealous about Brandon as she'd been about Tate?

Maybe Phoebe didn't know what she wanted. But she knew she wanted Aiden for as long as he'd have her.

CHAPTER 24

THE CONVERSATION FLOWED around the table, even drawing Aiden and Phoebe into it. His mind still lingered over what happened before dinner though. Aiden hadn't known what to say about Tate to Phoebe. He really didn't know what to say about Brandon, who had obviously been one of the many who had previously slept with Phoebe.

"Hey, Aiden. The dancing at this thing. . . ."

Aiden turned toward Claire's voice.

"Is it going to be more of this classical stuff they've been playing during dinner or will it be like a club mix after dark?" Claire took a sip of her wine.

They'd just finished dessert. Everyone had relaxed during dinner.

"They'll play some older standards to slow dance to, but as the night progresses, the DJ will play modern music." Aiden glanced at Phoebe, wondering if she would dance with him.

"I might need to have a drink then," Lacy chimed in. Her chair pressed against Jonah's as she leaned into his side. Jonah leaned down and kissed her softly.

Would Aiden ever be able to do that with Phoebe? Would she ever accept his love? Or would his love just drive her away faster? He sighed.

The general volume of the background noise had increased as they served dinner and more people got up to mingle. Overall the gala seemed like a success, even if they still had tables left for sale. The room seemed fairly full and people had been over at the silent auction tables all night.

The lights dimmed slightly and everyone quieted down as some of the organizers came onto stage to do their presentations. Aiden turned to watch Phoebe. He loved that everything she wore tonight he'd given her. His grandmother's diamonds had never sparkled quite as brightly as they did on Phoebe.

He'd never let anyone else wear them before. Never even thought of it. But after watching *Pretty Woman* with her, he knew they'd be perfect. She'd be perfect.

He captured her hand. Her soft brown eyes met his and he brushed his lips over her knuckles. There were so many things left unsaid between them. Things had gone so fast. But he didn't regret having her move in. Even if she thought it was temporary, he never wanted her to leave.

He enjoyed watching her play on her phone while she sat on his couch next to him. While he made them dinner, she would sit on the island countertop and talk to him. Showers were no longer a solo endeavor with Phoebe in the apartment. They didn't always fuck in the shower either, but they'd wash each other and talk. When they fell asleep at night, she would snuggle into his side. In the mornings, he'd wake to her beautiful face next to his on his pillow like she couldn't get close enough to him during the night.

He kept her hand in his as the speaker droned on. It had only been a month since they met but he couldn't imagine life without her anymore. Everyone clapped and Phoebe tried to take her hand from him to join, but he didn't let go.

She gave him a look that made his heart pound a little faster. He wanted to tell her he loved her. That he couldn't imagine his life without her in it. That he didn't care if Brandon tried to make a move because Aiden knew Phoebe would be going home with him tonight and every night.

The music started and the couples all left the table to go join in the dancing.

"Are you a dancer or a sitter, Aiden?" Phoebe quirked her eyebrow at him.

"I'll have you know I took ballroom dancing classes for a few years." Aiden grinned at her as he stood and pulled her to her feet, against him.

"Of course you did." She rolled her eyes. "Nothing should surprise me about you."

"Want to go cut a rug?" Aiden tugged her toward the dance floor.

She smiled at him as he led her onto the dance floor and held her in his arms as they swayed with the music. "I'm used to different music."

"Don't worry. I'm a fantastic lead." He gave her a crooked smile.

She laughed and it filled his soul. "You think you are the shit, don't you?"

Aiden leaned down and said in her ear, "I have you, don't I?"

He caught her smile before she rested her cheek against his chest. For now, Aiden had her and she was all his. He just had to convince her to keep him.

Dancing with Phoebe was like everything else he did with her: effortless and fantastic. He swept her around the dance floor, holding her tight against him. Her laughs and smiles were worth everything in his opinion.

"Aiden, I hate to be a bummer, but I need a drink." She looked up at him. Her dark eyes sparkled in the fairy lights hanging over the dance floor. "Preferably water?"

He kissed the side of her mouth to not smear her lipstick and stepped back. He held out his arm and she wrapped her hands around it. They walked to the table and Phoebe picked up her glass.

"You guys looked great out there," Morgan said from her seat at the table. Drew sat next to her, holding her hand and playing with her fingers.

"You want to hit the ladies' with me?" Phoebe asked Morgan as she reached for her clutch.

Morgan turned and pressed a kiss to Drew's lips before she grabbed one of his curls, pulling it tight and releasing it. He just smiled and shook his head at her.

"See you in a minute." Phoebe pressed up on her tiptoes and pressed a kiss against the corner of Aiden's lips. She grabbed a napkin and wiped the lipstick off, but he wished she'd left it.

He grabbed her hand before she took it away and kissed it. "I look forward to it."

Her smile warmed his chest as she strode away with Morgan. Maybe tonight he'd tell her the truth. Tell her he loved her and see what happened. She had to know. How could she not?

"Hey, man," a voice said behind Aiden.

Aiden turned and Brandon stood there. "I just wanted to apologize about earlier again. Phoebe and I have a bit of a history."

"Drew." Kyle from earlier came over to Drew at the table. "How's it going?"

"Can't complain." Drew leaned back in his chair.

Kyle's gaze moved to Aiden and he lit up. "Man, was that Phoebe Butler dancing with you earlier?"

"You know her?" Aiden kept his voice steady, even as his heart ricocheted in his chest.

"Know her." Kyle scoffed and came over to where Brandon and Aiden stood. "That girl is always ready to go. I'm pretty sure she misplaced my number because we were pretty hot and heavy before she ghosted me."

"Freebie is hot and heavy with every dude. You're not special," Brandon said in a laughing tone.

"Whoa, guys." Drew stood and rounded the table.

"Freebie?" Aiden repeated numbly.

"Yeah, that was her nickname in college." Brandon looked around before he grinned. "At least among the guys."

Kyle chuckled. "That's kind of funny."

It wasn't funny in the slightest.

Drew grabbed Kyle's arm. "Kyle, why don't we go—"

"I actually got to be her first. I consider it a badge of honor," Brandon said, puffing up like a peacock.

Aiden clenched his fist. The football player looking for the roommate. He never actually thought he'd meet that guy or really any guy Phoebe had sex with. He shouldn't be surprised, though, based on her number.

Kyle stepped forward and clapped Brandon on the back. "Well done, man. You know Phoebe and I had a thing going for a few weeks. I thought things were going great until she ghosted me. I figured she must be going for quantity over quality or something."

"Seriously." Drew stepped forward, but the guys ignored him.

"She never did anything half-assed." Brandon shook his head. "But I swear one guy could never keep her satisfied. Even that first time, she was practically insatiable."

"Guys, maybe now isn't the best time—" Drew glanced at Aiden and stepped into the middle.

"Did she ever do that thing with her tongue—" Brandon started.

Kyle finished, "That makes your eyes roll back in your head and makes you see fucking heaven?"

"Yeah, I taught her that." Fucking Brandon. The more he talked, the more Aiden had to refrain from punching his pretty mouth.

"Man, I guess I owe you thanks for that." Kyle held up his hand for a high five and of course, Brandon gave him one. Much as Aiden wanted to punch both these dicks, this wasn't the place for a fistfight.

Brandon turned to Aiden.

"But you're with her tonight, huh?" Brandon asked with a stupid grin. "Sorry if we gave you any spoilers."

Like Phoebe was a series finale. Fuck these guys. Oh wait, Phoebe already did.

"Yeah, man," Kyle added. He looked like he wanted to clap Aiden on the back, but he stopped himself. "Enjoy the ride."

"Did you ever think that maybe Phoebe has grown out of that shit?" Drew said, loudly.

The guys laughed like he made a joke.

"Man, last time I had her was a year ago," Kyle said. "We hooked up behind a fucking bar."

"Shut the fuck up." Aiden spoke through clenched teeth. "You are being disrespectful."

Kyle held up his hands and backed up a little. "Sorry, man. She's dressed all nice tonight, but that chick is a freak in the sheets. If you get her to a bed, that is."

Brandon actually had the balls to blush slightly and nod his head. "I don't mean any disrespect. Phoebe's a great gal."

"You guys can leave now," Drew said.

"I'll call you on Monday," Kyle threw over his shoulder to Drew.

Drew waved him off. Aiden's vision was still red.

"You okay?" Drew asked, looking toward the bathroom.

Thankfully Phoebe had missed that shit show. He'd been around men talking shit about women before. It shouldn't be affecting him, but this was Phoebe. He couldn't stop the pictures racing through his mind of her with them.

"Phoebe's different with you." Drew tugged Aiden back to the table and lowered himself into a chair before waiting for Aiden to sit. "She's been different for a while now actually. Sure she hooked up with a guy here or there, but that doesn't change who she is to you."

"What exactly is she to me?" Aiden lifted his gaze to focus on Drew's eyes. "She doesn't want a relationship. She has sex with me and for now only me, but that doesn't mean she's mine. She's not looking for the fairy tale happily ever after. She has one foot out the door, and if her place hadn't been wrecked, she probably would have moved on already."

"Fuck, man." Drew ran a hand through his hair and put his hand on Aiden's shoulder. "We need a drink. Give me a minute."

Aiden pushed his hands through his hair and leaned his elbows on his knees. Who was he kidding? Love may never be enough to hold someone like Phoebe.

Phoebe exited the stall and went to wash her hands. The bathroom was huge and not as busy as she thought it might be. She picked up her clutch and went to sit in one of the chairs to wait for Morgan.

A group of women came in. Their laughter echoed in the bathroom. Phoebe stiffened when she saw Tate among them. They broke off and most of them went into the stalls, but Tate saw Phoebe and headed over to her.

"I wanted to apologize." She sank down gracefully onto

the ottoman in front of Phoebe. This beautiful creature who should have been everything Aiden ever wanted. "I wasn't prepared to see Aiden for the first time after the breakup, and then I saw you standing with him. . . ."

"Okay." Phoebe wasn't sure what to say in cases like these. She'd never been in a relationship before to run into a guy later who had dumped her.

Tate smiled. "I really thought Aiden might have been the one. I mean the way his mother talked about him, what woman wouldn't want him?"

Again, never met his mother, so Phoebe was at a loss. But since the woman was opening up to her, why not ask. "What happened between you two? Was it just miscommunication?"

Tate leaned back on her arms. "Aiden and I got together at an event. His mother had interviewed me a few weeks prior as a potential date for him to this formal event. I was kind of surprised she picked me. I'm not as rich as they are by a long shot, but I have a good solid family so maybe that tipped the scales in my favor."

"His mom interviewed you?" That must be the legendary vetting process Aiden had spoken about. Phoebe didn't have any family. For a while she'd had her mom. To most people it would seem she had no one, but Phoebe knew Morgan and the rest of the office were her family now.

Tate gave her an odd questioning look.

"Yes. Anyway, we went to a few more events together over the next few months and one thing led to another." Tate straightened and looked at the stalls but none of her friends had come out. "We weren't a regular thing for a while. But he'd need a date and then we'd end up in his bed. After a year and a half, things took a turn and suddenly it seemed like we were going out more and I was spending more time in his apartment than my own."

"And that's when you decided to move in?"

Tate blushed. "Is that what he said?"

Phoebe nodded.

"I brought over an overnight bag a few times and then left a few things. Like an extra toothbrush, makeup, the little things that I need daily. Then I left a few pieces of clothing, but I never 'moved' in. One day, he called me over and handed me a box of my things and said we were through." She shrugged and her shoulders stayed down.

"That must have been hard." Phoebe had done the same thing when Aiden was at the hotel, but he hadn't seemed to mind. He kept asking her to stay. And she'd been grateful to have things at his place when the fire happened.

"Hard is walking in and finding the guy you used to love looking happy with a beautiful woman." Tate gave her a resigned look with a sad smile.

Morgan came out of the stall and headed to the sinks, glancing at Phoebe on the way. She paused as if she would come over if Phoebe needed her. Phoebe waved her off.

"Anyway, I should let you go back to your man." Tate stood. "I really think I was just convenient to him at the time. He needed someone to go to all those events and we had a little chemistry and I didn't put any pressure on him to move the relationship forward."

She shrugged. "I really hope you guys make it."

Morgan came over as Tate disappeared into a stall. "What was that about?"

"She used to date Aiden." Phoebe stood and moved toward the door with Morgan.

"I'm glad I haven't run into any of Drew's exes." Morgan gave a shudder as they walked through the door.

"Fortunately most of Aiden's are in Chicago, but it doesn't sound like he really tried to make it work with anyone." Phoebe's heart twinged a little. Convenient. He'd said it. Tate had said it. Was that all Phoebe was? Convenient?

"Phoebe." A man's voice startled her out of her thoughts as she and Morgan stopped.

Fuck. Her very own stalker. "Hey, Kyle."

Morgan stepped in front of Phoebe slightly, protectively. She'd been with her during the Kyle debacle. He was a first-class clinger who hadn't accepted the fact that she had moved on, so she blocked him everywhere and stopped hanging out where she knew he would be. Fortunately, she'd never taken him back to her apartment so he didn't know where she lived.

"It's been ages." He stepped forward and Phoebe stepped back. "Ran into your friend Brandon. Man, that guy is something else, bragging about taking your virginity and teaching you things."

"Maybe you should go now, Kyle," Morgan said. "You might have had too much to drink."

Phoebe looked closer at Kyle. Sure enough, he was weaving on his feet and had that smell of alcohol practically bleeding from his pores.

"I met your current conquest too." Kyle's smile was a little sloppy. "Or maybe you haven't tapped that yet, but I figure by the end of the night, he'll have your skirts over your head."

Morgan pulled Phoebe back and started to move her around Kyle.

"What do you mean my current?" Phoebe asked, braking hard so Morgan couldn't drag her away before Kyle answered.

"Aiden, right?" Kyle winked and stuck out his finger guns her way. "I'm sure he won't mind mine and Brandon's sloppy seconds, right? If he doesn't work out tonight, I'm always available. We had a good time together."

Fuck, what did they do? She didn't resist when Morgan pulled her away.

"Make sure to do that tongue thing though. I think we

intrigued him with that one," Kyle yelled, but there weren't many people nearby and the music was still really loud.

"How the hell did he meet Aiden?" Phoebe muttered to Morgan as they made their way back to their table.

"Maybe they were friends in school." Morgan shrugged. "I hated Kyle when you were fucking him, but I think I loathe him now."

"You and me both." Phoebe's brain kept spinning though. What was she going to walk into when she got back to Aiden? He had said he didn't care how many people she'd slept with, but being confronted with not one but two at a time had to be some extraordinary shit.

And then there was Aiden's ex. Tate had seemed a little needy when they first ran into her, but in the bathroom she'd just been defeated. Would that be Phoebe when Aiden finally left her?

CHAPTER 25

WHEN PHOEBE and Morgan made it back to the table, Drew and Aiden both had a glass of scotch in their hands. The guys sat back and watched the dance floor. Phoebe had no idea what mood Aiden was in, but this night could suck it for all she cared. She kind of wished she'd stripped him of his tux and fucked him all night instead of bothering coming here.

"If it isn't my girl Freebie," Aiden said as they approached. Her heart squeezed at the nickname. Phoebe had heard the nickname Freebie a few times on campus from non-discreet assholes. Brandon must have let it slip. She wondered what else he had let slip.

"Are you two drunk?" Morgan asked Drew.

"The bartender gave us the bottle." Drew gestured to the half empty bottle on the table with a sideways smile on his face.

"We've been gone like ten minutes. Did you do shots of scotch?" Morgan put her hands on her hips as she stared down at Drew. Drew nodded.

"Not drunk, just happily numb." Drew's smile was a little sloppy.

Phoebe watched Aiden. He slowly sipped his scotch while he stared at her. His eyes were emotionless voids right now and it made her chest feel like it was caving in.

She grabbed Morgan's arm and leaned close to say, "Could you take Drew somewhere?"

"You sure?" Morgan's eyes met hers and she placed a hand over Phoebe's. "Of course, whatever you need."

"Time for some air." Morgan took Drew's glass away and gave a quick apologetic look to Phoebe before helping him walk toward the door.

Phoebe grabbed a glass from the table and filled it with scotch before sitting in the chair Drew vacated. She took a few sips, staring out at the dance floor with Aiden.

"Ran into Tate in the bathroom." She kept her emotions out of her voice.

"We're fucked. Aren't we?" Aiden said as he reached for the bottle to refill his glass.

"Not sure if you're quite to fucked level yet." Phoebe turned her head to look at him. "Keep drinking and you'll likely get there."

"I'm definitely heading toward drunk." Aiden's scotch sloshed in the glass as he jerked his glass between the two of them as he said, "I mean we're fucked. You and me."

Phoebe took a deep breath and downed the rest of her glass before setting it on the table. Everything inside her screamed at her to stop this, but how do you stop someone you love from leaving you? "What do you want me to say, Aiden? Kyle told me you, and Brandon, and he had a nice discussion about me."

"Those guys really liked fucking you." Aiden's words shouldn't have hurt as much as they did. It was the truth after all. She had fucked them, but it felt like a lifetime ago.

Phoebe straightened a little, thinking of her own run-in

with Tate. "At least I'm honest with the people I fuck. Did you ever tell Tate that she was just a fuck?"

Aiden tossed back the rest of his drink. His green eyes almost burned when he met hers. "I never led her on or made her believe there was more to it. I told you that."

"Tate obviously didn't get the message. Ran into her in the bathroom. She was pretty fucking honest about what happened."

"And I haven't been?" Aiden shook his head. "There are two sides to every story."

"Yeah, and I told you mine." Anger burned through her. Phoebe stood and looked down at Aiden. "But Brandon and Kyle make all the difference, don't they? You said it didn't matter how many men I slept with, but you never counted on actually meeting any of them, did you?"

Aiden stood and closed in on her until she could barely breathe. His words were soft and twisted. "Did Tate tell you how much she liked it when I fucked her? Did she tell you that she showed me a thing or two? Did she tell you how she couldn't wait until I fucked her again?"

"I'm not fucking either of them—"

"But how long until you grow bored of just me? Phoebe, how long until I'm not enough and you crave someone else's touch?" His fingers trailed over her bare arms, sending shivers down her spine and desire pooling low and heavy. Even though his words were ugly, her body responded to his closeness and touch, wanting to lean into him.

She wanted to say he was all she ever would need. He made her feel things no one else could, but her pride wouldn't let her. There was no telling what his response would be. She couldn't tell him she loved him and have him throw it back in her face.

"I'm not some Barbie doll you can dress up so you can be seen in public with me. You put me in designer clothes and expect me to be one of them. Wake the fuck up, Aiden. I will never be on the same level as Tate or even fucking Rachel. I'm not going to be one of those women your mother approves of. Just because you enjoy fucking me doesn't mean I'll fit into your life."

Aiden's fingers tipped her chin back up so she would look in his eyes. "I don't need you to be one of them."

"But. . . ? Come on, Aiden. There's always a but. You wish I was more like them. That I only opened my legs for the right kind of guys before and not just someone who tickled my fancy. Maybe you even wished I'd saved myself for you and only you. But news flash, if I hadn't been the girl who goes for the guys, you and I wouldn't even be having this conversation. We fucked and couldn't seem to stay away from each other's bodies. That's all this is."

Aiden's mouth flattened and he took a step back for a moment.

Then he closed in on her. His hands on her hips, drawing her into him. He stole her breath. His head dropped and his lips found her pulse right next to her ear. She clung to his arms as her knees grew weak. Only for him.

Then he whispered, "You're right. That's all this is. The only thing I could possibly want from you is a good fuck, right? So let's go find a corner somewhere and I'll make you fucking scream until you're hoarse."

Phoebe bit her lip as his lips trailed over her neck to the spot where her shoulder and neck met. He scrambled her mind with his touch. She wanted what he was offering, but she couldn't do it. If they were just playing around, she'd be all for it, but he was angry. She was mad. They'd both said hurtful things and she didn't want it like this. She didn't want to just be the woman he fucked. She didn't want to cheapen what she felt for Aiden.

She wanted to be his. She wanted him to imprint himself

onto her soul. She wanted to matter to him. To connect with him like no one else in her life. To have him see her the way he always saw her.

Pulling away, she met his eyes. They were hungry for her, but they still had that burn of anger. The hate sex would be intense, but if the intensity and tenderness between them disappeared, she'd be broken afterwards.

"Not like this, Aiden," she said softly.

"Then how, Phoebe?"

Claire's voice stopped her from saying more. "Not going to lie, this place kind of sucks."

"We're going to bounce," Logan said. "How about it? You guys up to moving the party to a real club?"

Phoebe continued to search Aiden's eyes, but he'd closed off at Claire's words. He lifted his gaze from hers.

"Not for me," Aiden said. He crossed to the table and grabbed the bottle to pour more into his glass.

Fuck this. Fuck Aiden. "I'm in."

"Woohoo, my party girl is on board." Claire wrapped Phoebe in her arms and hugged her. "Jonah and Lacy are still dancing."

"I've got an Uber waiting." Logan held up his phone.

Phoebe started to follow them when Aiden's hand on her arm stopped her. She gazed up into his green eyes, hoping to see more. Hoping for a kind word or an apology.

"Leave the diamonds. I'll make sure they get home safe." He had that cold look on his face again. The same one he'd given to Tate. The one that was breaking her heart.

Fuck Aiden. She took the earrings out of her ears and set them on the table next to his bottle and then turned around so he could undo the necklace. His fingers brushed against her nape. When the catch released, he pressed a kiss against her neck. Shivers scattered down her spine and in that moment, she hated her reaction to him. Hated how easily he got under her skin.

He took the necklace and set it down before saying, "Don't fuck anyone else."

❧

Phoebe's "Fuck you, Aiden" still rang in his ears as he sat at the table by himself drowning himself in the bottle of scotch. Everything felt wrong. This whole night was wrong. He'd tried to leave this life behind in Chicago and yet here he was in a tuxedo surrounded by the wealthy and elite. Alone again.

"Where's Phoebe?" Morgan stood with her hands on her hips as she narrowed her eyes at him. Drew stood behind her.

He took a breath to ease the tightness in his chest. He'd pushed Phoebe away.

"Aiden! Phoebe?" Morgan looked pissed at him.

"She went to fuck more guys probably." Aiden lifted his glass and downed the last of his scotch. Phoebe wouldn't have to look hard. Aiden's money on her body looked fabulous.

"What the hell are you talking about?" Morgan tapped her foot.

"You have really big eyes." Aiden suddenly noticed. "Like really big eyes. Did you know that, Drew?"

Drew smiled and nodded. "I love her eyes."

Aiden reached for the bottle, but Morgan sat and moved it out of the way. "Not until you tell me what happened with Phoebe."

Aiden frowned. "I got mad at her for fucking other guys. She got mad at me for making Tate sad." Hmmm, that didn't sound quite right, but his brain wasn't exactly functioning properly right now. "Claire and Logan bounced and took Phoebe with them."

Morgan shook her head.

"I think I. . . ." Aiden shook his head to clear some of the fogginess. He reached in his tuxedo pocket and pulled out the diamond necklace that used to be warm from Phoebe's neck. Now it was cold. So fucking cold. "I think I fucked up."

"You need to sleep this off." Morgan rose and looked toward the dance floor. "Stay right here. I'm going to get Jonah and Lacy."

Drew started to follow her, but she pointed to a chair and he sank into it with a grin. "I love it when she takes charge."

Aiden set his glass on the table and struggled to make his brain work.

"What did you guys think?" Rachel popped up in front of him, surprising him.

"Think about what?" Aiden asked. His lips felt funny and he pressed his finger against them.

"I think my friend had a little too much fun," Drew said.

Aiden narrowed his eyes at Drew before glancing at the bottle of scotch. He'd had a lot to drink.

Rachel laughed. "At least you have a designated sober friend, right?"

"Morgan." Drew's face smiled again. "She's awesome."

"I guess I'll see you in the office on Monday to discuss next year, Aiden?" Rachel moved closer. She smelled like some flower, but it wasn't lavender. God, he missed his lavender girl.

"I'll let him know when he can remember." Morgan suddenly was there.

How did she do that?

"Have a good night then." Rachel faded off into the distance.

Suddenly Jonah was at Aiden's side and helping him to his feet.

"You guys all move super fast." Aiden grinned. "Wait until I tell Phoebe. She won't believe me."

"How much did he drink?" Jonah brought Aiden's arm over his shoulder and helped him stand.

"Probably most of the bottle." Morgan shook her head. "Diamond check."

Morgan came closer and she reached into his tux pocket and pulled out the necklace and earrings. They'd looked so beautiful on Phoebe. He'd wanted to strip her down to nothing but the diamonds tonight.

"I love her, you know," he said softly.

Morgan's eyes whipped up to stare at him. "What?"

"Did I lose her tonight?" Aiden's head rang with Phoebe's parting words and the hurt in her eyes.

"Maybe. Maybe not." Morgan sighed and dropped the diamonds back in his pocket. "Sometimes Phoebe can be reasonable and other times she goes apeshit. It all depends on how much she cares. She only goes apeshit when she really cares."

"Phoebe doesn't care about me. I'm just her fuck toy." Aiden let himself be led by the group.

"If you think that, you really are stupid," Jonah said.

Aiden swung his head to look at Jonah and immediately regretted it as the room spun around him. "I'll have you know I love Phoebe, but I can't tell her that because she'll leave me."

"That makes perfect sense." Jonah shook his head as they reached the museum doors. "Fear is crazy that way."

"I'm not afraid," Aiden mumbled, mostly to himself.

The limo was already pulled up to the curb as everyone settled into the back. Well, everyone that was left. The two couples snuggled while Aiden tried not to pass out on the back seat. He missed Phoebe.

After the others were dropped off, the limo headed toward Aiden's apartment, but Phoebe wouldn't be there. She was out clubbing. Probably hooking up with someone else. She might not even come home tonight.

Sobering up a little, he rode the elevator up to his apartment by himself and let himself in. She was everywhere and nowhere. This place wouldn't be a home without her in it. He put the diamonds back in the box and returned them to the safe before heading into the bedroom to take his tux off.

He'd dropped his jacket on the bed before his phone buzzed.

Meet me at the Indigo. The text was from an unknown number. But maybe it was Phoebe. Who else would want to meet at the Indigo?

He shoved his phone in his pocket and grabbed his wallet from his jacket before heading out the door. The cab ride helped him sober up even more, so by the time he arrived he wasn't really sure what to expect. Phoebe would have texted from her phone unless she wanted to humiliate him somehow. Maybe this was how she got her revenge.

She had threatened Drew with setting up a Tinder profile to get back at him, so maybe she'd done that to Aiden. It would explain the unknown number.

Images of Furries almost made him turn back around, but he went into the bar of the Indigo and immediately saw who had texted him.

He went over to the table for two and sat across from Tate Gray.

"I'm surprised you showed." Tate took a sip from her drink before crossing her legs.

"I didn't know who I was meeting." That didn't sound like

a great excuse, but he hadn't exactly been in his right mind for the past few hours.

"Drink?" She began to hold up her hand, but he waved her off.

"I'm done drinking for the night. What do you want, Tate?"

She smiled at him with that smile that always meant she wanted something. "I've missed you, Aiden. Can't that be reason enough?"

"I'm with Phoebe." He didn't allow any emotion to enter his voice, but he wasn't certain Phoebe still felt the same way. *Fuck you, Aiden,* still rang in his ears.

"I have to admit I was a little curious about your new plaything, but I couldn't find anything about Phoebe Butler." Tate tapped her nails on the table. "I mean she was dressed like high society, but very lowbrow in vocabulary. Still, she's a pretty one. But she has no name, no family, no money. I can only assume."

"And why does that matter?" The waitress brought Aiden a glass of water which he thankfully drank.

"It doesn't matter to me." Tate looked at her nails. "But it could matter to your family. After all, they were very protective of you. Had to make sure none of us were just gold-diggers, I believe your father once said."

"Cut the bullshit. What is this really about, Tate?"

"You need someone like me. Someone who fits all the lengthy qualifications your family requires of a life partner. You could keep her on the side if you wanted." Tate locked eyes with him. "But to all those concerned, I would be yours."

"What makes you think I want that?" Aiden tipped the glass in her direction.

"Your family made it perfectly clear what they wanted." Tate settled back in the seat like she'd won.

"Do you see my family here? Does it look like I care what

they think about who is in my life? Do you think I care what everyone else thinks? Did my mother tell you why I moved here?"

Tate pressed her lips together. Obviously not.

"I came to have my own life. Build something of my own. Have something that is mine. I don't need any other woman to come in and try to rule my life. I love Phoebe and she's the only one I'll ever have as my wife. If she ever forgives me."

God, he'd made a mess of everything. Every word he'd said to her in anger and jealousy pulsed through his head. He had to find her and make this right. He stood.

"Your mother will never approve." Tate didn't rise from the seat. She barely cared about this. It was almost a business transaction to her.

"My mother doesn't have to approve. That's the great thing about being a grown up. You should try it sometime, Tate."

He pulled out his phone as he walked out of the hotel. He could text Phoebe but she would probably ignore it. If she hadn't already blocked him. She had been pretty pissed He had Drew's number, but he didn't have Logan's or Claire's. Maybe Drew would still be awake.

Opening his text messages, he opened Drew's and started to text asking for Logan's number. But his phone buzzed with a text notification from Phoebe.

His heart stilled as he opened it.

Where are you?

He glanced over at the taxi stand and headed over to the man working there. "Can you get me a taxi please?"

Phoebe opened the door to the apartment. She'd only lasted a half hour at the club with Logan and Claire. The pulsing music. The hot bodies everywhere. The leering eyes of the men. She didn't really want to be there, but she'd needed to cool off before she spewed more vitriol at Aiden.

The lights were on and it looked like Aiden had been here. The jewelry box was gone from the counter. She strolled into the bedroom and his tux jacket lay across the bed. She searched around the apartment, but he was nowhere.

She sat on the edge of the bed and pulled out her phone from her clutch.

Where are you? She texted him and waited.

She waited a few more minutes before she texted Morgan. *Are you guys still at the gala?*

Not that she expected Morgan to answer because most likely she'd be occupied with Drew. Just thinking about it made Phoebe want to gag.

She figured she'd give it a little time while she got out of her dress and changed into some soft pajamas she'd found in one of the drawers. She didn't normally wear pajamas to bed. But she wasn't about to walk around the apartment naked while she waited for Aiden. She hung up her dress and his tux jacket and sat on the bed holding her phone.

Still nothing.

I'm sorry I was a dick. Phoebe typed but then erased. She didn't know what to say. She felt bad for the way things went at the gala, but she couldn't erase her past. She couldn't unfuck all the guys she'd been with. Of course, Aiden had said a lot of things that had hurt too.

But she was the one that trapped them both in this little box with no give.

She'd insisted from the beginning that she didn't want more than sex. He asked her to consider more, and she'd shied away from it. But he also let her move in with him when she had no where else to go. He assured her that even if they didn't have sex she could still stay here. He bought her clothes and found a way that she could accept them.

Tonight, they had fought, and now she wanted to experience what the other half did. Makeup sex after they have a discussion about what they really are to each other.

She hadn't stayed mad at Aiden. But they definitely needed to sit down and talk through some issues. Hopefully. They needed to have a conversation about feelings, but that filled her with dread.

Unless he decided she wasn't worth the effort.

Fuck it. She called his cell phone. It rang once before going to voicemail. She didn't leave a message. Maybe his phone died and he couldn't charge it. She stared at her phone blankly.

Okay, the tuxedo he wore was on the bed, so he had been here. And left the lights on, so he was probably coming back. She just needed to wait until he showed up. She stood and went into the living room and turned on the TV to distract herself.

She woke up to a different part in the series she'd been binging and paused the TV. Rubbing her eyes, she picked up her phone. It was three o'clock in the morning. No new notifications and it had been a few hours.

She tried his phone again, and it went straight to voicemail. Nothing good ever happened after two o'clock in the city. She stretched and made a lap around the apartment to make sure he hadn't just come through and went to bed or showered or something.

He'd been pretty mad at her. Maybe he decided to stay somewhere else for the night. Maybe he decided to hook up with someone for revenge sex. Nah, that didn't sound like Aiden. Maybe he went back to the hotel.

She figured it was worth a phone call. The night clerk answered at the Indigo Hotel.

"Can you tell me if Aiden Kingston checked in?"

"I'm sorry I can't give out that information, ma'am."

Shit. She should have known better. "Can I leave a message for him in case he is there?"

"Sure," the clerk's voice was wary.

"Tell him Phoebe called and is getting worried and to call her back, please."

"Is there anything else I can help you with today?" the clerk asked.

"No, thank you." Phoebe clicked off her phone and dropped it onto the bed, falling next to it.

She couldn't exactly call all her coworkers at three a.m. to see if they knew where Aiden might have gone. What if he wasn't hiding from her? What if he'd been in an accident?

Her heart tightened as she considered the possibility. It was late and he'd been drinking. She knew he came back here, but maybe he went to a bar. But what if. . . .

The *what if* dangled in front of her, tormenting her with memories of when her mother left that morning. At least the last thing she'd said to her mother was she loved her. The last thing she said to Aiden was, fuck you.

Her chest ached and she couldn't catch her breath. What if this was it? What if tonight had been the last night she had Aiden in her life? She curled into a ball on the bed as she stared at her phone, willing it to ring.

Of course, if he was in an accident, they wouldn't know to call her. After all, what the hell was she to Aiden besides his live-in fuck buddy.

He didn't even know that she loved him.

Why didn't she learn from her mother? When you love someone, you say it. Instead, she learned that if you love someone, they could leave you at any moment like her father left her mom. Like her father had left her. They could leave you aching in love with a hole in your heart from their absence.

She sat up and wiped her eyes. There were two scenarios running through her mind. One, Aiden wanted to be home with her, but couldn't because he was waylaid somewhere or, worse, hurt. Or two, he decided she wasn't worth the effort and had left her high and dry.

If she tried to call hospitals, they'd probably give her the same runaround as the hotel had. If he wanted her to know where he was, he would have called. Unless his phone wasn't working. But he had a rich person's phone so that shit always worked, right?

Phoebe held her hands to her head to stop it from spinning. It was still too late or early to call her friends. She could try Aiden again, but what was the point? He either left her willingly or unwillingly.

She stared down at the duvet and looked over the bed they usually shared. It was too big for one person and too cold without him in it. Sighing, she went back into the living room to the leather couch and drew a throw blanket over her. She pressed play on the TV for the company and lay down, but now her eyes were wide open.

She never told him she loved him. Would it have made a difference? Could she find it in her heart to tell him if he'd left willingly? To give him that power to destroy her?

Wiping her eyes with the corner of the blanket, she sighed. He already had that power.

Even if he left willingly, Aiden would come back. They would talk when he was sober. They always talked things out and if he didn't want to talk, she'd make him at least listen. Because she wouldn't be the one to leave without a fight.

PHOEBE WOKE to a gentle touch on her hip and a solid mass against her waist. She opened her eyes and immediately closed them against the sunlight peeking in the windows.

"Aiden?" Her throat was hoarse from crying last night.

"Hey." His voice sounded tired and weary.

She stretched a little on her side and opened her eyes again. "What time is it?"

Aiden sat on the couch in front of her waist next to her bent knees. She blinked her eyes to get the sleep out of them so she could see him.

"It's about six." His hand stayed settled on her hip.

He still wore his tux pants. His white shirt was untucked and had reddish brown stains on it. That woke her up as she focused on his face. A white bandage covered his forehead above his eyebrow. She pushed up and her fingers reached out for his bandage.

"What happened?"

He stopped her hand before it made contact and brought

her fingers to his lips. "Cab braked too hard. My head hit something sharp and my phone cracked against the divider. Not sure if it's broken or the battery just died."

She held his hand and stared into his green eyes. He'd been in an accident and she hadn't known. She hadn't been there for him. Her throat clogged with unshed tears.

"I could have lost you." It came out as a whisper.

"I'm here." His other hand cupped her cheek.

"The last words I said to you were, fuck you." She couldn't keep her tears in check as they rolled down her face.

"Hey, I'm here. It's okay."

"No, it's not." She tried to stop crying, but his face wavered in the unshed tears. "What if that had been it? What if I never saw you again? What if I never got to tell you that I love you?"

He smiled softly at her. "You love me?"

Her heart pounded in her chest. Loving him gave him power over her. Loving him could ruin her like it had her mother who had never moved on. But Aiden wasn't her father. He was so much more than the man who had fathered her. She had to let him know how she felt. She squeezed his hand and nodded.

"I said some pretty shitty things last night." Aiden's thumb smoothed over her cheek, wiping away a tear. "I don't care how many guys you've slept with. I really don't. All I care about is that the only guy you want to be with now is me. I love you and don't want to share you with anyone else."

Phoebe's heart swelled in her chest until she wasn't sure her ribs could hold it. She wiped away her tears. "I'm not just convenient for sex?"

"Oh, you're definitely convenient for sex." He pressed his lips against hers for way too brief of a second. He stood and swooped her up into his arms, carrying her to the bedroom. "I like you in my apartment—in our apartment. I don't want you to leave. I don't care if it's too quick or whatever bullshit you're going to throw my way. I love you and you love me. I have a big-ass apartment that feels like home when you're in it."

He lowered her feet to the ground next to the bed.

"How's your head?" Phoebe raised an eyebrow at Aiden.

"Honestly, it hurts, and I'm exhausted because I haven't slept all night." His hands lowered to her ass and pulled her into his erection. "But I just found out the woman I love loves me back and that gave me a second wind."

"Do you want to shower before or after?" She started undoing the buttons on his blood-stained shirt.

"Both?" He tipped her head up until her eyes met his. "I want you all the time. I want you sitting on the counter while I cook and telling me about your day. I want to snuggle with you on the couch while we watch movies and shows. I want you to call me on my bullshit at work and challenge me to work harder."

"Aw, even if we never have sex again?" She cocked up an eyebrow at him.

"Even if we never have sex again, I'll still love you." Aiden brushed a kiss over her lips.

"But we can still have sex, right?" She grinned up at him.

"That's the best part. I can have you all the time." He rubbed his finger along her bottom lip. "I want you in the shower with me, driving me crazy with your hands all over my body. I want you in my bed, on the kitchen counter, on the bathroom counter, on the couch, on the bed. Oh, in the tub. . . which reminds me."

He lifted her straight up, startling a squeak out of her. "I'm supposed to not get the bandage wet for a few days, so I'm thinking a bath would be ideal."

She wrapped her arms tightly around his neck. "Do you now? What happened to condoms don't work in tubs?"

"Who said anything about a condom?" Aiden raised his eyebrow at her as he carried her into the bathroom.

"We've never had that talk," Phoebe stalled. She'd never had that talk with anyone before.

He set her on her feet beside the tub and turned on the water. "We've had the I'm clean and you're clean talk. If I recall you said you were on the pill and I see you take one every morning."

Phoebe bit her lip as he slipped off his shirt and dropped it to the tiles. He closed the distance between them and wrapped his arms around her waist.

"What else do we need to discuss? I'm not planning on screwing around on you. You're not planning on screwing around on me." Aiden lips quirked up on one side. "I love you and trust you. I don't want anyone else but you."

She could feel the heat building in her cheeks. She stared at his chest and took a deep breath before revealing, "I've never had sex without a condom."

"Well, it's only fair then." He tipped her chin up. His eyes sparkled with delight and she just wanted to sink into him.

"Fair?" she asked. Her fingers traced the lines of his abs.

He sucked in a breath at her touch before claiming her lips with his. This kiss lasted a little longer and made her insides burn. He lifted his head only a slight bit and when she opened her eyes, he said, "You took my car virginity. I get to take your unprotected sex virginity."

She shook her head as a smile crept onto her lips. "You are a little weird."

"But I'm your kind of weird." He kissed her hard. "So, what do you say, Bee?"

"Yeah, no on that nickname either." She pressed her finger against his lips and gave him a stern look. "Not Freebie, not Bee, not Pheebs."

"Fine, Phoebe." His eyes sparkled. "Let me fuck you in the tub."

Her body softened and she nodded. He kissed her again, lingering on her lips, tasting her gently, taking her breath away. Her heart was in his hands. His to cherish or his to crush.

When he broke off the kiss, he brought his lips to her ear and said, "First the tub, then I'll make love to you on the bed."

He raised his head and she lost herself in his eyes. He lifted her pajama top off then pushed her pajama shorts and underwear down for her to step out of them. He pressed a kiss to her trembling stomach and looked up at her.

Everything she'd ever wanted lingered in his eyes. So much love that she couldn't believe she hadn't recognized it earlier. That tenderness and softness had always been there.

"Aiden." His name was soft. She put her hands on his jaw and lifted him until his mouth met hers. She wanted him to feel what he made her feel with every touch. She explored his mouth gently with her tongue. Her hands went down his chest to his belt. He lifted his head from hers, but his breath remained on her lips.

She breathed him in as she undid his pants, and he helped her take them off. He broke eye contact to turn off the tub. They stood there naked for a moment, just being with each other.

He stepped into the slipper tub and leaned back against the high side. He held out his hand for her and helped her over the edge. As she lowered herself down, she straddled his hips.

"Before we do this. . . ." Aiden's hands trailed over her body, dripping hot water over her breasts.

She pressed her hands on his pecs and waited for whatever he needed to say.

"I'm sorry for everything I said last night. I didn't mean it.

I was stupid and jealous. I know they don't have you now, but they'll always have a small part of you. But all that doesn't matter because I have the most important part of you."

"They never got a part of me." She shook her head. "They never touched my heart."

"I'm glad you saved your heart for me, Phoebe." Aiden pulled her into a hug. "That's all I ever wanted from you."

"You mean you don't want sex?" She sat up and raised her eyebrow at him.

He chuckled darkly. "I'll always want sex with you."

His fingers smoothed over the center of her as he leaned forward and captured her nipple with his mouth, teasing it to a hard tip. She'd been ready for him since she woke up.

Not willing to wait any longer, she took his cock in her hand and lifted up until he was aligned with her entrance. She waited until he met her eyes before she lowered onto him until he finally filled her.

"I love you, Aiden." She kissed him softly.

"I love you," he said as he held her hips to guide her back up, before slamming back into her.

She arched her back. Her hands gripped the sides of the tub as he set a rhythm that was guaranteed to drive her wild. His warm mouth closed over her nipple again as he continued to thrust up into her. Careful of his bandage, one of her hands sank into his blond hair to hold him latched onto her.

The water sloshed around them, adding a new touch to the mix. After Aiden had worshipped both of her breasts, he pulled back.

"Look at me," he said.

She met his eyes and just like that first time, she felt him inside her on so many levels. It had been too intimate that night, but she couldn't resist coming back for it again and again. Now watching him threw her over into oblivion. She rode him through her orgasm until his grip tightened on her hips and held her still. She watched his orgasm flow over his face and settled against him in the tub.

His arms wrapped around her and just held her against him, stroking her back gently.

"Can we just sleep right here?" Phoebe asked as she yawned. The warm water and Aiden's heat did everything it could to draw her into sleep.

CHAPTER 27

THEY DIDN'T STAY in the tub very long after Phoebe yawned again. Aiden brought her over to the shower to rinse them both off. He soaped every inch of her body as she soaped every inch of his. After they rinsed and dried each other off, he tugged her hand to lead her to the bed.

Last night had been one nightmare after another, but it had ended better than he could imagine. He lay naked in his bed with Phoebe sprawled naked on top of him. He wanted to make love to her right then, but the sleepless night finally caught up to him.

Aiden woke to darkness and a warm wet mouth moving down his body. The curtains were doing their job to hold out the daylight. Phoebe's hands stroked over his cock right before her mouth closed over him, taking him deep down her throat before backing off.

Her body was off to his side and he fondled her breast for a second. She came off his dick and gave him a smile. As soon as she did that, he tugged her hips over his face and waited. Her tongue darted out to taste him, and he did the same to her.

As she worked her mouth over his cock, he devoured her pussy. Like everything else, it almost became a competition over who could get the other one there first.

Phoebe sat up, delicately wiping the sides of her mouth. "You came first."

"You came longer." He dragged her lips down to meet his.

She rested against his body as they caught their breaths.

"I'm not like those other women at the charity event." Phoebe lazily drew circles on his stomach.

"Thank God for that," he said, stroking his hand down her back.

She propped her chin on her hand on his chest and looked him in the eyes. "Does that bother you?"

"That you aren't a prim and proper woman with a pedigree and trust fund?" Aiden wanted to clarify exactly what they were talking about here.

"A woman that could pass your mother's vetting process."

"My mother isn't dating you." Aiden tweaked her nose.

"What if she doesn't like me?" Real concern shone in Phoebe's dark eyes.

"She'll like you because I love you." Aiden pulled her down so he could kiss her full lips. "No one would be better for me than you, Phoebe."

"I was so afraid to tell you how I felt after saying I didn't want the fairy tale. But you are everything I've always wanted and more. I love you, Aiden. You make me want forever." She reached up and brushed his hair with her fingers.

His heart swelled inside him.

"I love you and want forever with you." He rolled her over onto her back and gazed down at her. "Now, be honest. You think I'll be enough for you?"

She laughed. "You aren't serious, are you? I don't think

I'm enough for you. I think I'm the one who had to call a time out that first weekend."

"That's true." He gave her a thoughtful expression.

"Give it up, Kingston. You know you're all mine." Her legs wrapped around his hips pulling him down onto her.

"And you're mine." He kissed her as he thrust inside her in one stroke.

She gasped against his mouth and her eyes met his. "I'm yours."

RUNNING LATE. Be there in fifteen. I swear. Morgan's text came across Phoebe's phone. Phoebe just smiled and set the phone to the side. She had her margarita and a choice table at the Indigo Hotel bar, she was pretty damn content to wait for Morgan to finally show up.

"Excuse me," Aiden said with an arched eyebrow. "But is this seat taken?"

She smirked at him. "What are you going to give me for it?"

He held up a finger. Taking off his jacket, he hung it on the back of the chair and then sat next to her.

She pursed her lips together waiting.

Finally he turned to her and said, "You must be tired."

She narrowed her eyes. "How so?"

"You've been running through my mind all night."

"Not bad. You got anything else?" Phoebe leaned back and took a sip of her margarita.

Aiden touched his shirt and said, "Feel this."

Phoebe smiled warily and reached out to feel the fabric.

"Do you know what this is made of?" Aiden asked with a straight face.

"Not really."

"Boyfriend material." His grin at his cheesy joke made her laugh.

"That's a good one."

"Thanks, I've been working on it all day." He wiggled his eyebrows at her. "Still waiting on Morgan and Drew?"

"They said they'd be here in fifteen minutes." Phoebe shrugged.

"Do you think they are. . . busy?" He lifted his eyebrow again.

"Ew, that's my best friend you are talking about." Phoebe smacked his arm with the back of her hand lightly. "But yes, probably."

"You know, I know a guy that could get us a room here while we wait."

She snickered at his hopeful expression. "You're the guy, aren't you?"

"I'm *your* guy, Phoebe." He leaned in and kissed her briefly to not mess up her lipstick. His forehead pressed against hers. "I love you. Only you."

Phoebe flushed with warmth as she said, "I love you."

ALSO BY AMY LARK

Just Ad Love Series

Not Quite Enemies

Not Quite Roommates

COMING SOON!

Not Quite Faking It SEPTEMBER 2022

ALSO BY AMANDA BERRY

L.A. Cinderella PUBLISHED BY HARLEQUIN

Fox Creek Series

Yours at Last

One Night with the Best Man PUBLISHED BY HARLEQUIN

More Than Friends

ACKNOWLEDGMENTS

For Not Quite the Boss, you can probably imagine how difficult Phoebe is to work with. ;) She was originally supposed to be book 2 but she kept insisting that was wrong. So she got her way. She really was a joy to write with Aiden, probably the only guy strong enough to take her on.

Thank you to Bria Quinlan for editing this book and making it the best possible book it can be. Your encouragement means a lot to me. MK Book Editing for providing copy edits and keeping me on track with my characters. Amanda Bonilla for proofreading and catching the things my eyes just can't find at this stage. Amy Halter for your excellent beta reading skills. And for the wonderful covers, thank you Sarah Kil Creative Studio.

My writing life wouldn't happen without Jeannie, Shawntelle, and Sela. We've been together since the start of this crazy journey for all of us. The encouragement and help we provide each other is necessary to keep me sane in this career.

To the Hermits! Our beach retreat helped me get back on task and a lot of the words in this series were made during our time together.

To the friends I've made during the pandemic and who kept me accountable for every word written. Who knew video sprints were what I was always looking for? To Carrie, Sarah, Holly, Selena, Danielle, Ivy, and a whole host of others: Thank you for being my daily push I need to stop procrastinating and do!

ABOUT THE AUTHOR

Amy Lark is a contemporary romance author. A Midwest girl stuck in the swamps of the South, she lives with her husband, her dog, and two cats. When not writing steamy romance, she's doling out advice to her children and bowing to her pets many demands. Find out more about upcoming books at amylark.com.